Caught in the Summer Flames

By Shivani Ladwa

EU Conformity Declaration
This product complies with the following safety regulations and standards to ensure consumer safety and product quality: Regulation (EU) 2023/988 of the European Parliament and of the Council on General Product Safety (GPSR): The Consumer Product Safety Improvement Act (CPSIA), Section 101. The Californian Safe drinking water and toxic enforcement act. (Proposition 65) EN71-Part 1: Mechanical and Physical Properties EN71-Part 2: Flammability EN71-Part 3 Migration of certain elements.

Published and Manufactured by Softwood Books
EU Responsible person: Maddy Glenn
Office 2, Wharfside House, Prentice Road, Stowmarket, Suffolk, IP14 1RD
www.softwoodbooks.com
hello@softwoodbooks.com

EU Rep:
Authorised Rep Compliance Ltd., Ground Floor, 71 Lower Baggot Street, Dublin, D02 P593, Ireland
www.arccompliance.com
info@arccompliance.com

Paperback ISBN: 978-1-0369-1719-7

Chapter 1

Sadie stared out the window, hoping for a glimpse of her. But hours had gone by and there was not even a sound of her laughter amongst the breeze. She missed her, it had been far too long. It was meant to be their last summer of sunset beach walks and dips in the ocean, memory making and pretending like the big wide world of adulthood wasn't just on the horizon. But Arya was nowhere to be seen. Their nightly calls became sporadic texts and their daily visits, stopped. They were completely out of sync. Boredom washed over Sadie and neglect started creeping in. She hated this feeling.

Throughout their 17 years together, Sadie had never felt so abandoned by the one person she claimed was her twin flame. But as sad as she was, she tried to keep her spirits up. Instead, Sadie spent her alone time adding to their summer scrapbook, a tradition they did every year without fail. Immortalising their year together. But this time it was just Sadie working on it. It left her with her own thoughts, pondering over what Arya was really doing, how there clearly was something more important than her, more important than their friendship.

Well, friendship has always been a funny thing. It's either a priceless bond that is unbreakable or fragile as a glass heart. Some friendships last the test of time, while others fade without a word. Despite the start of summer being a hiccup, Sadie still believed their bond to be unbreakable. It was practically written in the stars – since the day they were born. Born just hours apart, in the same hospital, only living streets away. It was a modern fairytale. The birth of something bigger. And from that moment on, they were a powerful duo.

Living in the iconic Cloudgham Cape meant there was always something new for them to discover. It was an exciting coastal city that had everything. From soft clouds shrouding the hilltops and breathtaking headland views to sandy beaches marking the end of the city. It was paradise to them and up until this summer, they spent every weekend exploring it. But when the last weekend came and passed, nothing happened. Sadie already felt like this summer was ruined, when it had only just begun. Dramatic was an understatement.

She had so many plans laid out for them, so many memories she wanted to make but there was so little time... This was their last summer together and she wasn't sure how she would cope when the future forced them apart. That thought kept her up for many nights the most. But she pushed it down, deeper and deeper until it was TV static at the back of her head.

To avoid the thought of the impending doom she conjured in her mind, Sadie dove into the latest books. Always creating an imaginary world, that only her and Arya could get lost in. Books were scattered across her room, like the thoughts in her mind, but she just couldn't part with them. Like most things in Sadie's life, if they were hers, they were for a lifetime. It didn't always work out in her favour though, but she was a possessive soul.

Arya, however, was the opposite. She thought endlessly about the future. Where her life is heading, what her next steps are, what new people she'll meet. She worried too much but didn't let them get the best of her. Instead, she let her worries fade away within her paintings. She painted every moment in her life, as if her brush was dancing to its own rhythm. She constantly changed her style, like shuffling through songs on a playlist. Sadie would read from her books, and Arya would paint the scenes. They complemented each other perfectly - like paint and the brush that holds it.

Right now, Arya was focused on manifesting her goals in life, and to fulfil her dream of using her creativity. She was passionate about creating and designing just about anything and if she were able to do this as her job, it would be a life well made. The project she was most proud of, was bringing life back into the small, old crumbly shed that lived at the bottom of her garden. And with the help of her carpenter Dad, she already had all the materials to hand to restore it and turn it into a new play den for her little brother Kiaan. Somewhere he could release his chaotic energy and free spirit.

It was painted with his favourite Disney characters. From clouds full of the Gods and Goddesses from Hercules with their brightly coloured attire in heroic poses, to Russel and Carl in his floating house. Then there was Mowgli and Baloo the bear stooped atop of the jungle trees grabbing mangoes. The rest of the cosy den was jungle themed with leaves and ropes that you could swing onto to reach the outside of the downstairs window. She felt truly accomplished.

To match her dream career, Arya needed a space to let her artistic nature be free, and that was her painting studio, her pride and joy. In the corner of her bedroom was a spiral staircase adorned with intricate leaves, that ascended through the ceiling.

It led to a small but wonderfully bright room, a place where it was quiet and peaceful. There was a giant window that let momentous light in, and it was where her painting easel was placed. On the side of the wall, were stacked shelves holding her beloved paints that were scattered around, with dripped paint that had now dried on the wood. From unfinished artwork and abandoned canvases to spectacular pieces of watercolour art and breathtaking mood pieces. Despite Arya's immensely clean nature, this was the only room where she allowed herself to be messy. Going as far as splattering paint on the walls. The only other person to see this room after it was finished, was Sadie.

They shared everything.

But things were about to change. As the school year went on, Arya's sense of independence grew. She loved Sadie, but she felt like something was missing. For the first time, Arya felt compelled to branch out of her usual duo and she found a new appreciation for others that felt like home and made her belly laugh. She wanted to make new friends, to make new memories with other people and to imagine a future where she wasn't always by Sadie's side. And she connected with a girl named Maya. Arya never had another friend before, especially a girl friend. She didn't know how to act or what to say around her, but Maya's aura quickly eased her nerves.

The one thing that connected both Arya and Maya together, was their shared Indian culture. Gaining another friend that had the same background as her, made Arya realise she had been squashing that part out of her all this time. And now Maya was helping Arya embrace her culture again. She felt valued. She felt like she finally fitted into this world.

But the joyfulness of this newfound friendship didn't last long. Despite having the best time with Maya, Arya couldn't shake off the guilt that crept into her mind. Guilt from hiding this new friendship from Sadie. She was deeply worried that Sadie wouldn't like someone else being close to her. And Arya's anxiety crippled her whenever she thought about it. Having another girl in their duo was uncharted territory for them, so she couldn't dump this on Sadie without warning. She wanted to gradually explain in person and slowly reveal their friendship in the hopes of Sadie understanding.

It was important to Arya that Sadie was okay with it. Because they were still each other's number one. Arya would never let anyone replace Sadie, but she just knew she needed to follow her own path. Even if it meant drifting a little further apart. But for now, she just wanted to enjoy her final summer with Sadie, before everything changed.

Because college loomed just around the corner, and with it, the uncertainty of what would come next. Sadie hated the idea of being apart. The thought of stepping outside their shared bubble felt terrifying. But one thing was certain: no matter where life took them, she wasn't going to let Arya go.

Arya, however, couldn't stop thinking about it. She talked about her college plans to Maya, but somehow never managed a complete conversation with Sadie. Something always happened to her when the topic came up. Arya knew Sadie dreaded it with every fibre in her body, but she couldn't help feeling eager to step outside of the comfort zone she'd always known. The thought of college, without Sadie, was weirdly exciting.

Arya wanted to explain everything to Sadie. To tell her exactly how she was feeling, but she was hesitant this time. Although Arya felt like her secrets were snowballing and the pressure had become too much. How could she tell Sadie? Sadie would hate her. Would she embrace Arya's growth and open her arms to Maya? Or would Sadie be angry at her? For the first time, Arya was unsure how her once best friend would react. But that was it, they were best friends. And friends don't hold each other back.

Arya didn't think Sadie would mind.

Chapter 2

Days went by and it was now approaching the best part of their summer break; their joint family holiday to Disney World. It was something they had been planning for a while and the girls couldn't wait any longer. It's what got them through the school year. To Sadie this was the most important time of their lives. It had been a little boring at the start, but she knew they'd be reunited soon and everything would be okay.

It was now a week before their getaway where they were going to be what Sadie called "theme park crawling." She had stayed up night after night, obsessively planning each and every day, leaving no room for adjustments. Every aspect of the trip had to be planned precisely. Nothing was missed; nothing was to be changed.

One morning, Sadie was lying on her unkept bed staring at the old glow-in-the-dark stars stuck on her ceiling, when Arya appeared at her door.

"Hey Sades. Missed me?" said Arya.
Sadie got up so fast, she fell off her bed.

"Oh my god! Where have you been?" she screamed, trying to get back up. "It feels like it's been forever. Please don't go this long without seeing me again!" she jumbled out.

"It's only been a week, silly. I can't be with you forever," replied Arya, helping Sadie get back on her feet.   "Besides, we've got the next two weeks with each other, remember? Are you sure you won't get sick of me then?"

Sadie gasped "Of course I won't. I could never get sick of you."

Arya thought Sadie was such a drama queen, but sometimes it could be sweet.

"How have you been, Sades?" asked Arya.

"Oh, just fine. Absolutely fine, never been better!" trying to hide her sadness. "Just been thinking about our holiday, super excited."

"I don't think anyone is more excited than Kiaan. He's been talking about it in his sleep! He wants to meet everyone. Every. Single. Character. It's going to be exhausting," laughed Arya.

Arya had been desperate to find new inspiration to connect with for her art. Being in a different environment, surrounded by electrifying excitement, would help with fresh ideas. Besides, she couldn't possibly go on roller coasters all day every day for two weeks; she'd be sick. Everywhere.

"I've already started to pack my drawing materials," said Arya. "Had to sacrifice a few clothes, but it was totally worth it."

"I've bought five more books," added Sadie, excitedly.

Talking about the holiday made them realise how impatient they were, it took every ounce of them not to throw everything in a suitcase and run to the airport right then and there. But there was still a whole week to go, and the waiting was torture. There was still so much to sort out - like finding someone to watch Bailey, Arya's ever-adorable but totally spoiled dog. Turns out planning a big holiday was a lot more work than they'd thought.

While the girls were busy upstairs, Sadie's Dad came home. Her Mom, Rose, had already been downstairs sipping on some wine. Her parents were very easy-going, joyful people. Rose always walked around with a spring in her step and felt like a breath of fresh air. Rose was a constant summer and as sweet as her namesake.

Sadie's Dad, Noah, was an English professor at the university, which was probably where Sadie got her love of books from. He was a very lively professor, incredibly witty too, and was much more innovative than most.

"Hey, it's my favourite girls," he smiled as soon as he saw them. "Are you guys hungry? I'm going to make my famous spaghetti bolognese. Do you want to munch with us?"

"Duh, I wouldn't miss your speciality!" beamed Arya. She absolutely loved his food. "What's your secret to making your spaghetti taste incredibly marvellous?" said Arya theatrically.

"Something sweet, something spicy and a bunch of fresh basil. Can't tell you my secret, can I?" he replied.

Arya rolled her eyes playfully. She had been wanting to know his recipe for ages, but he would never let it out.

13

As Noah cooked, the smell of the food began to make her stomach growl ferociously. And if her favourite dish wasn't enough, she still had dessert to look forward to. Every Friday, Sadie's family would always have something delicious. Whether it was something homemade and delicate or shop bought and heavy, it was a sweet treat to end the week.

While Noah bustled around the kitchen, Rose continued happily sipping on some red wine while chatting to Arya about what she had been up to. Arya replied with so much enthusiasm, that she didn't think before she spoke.

"My friend Maya had a family wedding last week, so I was with her, helping her organise her outfits and jewellery for each event. I even dressed up in a few of them myself!" she started.

As soon as she said this, Sadie's normally bright and cheerful face dropped into an intense glare. This was new, she thought. Seeing Maya outside school was something Sadie had never imagined, and she didn't like someone else spending so much time with Arya. With or without her, Arya was only *her* best friend. Sadie hoped this would never happen again. She didn't think she'd be able to stomach it. No one could take her place.

While her mind was racing a mile a minute, Arya hadn't noticed Sadie was upset and carried on.
"Oh! She also invited me to the henna night. All the girls got it adorned on their hands. Here's mine! Although, it's kinda faded a little." Arya showed Rose her hands. "I haven't been to one in a while, so I've really missed the wedding hype."

"Wow, that still looks beautiful! I bet Indian weddings are so much fun. I've always wanted to go to one...maybe yours, eh?" winked Rose.

Arya laughed. "You'll have to wait a long time yet! I wouldn't wait around for a little old me."

Sadie got up abruptly "Excuse me. I'll be right back," she in a monotone voice.

She rushed to her room and slammed the door. Now standing in the middle of her room, Sadie tried to compose herself and took a few deep breaths.

"Come on Sadie, snap out of it. What's come over you? Arya isn't yours. You don't own her." She stared down blankly at her hands. But her mind protested.

"No. She is *my* best friend, and I can't lose her... She can't have anyone else." she mumbled.

Sadie continued arguing with herself, with back-and-forth remarks. Reassuring herself that Arya wouldn't leave her but then being so paranoid that Maya was worming her way in and pushing Sadie out.

After a while, her mind started clearing a little and she thought that if they had only met up a few times then it wasn't really any competition. So, why was she getting so worked up over it? Finally, she realised she was overreacting and reassured herself that nothing could come between them. Only when she felt fully calmed down, she was ready to go back.

As Sadie walked down, she noticed Rose and Arya eyeing her cautiously as they watched her approach.

"You alright bub?" asked Rose.

"Yeah. I just…er, I needed to put my phone on charge." She looked at Arya and plastered a fake smile on her face.

Arya smiled back but had a feeling that Sadie was lying, that she was upset about Maya. She was so frustrated with herself for letting it slip, without talking to Sadie first. What if she had just ruined everything? It was a silly mistake, but she couldn't turn back time. All she could hope for was that Sadie was actually okay with it.

Arya thought that going forward, she should name drop Maya every now and then, so Sadie would slowly accept their friendship. And hopefully not feel threatened.

A while later, dinner was ready. Suddenly, Sadie's mind totally cleared, and her stomach growled. The alluring smell of dinner embraced every corner of the kitchen. The tomato sauce glistened, the hints of basil hit you effortlessly and the cheese just oozed into every space it could find. Soon enough all the food had been eaten. Not a single morsel was left.

After they all indulged, they dispersed before they were ready to sink into dessert. Arya was happily watching their favourite show, but hadn't noticed that Sadie wasn't paying attention at all. She was lost in a world of her own, but this time it was a calamitous place. Incessant thoughts constantly replaying repeatedly.

How much time had Arya really spent with Maya?

Was it just a few days or had it been weeks?

Did they call each other every night, like Sadie and Arya usually did?

Because without fail, every night they would call each other, whether they had spent the day together or not. But that hadn't been the case in the last week, and Sadie took that very seriously. She didn't like change. She didn't like people not keeping to their word. And she was now paranoid it was because of Maya. All because of her.

A thought crossed her mind, maybe Arya just wanted a friend who was Indian too? Someone to bond with. What if this was the beginning of being replaced as a best friend too? But she felt guilty thinking that and moved on.

It wasn't like Sadie and Maya didn't get on; she did like her at school. Although that didn't count, not in the real world, Sadie thought. And now it seemed like Arya and Maya had gotten closer, and Sadie now saw Maya as a threat. How could Sadie compete with someone who shared something so personal with Arya?

A new feeling erupted within Sadie. Fear. The thought of Arya leaving for someone she knew for a short year, made Sadie feel sick, physically sick. And her stomach started turning at the thought. She needed to do something to stop this from happening, to stop Maya from taking her place. Because three was a crowd after all.

But, yet again, her mind changed course, and her frantic thinking reined in. She was being overdramatic. It wasn't like that at all. It felt like there was a war raging in her head, and she couldn't decide which side she was on.

Finally, Arya noticed Sadie's glum expression.

"What's up?" she asked.

"Oh, nothing. Sorry, I was just thinking," laughed Sadie, awkwardly. She paused. "So how was your time with Maya? Did you see each other all week or...?"

Arya paused for a second, initially surprised that Sadie had asked about Maya. But then she thought, maybe this was a good thing. Maybe Sadie wasn't bothered after all?

However, Sadie was only digging for more information. Finding out how much of Sadie's time Maya took and calculating how much of a threat she was. The only way to do that, she realised, was to feign interest.

Arya shrugged.

"Yeah, we saw each other most of the week. She wanted help choosing her outfits but then ended up borrowing one of mine. Different states have different styles, so Maya liked mine."

Arya stopped there as she tried to gauge Sadie's reaction. But Sadie just looked at her blankly. Arya wasn't sure whether to carry on, but there was no time like the present. Maya's name had already been mentioned now and even if Sadie hadn't been paying attention, she also couldn't accuse Arya of never bringing her up. She cleared her throat and continued. "Ahem."

Sadie was thrown back in focus and blinked a few times. What did she miss? She didn't really care about what they did together, all she wanted to know was how much time they had been spending together. Anything else was useless knowledge.

"...and before the wedding, there was a party where the women get henna done, play games with songs and just celebrate together. I was invited to that, and we thought it would be cute to wear similar colours. I have so many to choose from, so it wasn't hard to find the perfect dress." Arya laughed awkwardly, feeling like her words had become overflowing water spilling out of her mouth.

"Oh...wow. That sounds fun," replied Sadie, feeling a little deflated that Arya and Maya had seemed to spend so much time with each other. She felt left out that they had even gone to a party, especially as an inseparable pair. It made Sadie feel weird and sad, or was it anger and jealously? Either way, she needed to stop this conversation and move on to herself. She was done listening about Maya.

"Are you going to show me these new outfits or? I mean, I would love to see them too," she said with a strained voice.

"Of course! I only got them a couple of weeks ago, but I put them away because I didn't have anything to wear them to. And Maya asked me to her cousin's party at the last minute. I'm sorry. I was meant to show you, why don't you come round tomorrow after your lesson?"

"Okay!" Sadie smiled now, feeling slightly happier.

After that strained conversation, Sadie asked every question under the sun about Indian weddings, because this she was actually interested in. Then it was dessert time. Rose had brought out four delectable molten lava chocolate cakes. fresh out of the oven; it was the most delicious dessert they had. After everyone indulged a second time, the girls went to Sadie's room.

"Urgh, I am so full. I have a food baby," laughed Arya.

"This will be us every day soon."

"I cannot wait to try the grey stuff," said Arya.

"You sure you're not going to draw it instead?"

"Very funny. Although…" thought Arya.

Sadie interrupted, laughing. "Please tell me you're not actually thinking about it…"

Arya playfully pushed Sadie over. They laughed and joked around for hours, and Sadie started to feel the tension slightly melt away. But the new friendship was still at the back of her mind, like a nagging thought.

However, she was determined not to let it stop her from having the best summer. Because it would be the best, she would make sure of it. She was soon to be holidaying with her best friend and nothing in the world could ruin that feeling. Not even a third wheel to their friendship. There was no competition, Maya had nothing on her.

Chapter 3

Sadie woke up lazily, gazing at the bright sun rays seeping through her curtains. She loved the warmth on her face. It made her feel right and ready for the rest of the day. It was only 9am so she decided to lounge in bed for a while. And like clockwork, she went on her phone. She was addicted to social media, glued to it every morning without fail. As she scrolled through her newsfeed, she suddenly came across Maya's account as a 'suggested friends'.

Ha, friends, Sadie thought.

A funny feeling arose in her stomach. Just seeing her name appear on the screen agitated Sadie now and she couldn't shake it off. She really did not like Maya one bit. But her curiosity got the better of her. Sadie clicked on her profile. Big mistake. Maya's most recent post was a carousel of pictures, all from her cousin's wedding. Sadie had to admit; it looked amazing.

Everyone was dressed up to the nines in their Indian attire, the girls in saris and dresses that shimmered and sparkled with brilliant and alluring colours. All were decorated with embroidery that was gorgeous to the eyes. And the guys were dressed in coloured sherwanis that matched the girls. There was also a picture of what Sadie assumed was Maya's cousin in a lehenga, an Indian bridal outfit. It took Sadie's breath away; she looked magical.

Sadie swiped to the last image and saw it was of Maya and Arya. Her heart stopped. They were both dressed in aqua coloured Indian dresses with

21

matching bangles, sitting down with their hands faced towards the camera to show their hands decorated with beautiful and intricate henna patterns.

They looked happy together.

Sadie opened the comments and saw everyone's reaction to the wedding pictures. How amazing the bride looked and how cute and beautiful Arya and Maya were. How they looked like sisters. How amazing their matching looks were.
Sadie felt sick in the back of her throat. She was livid. But she couldn't stop reading them, over and over, obsessing over everyone's kind words. She ended up staring at that picture the longest. Through her anger she tried to find something to say, calculating in her mind. But she couldn't find anything to say. For once she was speechless.

Hurt so deeply that she couldn't mutter a single word and she closed her eyes in defeat. But only for a split second, because she had much more to show on her own page. Her friendship with Arya was infinitely special.

She outdid Maya tenfold with the countless moments she had with Arya over the many, many years they had together. After she scrolled through them, she felt her smile come back and finally felt ready to get up. Pulling the duvet off her, she slipped her feet into her fluffy unicorn slippers and clambered out of bed. As she walked around her room, having a good stretch, she remembered she was going to see Arya after her lesson, and she burst with glee.

Her piano teacher, an elderly man named Arthur, only lived a couple of streets away. Sadie enjoyed his company, so her lessons were always fun to go to. But she mainly loved going to his house because he had two adorable fluffy Samoyed dogs.

As Sadie walked up the driveway, she could hear them barking and see them bouncing up at the window, and before she could knock on the door, Arthur opened it, and the two dogs bowled Sadie over and she fell to the floor.

Arthur tried to pull them off Sadie, but then he thought. "Y'know you kinda smell like bacon. Maybe they just want bacon."

"Very funny. Sorry I haven't been over, I know I'm meant to be walking them this summer... But I promise I'll walk them every day this week! Then I'll be going away for two weeks."

"Atta girl. God knows I need a little bit of a break from these pair of floofs."

Sadie laughed. Floofs.

She knew he adored those dogs more than anything. He and his late wife had adopted them just before she passed away. Now he took care of them more than himself. It was heartbreakingly sweet. One was called Candy and the other called Floss. It was the perfect name for dogs who had fur that was soft to the touch, and it also reminded Arthur of his wife's favourite sweet treat.

As Sadie walked into the house, the familiar smell of madeleines filled the air. She couldn't wait to have one. The first time she ever tasted them was here, and she couldn't believe she'd spent so much of her life without the taste of buttery goodness. He always made them at the start of each week in preparation for their lesson. Because if it was a difficult one, it would be a pick me up. But she hoped this lesson would go well for once. She needed a win.

Before Sadie began, Arthur let the dogs out in the garden, so they could be left in peace. He was going to teach Sadie a new piano technique, so he needed her full attention. As a beginner she was having a hard time understanding the different keys and moving her fingers. She wanted to learn how to make them dance, not fumble and make the wrong sounds. Her childhood dream of learning how to play the piano couldn't be tarnished by her lack of rhythm. Sadie always put too much pressure on herself.

After she took a deep breath to lighten the load, the lesson commenced. An hour later and it was over. To her surprise, it went better than expected. Maybe the little break had helped her piano skills. Feeling cheery now she played well, she treated herself to some delicious cookies and listened to Arthur talk about his dogs. Being a family friend, she didn't mind staying a little longer. She loved them and wanted to help Arthur out, especially since he was alone.

After he finished, Sadie gave both the dogs a scratch on their tummies and lots of cuddles and left. She leisurely walked past rows of houses, admiring each one as if it wasn't something she saw every day. This neighbourhood wasn't your average one, with green lawns, white picket fences and small driveways. They were bright, colourful and eccentric. Many people had even converted their attics into different things like game rooms, cinema rooms, workout rooms. Some even had libraries.

She then turned into Arya's street, which always calmed Sadie. Along the entire stretch was a row of flourishing trees, branching over into the middle of the street, creating a beautiful archway that was adorned with the tiniest blue flowers that Sadie had ever seen. When they bloomed, they illuminated the entire street and as summer began the petals fell gracefully, gently caressing your face and settling in your hair. Sadie felt like an enchanted fairy whenever this happened to her.

She beamed as she passed the towering trees and effortlessly caught one of the flowers blowing in the breeze. Whenever she managed to catch one, she'd make a wish and this time she wished she and Arya would always remain friends. No matter what may come their way. Then she blew it away and it landed amongst the hundreds of other flowers.

A few minutes later she reached Arya's house. It had a bright, sunshine yellow door that always warmed Sadie's soul, reminding her of the warmth Arya radiated. Arya was Sadie's sunshine. Sadie skipped up the drive, creating an energetic wind that moved the wind chimes dangling delicately in the porch. They created the most hypnotic tone; you could stand there and listen to the chimes resonate in your bones. Sadie rapped on the door to the rhythm of the music and within a couple of seconds, Kiaan opened it.

With floppy black hair all over his face, which today was covered in paint for some reason, and big sparkling brown eyes, the little six-year-old looked like he was going to keel over.

Taking in deep breaths, Kiaan panted out, "Oh...hi...Sadie..."

"Uh, are you okay?" asked Sadie, concerned.

Kiaan shook himself, rubbed his face and hid behind Sadie.

"Hide me! Arya's chasing me because I ruined one of her paintings! I just thought it would look nicer with my Kiaan print. She never lets me paint with her!"

Then Arya came rushing down the stairs.

"That's because you paint your whole face and then hug people!"

"But that's my art!" he yelled.

Once Arya reached Kiaan, she pulled him from behind Sadie and brought him into the tightest hug because she knew it would wind him up, even if it meant getting paint on her. It was worth it.

"Ew, no, stop hugging me!" wiggled Kiaan, elbowing Arya in the stomach to get her to let go.

"Jeez, you two are like a pair of animals. I swear every time I come round, something has happened," laughed Sadie.

"It's just the norm, isn't it?" winked Arya.

Sadie wouldn't know, she was an only child.

After Kiaan escaped her grip, Arya let Sadie in and sat in the living room. Arya watched Kiaan run out of the house into the garden, wondering

26

how he always had so much energy. Then she grabbed a clean t-shirt from the laundry pile and quickly changed, as Sadie looked away blushing. Arya plonked on the sofa and eyed Kiaan as she knew what he was about to do with the football.

"If you start kicking that ball against the window, I'll spray you with the hose. And eat all your favourite treats." They stared daggers at each other.

Sadie shook her head; this happened every time. They always had a stare off and whoever won had to listen. She could see Arya's eyes starting to water, but she was very competitive and never gave up. Kiaan on the other hand looked like he was about to cry.

"OW! Okay fine! I won't. You never let me have fun." Kiaan rubbed his watering red eyes.

"Ha. What a loser," laughed Arya, triumphantly.

All the commotion had woken her dog up with a start. He was a golden retriever called Bailey and was the most energetic, but sweetest boy. You could hear him run from anywhere by the sound of his paws. He looked at the girls and then at Kiaan playing with the ball and got so excited, that he bolted outside. Sadie gazed at Bailey with so much love in her eyes, she was so jealous that they were allowed a dog. She always wanted one.

"He's so funny. Hey, I just saw Candy and Floss too! I wish every day I could be surrounded by dogs, there's no better way of spending my time."

"Aw, I love them. They always look so soft. But I would hate to wash their fur. Could you imagine if they played in a muddy puddle? No thank you!"

"Remember when Bailey was a puppy and jumped into the deepest mud puddle you'd ever seen? I can still remember you bawling your eyes out because it took so long to wash out. You know you love muddy dogs," giggled Sadie.

Bailey came back in, plodding his paws on the floor. He looked at Sadie with his brown puppy eyes and then jumped on Arya.

"Oof, Bailey, get off you big lump," said Arya, pushing him off.

After giving him a belly rub the girls went upstairs. When Sadie walked in, she noticed there were a few Indian dresses sprawled on the golden, plush bedspread. Thinking how sweet it was that Arya had it ready to show her. She sat on the floor and started running the material through her fingers. It was so delicate and beautiful. One of them was her favourite colour: green.

It had a gold blouse and alternating dark and light green sections to the skirt. The bottom of the skirt had heavy embroidery: elaborate and huge, teardrop-shaped sequins along the bottom, golden threads in an array of different patterns protruding out of the teardrops and silver and gold sequins dotted around the border. On the dark green sections of the skirt, there were light green flowers stitched in the fabric and dark green flowers in the lighter sections of the skirt. Sadie hadn't seen anything like it before, and she wished it could be hers.

"That's yours," confirmed Arya, looking at Sadie admiring the dress.

"Really? No... I couldn't take this Arya," replied Sadie, with her eyes wide open.

"No, honestly. I asked my aunt to get an outfit for you specially, in your favourite colour, and I made sure it had flowers on it. Let's say it's an early, early birthday present," Arya smiled.

Sadie was lost for words. She kept looking back and forth from the gorgeous skirt to Arya and she suddenly welled up.

"Oh wow, this is the best gift I've ever gotten. I can't believe you got this for me, I don't know what to say!"

Arya giggled. "Oh, don't be silly, I wanted to get you something beautiful because you're the bestest friend ever and I know how much you've wanted one."

Sadie jumped up and bear-hugged Arya, swaying her from side to side. She hadn't felt this special in what felt like a while.

"Can I try it on?!" asked Sadie.

"Yeah of course! I need to see if it fits you anyway, it might have to be altered if not. Mine always does," replied Arya.

Sadie excitedly got changed into the skirt, while Arya helped clip her blouse together. Arya then draped the delicate Indian scarf around her, as Sadie tied the waist securely and as tight as she could so it wouldn't fall. It clung to her in a flattering way. Arya helped her with the rest of the outfit and as soon as it was all put on, Sadie felt the heaviness of the dress. She hadn't worn something this heavy before, but it didn't stop her twirling around the room, feeling like a princess. The jewels and sequins glimmered as she twirled through the sun rays that seeped through the window. She danced towards the mirror to admire the outfit on her and how the skirt flowed graciously around her waist, the colours complimented her so well.

"This is beautiful. I've never worn something so elegant before. Thank you so much!" gasped Sadie.

"I'm glad you like it. You look gorgeous in it. The dress suits you so well!"

"I don't want to take it off now, but my god is it heavy!" laughed Sadie.

Arya just watched Sadie prance around in a world entirely of her own. She just loved making Sadie feel special. As Arya watched her run her hands down the skirt, Sadie's expression changed to surprise.

"It has pockets!!!" Shouted Sadie. As she placed her hands inside. "I can't believe an elegant skirt like this has pockets, and yet I struggle to find any in my jeans!"

"Looks like the designers knew what women really want," laughed Arya. "Anyway, it doesn't look like it needs altering for you at all! Do you want to keep it here or take it to yours?"

"Would you mind keeping it? My room is a mess... I don't want to crumple it or anything," admitted Sadie.

"I was actually hoping that you'll wear that for Diwali.".

"But aren't you just going to see your family? Why would I wear it?" asked Sadie.

"Oh, we're having a party this year! We're asking all the family to come to ours. We'll have all sorts of food there, drinks and family fun! We wanted to invite your family too."

"Yes! There's nothing I'd love more than to party with you and be involved in your celebrations!" replied Sadie, happy that she now got to party with Arya.

Arya paused for a moment, wondering whether it was worth mentioning something else. But no matter what answer Arya came to, she always came back to the same conclusion; that she shouldn't hide her friends and decided to mention Maya, again.

"I was also thinking of inviting Maya too... I thought it would be really nice to have us all together. You're both important to me. What do you think?"

Sadie's gleeful face changed in an instant. Why was Arya so obsessed with Maya all of a sudden? It aggravated her so much. Trying not to roll her eyes and let the scowl on her face show, she turned away, taking a few deep breaths to steady herself. October was a while away, things could change before Diwali comes, Sadie thought. Maybe Arya wouldn't be friends with Maya by then, maybe something will happen that will break their friendship. Maybe she could do something…

This was the only reassurance Sadie could give herself and she was hopeful that by the end of it all, Maya will just be a blip in their friendship and nothing more. Feeling satisfied with her own words of comfort, Sadie turned back to Arya and simply smiled.

Arya smiled back. Another successful name drop. She was happy her plan was working and hoped that in due time they could all be friends. That's all she wanted. The more Sadie got used to the idea of Maya, the more she'd accept that Maya was a part of her life. Arya felt like Maya was a one in a million friend, and she wasn't ready to lose someone like that. So, Sadie had to deal with it, in whatever way she needed to. Arya just hoped that Sadie would understand.

Again, Sadie was in a different world than Arya. It was chaotic and sad. Desperately wanting to change the conversation, Sadie started to scan through all the other dresses sprawled on the bed. Holding each one delicately in her hand, wishing she could keep them all. She made Arya wear one and then they danced around the room like two queens dancing through a royal palace. Roleplaying a Romeo and Juliet style scene off Arya's spiral staircase. Sadie's mood lifted once again, and she was back to normal.

Arya always appreciated the enthusiasm Sadie showed towards her culture, even if she hadn't any herself. But she was learning too and so was Sadie. On occasion, Sadie would ask Arya's parents a thousand questions: why they celebrated different things, why there were so many Gods and whether they could teach her how to make an authentic Indian dish. Arya's parents adored Sadie and answered every single one.

After Sadie dressed back in her clothes, she and Arya took Bailey out for a walk. He zoomed as soon as he saw Arya grab his lead off the hook and started whining when she took too long.

Eventually, they arrived at their favourite park and spent the rest of the afternoon there, relaxing by the lake and soaking in the rays while Bailey played fetch with them. Sadie felt at peace, looking over at Arya who was beaming, taking in the warm summer sun. Life couldn't be better. What was she even worried about? Nothing could come between them.

Even though they spent the entire afternoon together, Sadie still eagerly waited for their nightly call. Hoping that now she had seen Arya after all this time, she assumed they'd return back to their routine. But Sadie had been waiting for an hour now, and Arya hadn't called.

Time moved on and as the seconds ticked by, Sadie began to feel increasingly irritated. and her temper started to rise. Where had Arya gotten up to? Why was she way off schedule? What was more important than Sadie? Feeling impatient, and fed up with waiting, she called instead but it was swiftly rejected. Sadie was shocked, thinking about who else Arya was calling when she received a text soon after.

Hey, sorry I'm on the phone with Maya atm. Hope that's okay... I can call you later?

Sadie screamed into her pillow with pent up rage. Questions now flooded her mind. How could Maya think it was okay to come between two best friends, between a friendship that was already complete? Why was Maya determined to mess everything up? Why was Maya even around?

Not only was she angry at Maya, but she felt bitter and annoyed towards Arya too, for allowing this to happen. How could she let someone else in? They were perfect the way they were, Sadie believed she was enough.

And just like that, toxic thoughts started to sprout in her already clouded mind. After a while, Sadie laid down on her pillow, feeling crestfallen. Eyes wide open, staring into the dark. Finally, she fell asleep with a heavy heart and a mind full of tumultuous storm clouds.

Chapter 4

The next day came, and Arya decided to see Maya. It had felt like a millennium had passed since they last met, which was exactly how Sadie had felt when she hadn't seen Arya for a while.

After Arya got ready, she went downstairs to have breakfast. Her go-to food was porridge with honey and blueberries. Bailey did his tippy taps with his paws on the floor watching her eat. She knew exactly what he wanted; a burst of blueberry sweetness. Arya threw three blueberries towards him, and he caught all of them in his mouth without a beat.

It was a delightful, fresh and summery day, so Arya decided to bring Bailey with her. She updated Maya on the plan and carried on being a busybody, while she waited for a reply. Arya washed up and while she was thinking about the upcoming week, her phone pinged. It was from Maya.

Yeeees, I need a Bailey hug! Who wants to see you anyway? Just kidding!

Arya rolled her eyes playfully as she replied and made her way towards the front door. Clasping Bailey's leash on, they were ready for their day. As soon as Arya stepped out of the house the sun wrapped around her like a comfort blanket. The warmth of this summer day lifted Arya onto cloud nine, feeling within her that this summer would have a lifetime of memories. With a spring in her step, they both paced down the street. Bailey led in front, with his golden head cocked to the side watching a butterfly flutter ahead of him. He started huffing when he couldn't catch up with it and it flew away, looking back at Arya as if he blamed her, she found it hilarious.

She received another text, but this time it was from Sadie.

Fancy hanging out? Was thinking of heading to the pier for a dip in the sea!

Arya sighed, knowing she would have to say that she couldn't. She hated saying no to people. Arya was very much a 'yes' person. She quickly text back saying that she was busy but would see her tomorrow. Arya definitely did not mention Maya, feeling like her name had been mentioned a few too many times in the last couple of days. She didn't want to push her luck. Then she put her phone away and turned into Maya's street. Arya got a text back from Sadie but ignored the reply. Standing at the foot of Maya's house, she knocked on the door. Trying to ignore Bailey's incessant pulls on his leash, as he was desperately trying to get away and run towards the park.

"Bailey, sit still!" Arya told him.

He gave her the puppy eye look but listened to her and sat down looking sulky. Arya thought that he was such a diva and was about to ruffle his fur when Maya opened the door.

"Hey Ari! You ready? I packed some smoothies for us. It's strawberry and banana!" said Maya excitedly.

Arya smiled at Maya's new nickname for her. She liked it.

"Ooh can't wait to try it." with a smile on her face.

As soon as Bailey saw his new friend, he started barking and bouncing up at her desperate for attention. He was so excited to see her, his tail was no longer visible anymore, it was moving that much! Maya crouched down, brought him in for the biggest hug ever and rubbed his belly, that's what he was looking for the most. Bailey was so content with his rubs, he started drooling all over his fur.

"So, which park does Bailey want to go to?" cooed Maya.

Arya rolled her eyes laughing.

"You're the one I learned this from! Besides, he is a baby. My fluffy baby."

Arya playfully pushed her. They then chatted about Arya's upcoming trip and wandered into Crimson Lake Park. The park acquired this name due to the brilliant appearance of the lake in the autumn. When the once golden leaves turned orange and a deep red, they gracefully fell from the towering trees and landed atop the surface of the lake. Making the water look like it ablaze with flames. It was incredibly breathtaking and such a memorable sight to see. It even became famous nationally; people would flock to the park at the end of September to October to see the lake in its red glory. And then when the end of the month dawned, the park became the place to be. It had become the perfect Halloween attraction. The trees also had the sweetest smell and the darkest bark of all trees.

They wandered around the bank of the lake, gazing at the shimmering water reflecting the glorious sun rays. The air around them was transcendent and peaceful. And when Bailey became impatient with being on the lead, the girls settled down under the sweet trees and let him roam free for a while. Taking in the surroundings and its sounds. Like the gentle sway of the lake's waters to the booming barks of all the dogs on a chase and the cheering of a Mommy and Baby class.

Arya took a deep breath and felt a wash of serenity fill her with glee. Summer was her favourite time of year. She gazed lovingly at Bailey walking back to her, his ruffled fur aglow with the sun, looking like a lion. But he wasn't alone, a little puppy was following him. As Bailey laid next to Arya, the puppy copied him.

"Hey little one, where did you come from?" questioned Arya, scratching its head. She checked whether it was a girl or a boy. It was a gorgeous, chocolate brown girl, with piercing blue eyes, but she had no collar. Arya wondered whether she was a stray.

"Aww, look at this little nugget. Such floppy ears too!" laughed Arya. "Hey Maya, isn't she adorable? I can't see anyone around though..." she wondered, gazing in the distance.

But there was no one around, other than the moms in the class.

"Should we see if anyone owns her?" asked Arya.

"Sure!" replied Maya.

They asked, but to no avail. They wandered around the whole park, but no one claimed her.

"I think we should take her to the vets. She doesn't have a collar, but she might have a chip?" wondered Maya.

Arya nodded in agreement.

The girls took her with them. Maya put Bailey back on his leash and Arya held the chocolate lab in her hands, who laid there calmly and started licking her fingers. Just as they were walking out of the park entrance, Sadie was walking across the road with Candy and Floss.

Sadie glanced across the road and her body suddenly had a rush of cold air coarse through her. In front of her eyes, she saw her supposedly *busy* best friend and Maya together. It made her blood boil, and her body feel like ice at the same time. They were slowly reaching the same spot and her heart felt like it was erratically beating.

Sadie approached Arya and Maya.

"Hey Sades! What are you doing here?"

"Oh, taking the dogs out for a walk. Since I had nothing else to do today. Didn't you say you were busy?"

"Yeah, I was busy with Maya."

"Yeah, sorry Sadie! I just wanted to spend some time with Ari and then she brought Bailey along..." chimed Maya.

Sadie scrunched her nose up at "Ari". She felt grossed out at this name. How someone else felt they were close enough to give her best friend a nickname. Arya was already short as it is.

"Didn't you just spend the entire wedding together?" questioned Sadie.

This took Arya back by surprised. It seemed petty.

"Well, Indian weddings are a bit chaotic, you wouldn't understand. So, no, we didn't spend every minute together," replied Arya, matching Sadie's tone.

That stung Sadie. But Arya carried on.

"We already had plans to just hang out. I decided to take Bailey with us to the park and then we found this little girl all alone with no collar. We're just going to see if she's chipped. Do you want to come?" asked Arya.

"No thanks. I'll leave you be. You seem to be *so* busy," said Sadie, side-eyeing Maya, who was busy stroking the puppy to defuse the tension. "I've got things to do anyway. Bye." Sadie walked off and left the girls. Once she was out of earshot, Maya piped up.

"Wowwww. So, that wasn't awkward at all. What's got into her? Also, what was up with her face? It looked like she smelt poo right under her nose."

"Umm, I don't know what came over me. I've never been so snappy with her before..."

"Well, she kinda deserved it. She was being petty, Arya," replied Maya.

Arya stood with deep thought. "She probably just thought I was doing something more important. It'll be fine."

"Still, she doesn't need to be like that. You're just with someone else; it's not like you lied either..."

"Yeah, but I think that might be what the problem is. Me being with you. I don't know how she feels about it. Since we're like best, best friends and there hasn't been anyone else before," started Arya.

Arya paused for a moment and then took a huge, deep sigh and felt something in her to carry on talking. Maybe it was her conscience telling her to unload her worries off her chest, or maybe Arya just couldn't hold it back any longer. Either way, she knew she could trust Maya and she wouldn't judge her. So, she let it all out.

"To be honest, I'm feeling really uneasy about all of this. Like I don't want to keep hiding our friendship, which is why she knows about it now. But I was so scared to tell her...how is that normal? And when it was finally out, I don't know, I just got a weird vibe from her and could tell she was holding something back. I don't know whether it's because this is all new to her. Since we never really felt the need to spend time with others, because we were enough. But since I made friends with you guys, it's just been so much fun. Maybe she just doesn't feel the same... I'll ask her one time. I can't always be her only friend y'know? I just hope that she doesn't find it too hard without me when the time comes."

Arya finally took a breath. It was cathartic.

Maya blinked a few times, clearly not expecting Arya to have unloaded all of this. "I didn't realise you felt this way... Friendships are meant to be easy, especially if you've been best friends for as long as you two have. Are you ever going to tell how you truly feel?"

"I honestly don't know. I thought we understood each other so well, but right now...I can't read her. For the first time, I feel like we're not on the same wavelength. And our friendship feels a little weird. Maybe I'm overthinking it. Or maybe we're just growing up now...".

Sadie felt flustered as she walked through the park, completely ignoring the struggle the dogs were facing trying to keep up with her. She was supposed to have a relaxing stroll under the sun, but that was no longer happening. A horrible feeling of betrayal was sitting in the pit of her stomach, knowing that Arya had lied to her just to hang out with Maya.

Now, having angrily powered through the park to the other side without realising, pure annoyance filled her mind. All towards how ignorant Arya was. Ignorant about how Sadie should be her only best friend and no one else. Why did she even need Maya?

Sadie stopped walking just as she was about to turn the corner on the street and took some deep breaths to calm herself down. The dogs sat down panting as they exhausted themselves. After a few deep breaths, she felt calmer. Her holiday with Arya was coming up, so she decided to think about that instead. Reassuring herself that it would just be her and Arya together having the time of their lives and no one else would be stealing her away. After repeating this over and over, it sank in, and relief washed over her. Soon it was going to be a blissful two weeks, with no third wheel.

And like that, a switch was flipped in her brain, and she was her bright self again. Now with a spring in her step as the anger blew away, Sadie turned a corner and noticed a new shop. She casually walked over to it, her curiosity leading the way and saw it was a cute boutique shop called Daisy's. Intrigued, she decided to have a look. Maybe she could buy something for herself as a pick me up. Quickly tying Candy and Floss's leads outside, she walked in.

"I won't be long girls, don't miss me too much!".

As she opened the door, a sharp ring sang through the shop and a cinnamon smell swept over Sadie. She breathed in and felt like her body lightened up and her shoulders relaxed. The smell of cinnamon instantly reminded her of Christmas; her favourite time of the year and she also loved the smell of the spice.

"Hiya, welcome to Daisy's! Can I help you with anything?" chirped a cheery, small woman. She had blonde ringlets that were half tied up with daisy clips dotted around her hair. She smelled sickly sweet, and her cheeks were enhanced with a rosy blush.

"Oh hi. I'm alright thanks, just looking around."

The owner deflated a little but managed to smile and let Sadie wander around. Sadie thought about whether many people came here. It seemed pretty well stocked and the shop was empty. Her eyes wandered over the shelves that were filled with floral candle holders, coasters, vases, napkins and teddies. The shop was flower power heaven and Sadie loved everything about it. The vibrant pinks and yellow colours adorned the shop and everything in here screamed "buy me!".

She noticed a stack of shelves with sequin pillows that revealed something underneath when brushed the other way. Sadie was curious so she picked up a turquoise sequin pillow and started brushing them over and a blue flower was brought to life.

"That's a blue hydrangea, they're beautiful flowers! Each pillow has a flower corresponding to the colours of the sequins. Isn't that neat?!" the rosy-cheeked lady squealed.

Sadie edged away.

"That's err lovely, thanks for telling me that." She said and walked hurriedly towards the back end of the shop. Sadie was getting slightly irritated with the owner as she kept watching over her shoulder every time, she went to pick something up.

As she was about to make her way out of the shop, something glistened in the corner of her eye and grabbed her attention. Sadie turned back and wandered towards a shelf that held dainty bracelets with jewels adoringly placed in the middle of a daisy, on a chain. They were called 'Daisy Chains', this made Sadie smile.

They were either gold or rose gold and the jewels were the colours of each birthstone. Sadie searched through the bracelets until she found sapphire, which was the birthstone for September. The month that she and Arya were born. The deep blue dazzled her eyes and grabbed her heart. She had to get it. Without a second thought, she grabbed two, so she could gift one to Arya as best friendship bracelets. She knew that Arya was going to be stunned by it just as much as she was. But secretly Sadie had another reason for buying it: to show everyone that the two of them were the best of friends.

She gently held them in her hand as she walked back through the shop to the counter. The owner quickly dashed behind it and beamed as she took the bracelets off Sadie.

"Oh, these are gorgeous! I love sapphire, such a beautiful and tranquil colour. Who are these for?" she asked.

"They're for me and my best friend. We were born on the same day, in the same month! She's going to love this," answered Sadie. Feeling like she had to tell the whole world that she has a special best friend.

The owner just smiled sweetly and delicately wrapped them in cotton and popped them in their own individual plush grey bags. Everything about the bracelet and the wrapping was delicate and gorgeous to look at. Sadie paid for the bracelets and placed them carefully in her shoulder bag. And as soon as she stepped back out into the warm, gentle breeze, she felt repurposed. Sadie took the dog leashes off the post and walked down the street, heading towards Arthur's. Now beaming under the sun, knowing she had the best present ever in her bag. Feeling content within herself for once.

Chapter 5

Arya and Maya walked in silence back to Maya's place. The vets found no chip, so Maya took her back instead of leaving her there. They'd put up posters tomorrow, in hopes of reuniting the puppy with her owner. Arya hoped Maya's parents wouldn't mind keeping her for a few days.

On their walk home, Arya hadn't said much after bumping into Sadie. She only spoke to the vets, and after that she seemed lost. Like the whole world was on her shoulders.

"Are you alright?" asked Maya.

"Yeah. I'm fine."

"*Fine?* Come on, we all know what that means," persisted Maya. "Are you still thinking about Sadie?"

"I don't know...just got a weird feeling in my stomach. I know she was upset when she saw us, and it'll probably be awkward when I see her next. We also have the holiday coming up next week, god knows what that's going to be like..." Arya stopped talking, her emotions started bubbling and she couldn't compose herself any longer.

Sadness started to set in, her eyes started to tear up and her lip quivered ever so slightly. Maya noticed this sudden change in Arya and stopped her from walking, brought her in for a tight hug, reassuring Arya in the hope of calming her down.

"Hey, it's okay! It'll be fine, she will be fine, I promise. You're best friends, it'll blow over and will be like nothing happened. And if it's not, then you've got me. I'll always be here for you no matter what. But...maybe you should mention this to her," suggested Maya, "if it's stressing you out this much?"

Arya felt safe in Maya's hug, it eased her mind, and it stopped buzzing. Her heartbeat stopped beating erratically and once she took a deep breath, it felt like she exhaled out all the negative energy.

"Thank you. That really means a lot. I thought she was okay with it yesterday, now I'm not so sure. And I feel like if I talk to her, it'll just end badly. Maybe I'll talk to her after the holiday, I really don't want to ruin things for anyone."

Arya felt better after talking about her worries. Her new friend had been so supportive and helpful in trying to clear her worried and tired mind, she could see them being friends for life. Maya also tried to make Arya understand that she shouldn't be worrying about it so much. Having other friends wasn't the end of the world and Sadie was the one at fault. But then again, being told to stop stressing was always easier said than done. After a couple of minutes of being so lost in her thoughts, Arya realised that she had completely forgotten about the chocolate lab that was sleeping in her arms. Looking down at her breathing silently, Arya felt much happier.

"Animals really are good de-stressors," she sighed.

They carried on walking to Maya's with a tired Bailey in tow. As they approached the door, Maya's Dad, Rahul, pulled up on the drive, beeping his horn to scare them, but it startled the puppy instead who started yapping at the noise.

"Who's this little one?" asked Rahul as he was getting out of the car.

"We haven't given her a name yet, but we think she's a stray! She came up to us at the park," answered Maya.

"Soo, what is she doing here?"

"Oh um, I said to the vets that I'd take her home while I try to find her owners and if she didn't have any...I was hoping we could keep her." Maya gave her Dad her own puppy dog eyes.

Rahul walked around the car to them and took the puppy out of Arya's arms. She started to lick his face but then got bored and tried to bite his nose.

"Hm... It's a lot to take on, as well as all the other pets we have. But...I have to say she really is adorable, and I've always wanted a dog. Although, you'll have to ask your Mom first."

Maya gave a big sigh of relief. "Okay!"

Arya wondered if her Mom would be easy to sway. They walked into the house to the sound of erratic chirping and bells ringing. Maya's cat was winding up her budgies in their cage, trying to swat at them, and they were trying to nip him back.

"Hey! Leo stop that!" shouted Maya.

Bailey started barking at Leo, making him jump with fright. Maya left Bailey in the hall and hurried over to check if her budgies were okay. As she opened the cage door, they flew out onto her shoulder. One was a fluorescent yellow, with blue flecks dazzling the neck, orange feathers interlaced into her yellow wings and a vibrant red beak. Her other budgie was a soft baby blue with white and black freckles dancing along with its feathers.

"Are you okay Blue? What about you Banana?" cooed Maya. Both the budgies chirped away musically and nudged her cheeks, gently nipping them to show her they were okay.

Arya then put the chocolate lab down, who immediately ran to Bailey.

"We should give her a temporary name, don't you think?" asked Maya. "Ooh, how about Choco, like chocolate chip?"

Arya side-eyed her. "Umm, no. That's the most unimaginative name you could think of."

"Urgh, fine. You come up with one then!"

Arya thought for a while. "How about Coco?"

"Like that's any better," argued Maya, playfully.

But the puppy barked at this name, and the girls knew that it was meant to be.

"Well, I guess she likes the name," said Maya. "That's that then!"

Arya went to pick Coco off a very patient Bailey, who had just let her bite his ears as he was trying to rest.

"Hey little Coco, this might be your new home," she whispered. She snuggled Coco for a moment before putting her down again. Then she grabbed Bailey's leash and headed for the door.

"I'm going to leave now. Bailey's probably hungry and needs a bath. He's starting to smell. Maybe he got it from you?" joked Arya.

Maya rolled her eyes. "You're sooo funny. Anyway, I'll print off some posters for Coco and then we can put them out tomorrow?"

"Sounds like a plan. See you later! Come on Bailey bear. Let's go home."

When Arya arrived home, she heard a bustle of conversation coming from the living room. She wondered who had come round. Before she went inside, she let Bailey go and he scampered to his water bowl.

Arya walked into a conversation with her Mom and Sadie. She didn't know Sadie was going to be here; she hadn't told her. After how bitter she'd acted towards her and Maya, Arya didn't think she'd see Sadie for a couple of days, let alone a couple of hours later. It felt like Sadie couldn't seem to make her mind up about whether she was annoyed with Arya or not.

"Hey Arya! Been waiting for you!" beamed Sadie.
Arya was so confused.

"Er...hi? I didn't know you were going to come over...".

"I just decided to come over, I've got a surprise for you," hinted Sadie.
Arya smiled and sat beside her, to avoid any awkwardness in front of her Mom, who was busy talking about their holiday.

"Not long till we go away now. Are you girls excited?" asked Arya's Mom, Aashi.

"Oh yeah! I just want to buy all the Harry Potter merch!" replied Sadie.

Sadie and Aashi chatted excitedly about their upcoming trip, while Arya sat there with a blank stare, but a smile on her face. Utterly baffled at how Sadie was here acting like nothing had happened, after showing such icy behaviour towards her and Maya. Was it even the same Sadie? Arya quickly text Maya to tell her what was going on.

Sadie is at my house right now. She didn't even tell me she was coming round. And she seems totally normal too... Bit weird, right?

When she looked up, Sadie was staring at her with an intense glare.
"You alright, Sades?" questioned Arya.
"Yeah, just waiting for your answer."
"What answer...? Sorry, did you ask me something?" replied Arya.
"I asked what you were more excited about."
"Oh! Oh...sorry. Umn, probably getting to sketch new things. Like the castle in Magic Kingdom or something from the Harry Potter World. I don't know," mumbled Arya, shrugging her shoulders.

Arya wondered whether she was being too paranoid and stubborn, because Sadie had clearly moved on from earlier and maybe she should too. It's not like Arya did something terrible, although Sadie did seem to be more possessive now. Before she could think anymore, Aashi wandered out of the room and left Sadie and Arya in silence, alone. Arya decided to ask Sadie whether she was okay, to break the ice a little.

"How're you? How was your walk with Candy and Floss?"

"It was tiring, but we found this cute little boutique that makes these lovely floral trinkets," said Sadie. "I actually got you a bracelet from there. Here."

She let the bracelet fall from the plush bag into her palm. With shaky hands, she delicately clasped the lock of the bracelet around Arya's arm. Positioning the sapphire jewel to the centre of her wrist, so it would catch Arya's attention first and dazzle in her eyes.

A gasp escaped Arya's lips.

"Oh wow, this is so beautiful. Sadie, you shouldn't have. I don't know what to say..."

Sadie beamed.

"It's nothing. I got one too! They'll be a token of our friendship. The best friendship around and everyone can see how interlocked we are and will always be."

Something about what Sadie said made Arya feel weird, but she quickly let it slip from her mind. She couldn't stop staring at how beautiful the bracelet was. It was so dainty and intricate. Looking closer at the chain, she noticed it had a swirl pattern etched in it. It looked like two branches entwining themselves around each other. When the rose gold chain caught the light of the setting sun, it glimmered and twinkled, and the sapphire jewel shimmered like ocean waves. Arya fell in love with it and her worries about Sadie began to melt away. And she gave her the biggest hug she could muster.

"I love it! Thank you, so much!" beamed Arya.

Sadie just smiled back and was about to ask Arya if she could put the other bracelet on her, but Arya spoke first.

"Hey, I need to go wash Bailey bear, you wanna help?"

"Yes! Nothing is more fun than Bailey bath time. But you have to catch him first!"

"That's why I need your help," winked Arya.

She carefully took off the bracelet and placed it back in the bag, because she didn't want it to get wet. The girls then started walking to the kitchen where they last saw Bailey, but he wasn't there. Arya wondered about whether he heard the word 'bath' and bolted for it, hiding somewhere in the house. She decided to go to his hiding place and motioned Sadie to follow her upstairs. However, Sadie heard a ping and glanced down at Arya's phone that had lit up and saw Maya had text Arya.

That is weird...she makes you feel guilty and then pops up at your house? What did you say to her?

Sadie frowned, which then turned into a scowl. Her poignant voice echoed in her mind. Why were they talking about her? And she didn't make anyone feel guilty. That was Arya's own guilt for choosing Maya over her.

53

Without thinking, she unlocked the phone and deleted the text with a quick swipe. Arya wouldn't know any different. Sadie had figured out the pin code a while ago; Arya had no idea. The problem with Sadie was that she never thought of the consequences of her actions.

There. Dealt with.

After positioning the phone in the exact position it was left in, Sadie hurried after Arya.

The mission to wash Bailey was always a tough one because he didn't like to be washed. He liked playing in the mud and jumping in puddles on his walks or chasing cats down the street and up the tree. But he never liked being clean. Once Arya spent an hour trying to find him, and it turned out that he was hiding behind a huge plant pot in the garden, how he got out to the garden is still a mystery. This time, however, they were determined find him and make sure they have no trouble in washing him. The girls went into Arya's parent's room and found a bulge under the bed covers.

"Hm," said Arya loudly. "I wonder who's under the covers."

There was a slight movement, meaning Bailey heard them and his tail started wagging. Arya went along one side of the bed and Sadie the other, then they both jumped on the bed and started kissing Bailey. He started barking, the sheet now being pulled off him and he excitedly licked their faces. With all his might, he quickly jumped off and ran, but Sadie bolted towards him and grabbed his collar. He looked at her with sad eyes and before you know he was in the bath all suds up.

About thirty minutes after what was apparently the longest and most traumatic bath of Bailey's life, Arya dried him with a hairdryer. Sadie looked longingly at her. She gazed at Arya's empty wrist where the bracelet had briefly been and then glanced at Arya's odd facial expressions she made trying to dry Bailey. Arya noticed Sadie looking at her and lifted her eyebrow.

"Sup Sades?"

"Oh, nothing. Just wondering when you'll put your bracelet back on. It's so beautiful and I don't want it to stay in the bag," answered Sadie. "Also, would you mind putting mine on for me? I couldn't get it on myself…"

"Sure… let me just finish drying Bailey. I'll put yours on and you can put mine on."

Arya smiled at her. She then burst out laughing watching Bailey attack the hot air blowing over him, with his lips and ears flapping in the wind. Once he was released from the bath time shenanigans, he sprinted off downstairs to his favourite teddy; a cuddly, once baby blue teddy bear, that squeaked and smelled like blueberries. It was now faded, no longer squeaked and smelled like Bailey's stinky breath. However, he still cherished the teddy as if it were the only toy in the world.

Arya and Sadie followed him down, so they could get their bracelets. Arya looked at him, chewing his bear.

55

"One time I hid that bear at the top of my wardrobe before I went to school, just to see whether he'd find it. And when I got home, I found Bailey in my room looking up at my wardrobe. Whining with his leg in the air as if he was trying to paw at it. I felt so bad." She grimaced. "I don't know why he loves it so much, he can sniff it out like a bloodhound!"

"Who cares about the dog," scoffed Sadie. "Let's put our bracelets on!"

Arya looked taken back. Sadie had never called Bailey 'the dog' before.

"You mean Bailey. Not 'the dog' and I care," replied Arya, coldly.

Sadie looked heartbroken at Arya's tone and was about to say something when Aashi walked in.

"He loves it so much because it reminds him of you. We won it at an arcade when you were little, and you never let it out of your sight. You slept, ate and you even tried to bathe with it," said Aashi.
Arya smiled at this and kissed him on his soft, golden hair. "I love you Bailey bear, never change."

Bailey started licking her face and wagging his tail. Suddenly, Arya felt Sadie watching her and she then remembered what she was waiting for.

"Oh. Forgot about your bracelet," said Arya.

She went to get the bags and tipped them to drop the bracelets into her hand, then tied Sadie's around her wrist quickly and tried to put hers on by herself. Sadie reached out to help her, but Arya stepped back and fastened it herself. Sadie just silently stood there, looking crestfallen and put her hands awkwardly by her side.

"There, all done. Thank you for the bracelet, it's really lovely," smiled Arya tightly. She looked around, sighed and said, "Umm, I have some important things to do, so I'll catch you later?"

Sadie paused and blinked a few times. "Yeah, yeah sure. I'm glad you liked the bracelet."

Arya then walked her to the door and let her out. As soon as the door closed, Sadie burst into tears and her hands started shaking. She felt so frustrated that she didn't think before she spoke. Fists balled up with anger, her tears continued to fall, drop after drop. With a sharp tone, she told herself off and to grow a backbone. That it wasn't that big of a deal and Arya didn't mean it.

After a few moments, she took a deep breath and looked up to the sky. Just like her darkening mood, she saw threatening clouds slowly conceal the warm, golden sun. A dark shadow cast over her face and an ominous silence echoed through the air. Her tears had vanished, and she slowly walked home.

Chapter 6

Arya laid on her bed. It was 9pm and she was studying the bracelet, her arms held in the air, twisting it side to side, watching it move up and down her wrist. It was beautiful and thoughtful. However, she couldn't help thinking why Sadie would all of a sudden buy expensive matching bracelets. And right after being angry about her being with Maya.

They hadn't needed anything to prove they were best friends before, so why did they now? Paranoid thoughts started to creep in again. Maybe Sadie had an ulterior motive for this gift? Maybe she was trying to prove something?

But Arya tried not to let this thought get the better of her, paranoia wasn't good for anything other than ruining friendships.

Then again, Sadie was the reason why she started having them. They had always felt so secure in their friendship. Until now. Arya sighed sadly. Wondering if it was all her fault. She placed the bracelet back in the bag, turned over and grabbed her phone from under her pillow. Wondering why Maya hadn't texted her back, it had been hours now.

Hey, did you get my text?
Within a few seconds, there was a reply from Maya.

I did! I replied back, didn't you get it?
No, I didn't get it! When did you text back? What did you say?

She tapped her phone in thought, pondering over why she didn't get her text. It didn't make sense. But was she overthinking it? It was only a text after all, and sometimes they just don't come through.

Maya wrote, *I said how it was odd for her to make you feel guilty about being with me and then turn up at your house. And literally not that long after you text me!*

Like clockwork, another paranoid thought slithered its way back into Arya's mind. What if Sadie saw the text before she did and deleted it? Arya paused and contemplated this for a while. It was possible but also was out of character for Sadie.

It was getting so frustrating having these thoughts. She needed it to stop. Sadie didn't even know the pin, and she wouldn't ever invade her privacy. Sadie was turning into a lot of things, but Arya could never believe that she was sneaky or a liar. And yet, Arya just couldn't shake this weird feeling. She let out a huge sigh and replied. She placed her phone back under her pillow, pulled the covers up to her face and went soundly asleep.

As Arya slept, Sadie was wide awake, pondering what happened at Arya's, thinking about what Maya had said, and what she should do next. Her thoughts flitted back and forth. Was she on Arya's side or not?

I just bought her a beautiful bracelet, and she treats me like that! When did I make her feel guilty?

Through her anger and frustration, Sadie did have to admit that she had been cold and wasn't thinking when she said she didn't care about Bailey. Sadie knew how much Bailey meant to Arya; she shouldn't have been so careless. As that thought was settling into her head, something switched and she began focusing on Arya and Maya's friendship again, and how much she loathed it. Questioned flooded her mind.

What was the need for another girl friend?
Wasn't she enough?
Did Arya now find her boring?
Did Arya not like her anymore?
Did she need to seek validation from others?

Negative thoughts were firing in all directions in her mind. One after the other, over and over, the tension tore into her mind, and she needed to release it.

Knowing exactly what would work, she grabbed her book from the nightstand and dove headfirst, wishing she could transport herself into whatever imaginary world she wanted and stay there. And then she could live without the drama, without the troubling friendships and the pressure of the impending future. But the more she read her beloved fantasy books, the more disconnected she felt from the real world. Especially when she wasn't in the right frame of mind. But it was the only way she could magic away her bad thoughts.

Sadie had started to notice that the more negative she thought, the more hateful it made her on the inside. And she was already in Arya's bad books because of today. Buying those bracelets was to make up for one thing, but what could she do to make up for this? Or should she even make up anything? Sadie pondered over what she could do to apologise to Arya and then she thought that she should do just that. Apologise. She whipped out her phone and started texting ferociously like she had no time left in the world to write this one apology.

Hey, I'm really sorry about earlier, I was just too excited to get our bracelets on, I shouldn't have said that. I love Bailey too! Hope you're okay. See you soon?

She wouldn't be able to go to sleep without getting a text back, so she decided to stay up. But hours had gone by, and she hadn't received a reply. Her eyes were starting to droop and she couldn't keep them open any longer and soon enough she slowly drifted off to sleep.

The night wasn't peaceful though. Her clouded mind led to nightmares. It began with her on an isolated bridge with Arya. It was stormy and dark; the wind billowed around them and tensions seemed high. Hatred was pumping through Sadie's veins, and she wanted to hurt Arya. But before anything happened, she woke up with a start. Feeling really unsettled, she didn't dare close her eyes again, so she decided to lay awake in bed. Eventually, the sun appeared and shone in her bloodshot eyes. It felt cold. And she didn't feel like getting up and decided to stay as she was, not moving a muscle, for hours and hours.

"Sadie, come down! Arthur is here for you to walk the dogs," called Rose.

Sadie groaned and rolled off the bed, feeling exhausted from no sleep. She was also slightly annoyed that he was at the door so early. She wasn't in the mood to walk the dogs right now. But then she noticed the time; it was one in the afternoon. Sadie's mouth dropped in shock, she didn't realise how late it was and rushed downstairs.

"Woah, you look ruff," laughed Rose. "Get it? Ruff?"

Sadie rolled her eyes. "Wow Mom, good one."

Candy and Floss started barking and pulling on their leashes to get to Sadie.

"I'm so sorry I'm late," mumbled Sadie, guiltily. "I didn't realise the time, I'm really sorry."

"It's alright, Sadie," he winked. "You can make it up with a harder piano lesson!"

She faked a laugh and took the dogs off him. He then left and she flopped onto the floor, but this just made Candy and Floss jump on her.

"Oof. Alright, I deserved that," admitted Sadie.

"You'll have to put them in the garden while you get ready bub, I can't have them running all over the house." said Rose.

"Yeah, that's fine. I'll just go get ready."

Sadie begrudgingly retreated upstairs and got ready when she suddenly remembered that she hadn't checked her phone. Hoping that Arya had replied, she grabbed it from under the pillow but saw no text. She sighed and her stomach churned. Sickness started to squirm in her stomach again, and she desperately wanted to stop feeling like that. An idea then struck her. Now she had the dogs with her, maybe she could visit Arya with them, and they could all go on a walk together! They could go to the park and then she could show Arya the cute shop. Thinking it was such a brilliant idea, Sadie rushed back downstairs, startling the dogs who began jumping up at the window.

"Oh Sadie, they're getting impatient, take them out!" shouted Rose.

"Alright, alright! I'm just going to Arya's."

"That sounds lovely bub."

Sadie grabbed their leashes and took them outside. The sun was shining again. She hoped it would make her feel better, but it didn't. It felt irritable and cold. But at least she was with Candy and Floss, who always put a smile on her face, and she prayed it would do the same for Arya. She also hoped it might get her off the hook. As she turned into Arya's street, she walked past the quaint houses, under the blue flowers bustling in the trees and inhaled the smell of freshly cut grass. She saw someone walking down the street towards her and started to hear a booming bark. As she got closer, she felt her heart somersault, it was Arya and Bailey. They stopped short when they saw Sadie.

However, Candy and Floss had other ideas and bolted towards Bailey, pulling Sadie with them.

"Girls slow down!" shouted Sadie, nearly tripping up, but Arya caught her and stood her back up. Greeting her with a smile.

"Hey Sades."

"Hey."

The silence was killing Sadie, but before she could apologise, Arya spoke first.

"I'm sorry about not replying to your text. I was going to, but thought I'd come to you instead." She then gestured to Bailey. "Also, sorry for being short with you yesterday, I was just upset."

"No, I'm sorry. Not everything is about me, and Bailey bear is important," replied Sadie.

They both smiled at each other and hugged. As they let go, they saw Candy and Floss licking Bailey and messing up his fur. His eyes were on Arya, begging for her to rescue him.

"Hey, so I was thinking," Arya began, "Maybe you could help us put up posters to find Coco's owner? You know, the chocolate lab that found us yesterday? I know this is all new to you, but it would be nice if you spent some time with Maya. You guys did get along in school and we've become good friends now and I want all of us to get on." Arya looked at her hopefully.

Sadie thought for a few seconds. It wouldn't hurt to spend time with Maya, and if she meant that much to Arya then she should try. And as Arya said, they did get on at school.

"Sure. That would be nice," Sadie finally said.

Arya smiled, feeling relieved.

The girls walked side by side in silence, with their dogs yapping at each other, breaking the tension. Sadie realised their trip was only a couple of days away.

"Oh jeez, I forgot that I need to start packing! Have you started yours?"

"I haven't even thought about it to be honest. And now you've mentioned it, we don't have long left at all. Should we start this evening?" suggested Arya.

"Great! I'll definitely need help with what clothes to pack. I have more than I need!" laughed Sadie.

With a plan in mind and knowing her whole day was going to be spent with Arya, Sadie's mood lifted so high. Arya was all she needed.

The sun soon started to grow hotter as Arya walked, and she began to feel thirsty and needed something to cool her down. Luckily, they saw a pop-up truck with some slushies in a car park that was now a street food marketplace. Someone was finally making use out of the deserted car park, with the sole intention of bringing more character into the neighbourhood and it did so well. Especially in the summer. They had all sorts of food trucks there that served all types of food from spicy tacos and refreshing smoothie bowls, to sweet treats that were every colour of the rainbow and mouth-watering mac and cheese.

They changed every month and Sadie and Arya tried to go each time, so they wouldn't miss out and could try everything. This time though they just wanted something to quench their thirst, so they wandered over to the slushie truck to see what flavours they had to offer.

There were four flavours: Bashful Berry, Tongue-tied Tango, Green with Envy Grape and Cool As Ice Cola. Arya liked the names; they made her giggle. She grabbed a Bashful Berry and Sadie bought a Green with Envy Grape and sat down on the bench in the middle of the car park. The three dogs were following each other round and round the bench while the girls slurped on their slushies. Arya smiled at them, while Sadie quietly watched Arya beam. She loved the way Arya's cheeks would crinkle when she smiled, how her eyes glowed with happiness and the cute little laugh she made. Arya glanced over at Sadie, and she quickly looked away.

"You know I love you, Sades. No one could ever replace you. You know that right?" asked Arya. She knew it was something she needed to say to reassure a paranoid Sadie.

"I know, I know. But thank you for saying that it means a lot."

She didn't want to tell Arya how she really felt right now. They had only just mended bridges and she didn't want to destroy them already. Arya was now scooping up the last bit of her slush with her tongue sticking out and her face full of concentration. Her tongue was coloured purple from the slushie, and Sadie wondered whether her tongue was green. She began sticking her tongue out, so she could see what colour it was, sliding it left and right to get a better view, when she heard a burst of laughter. Arya had been watching and recording her too.

"Hey look! I put a cat filter on you!"

"Oh my god, let's see!"

Sadie moved next to Arya and watched the clip of her with pink cat ears and whiskers and couldn't help but laugh. It felt like old times, and Sadie's heart burst with glee.

"Don't post that!" moaned Sadie, jokingly.

They spent the next ten minutes messing around until Bailey started whining and getting fidgety. So, the girls threw their empty cups away and started making their way to Maya to pick up her and Coco. All three dogs walked in front of the girls, tails wagging in sync and barking to each other as if they were all in conversation. Candy started trying to eat a bee, Floss was trying to push her over and then Bailey strutted forward like he didn't know them. He then stopped short, crouched down and his tail became still. Arya nearly fell over him because she wasn't watching what he was doing.

"Oof. What is it? Is it a squirrel?!" asked Arya.

As soon as she said the word 'squirrel', his bark boomed, and he started jumping up and down with such eagerness to chase it. He bolted before Arya could say no, with the leash just slipping through her fingers. She started chasing after him, with Sadie, Candy and Floss in tow, the dogs were loving the chase. As Bailey turned the corner of the street and before Arya could grab onto the leash, she heard a small yapping noise growing louder and louder. She saw Bailey had stopped abruptly. His tail wagged excitedly; he had spotted Coco with Maya. It was amusing watching Coco trying to nip at Bailey, like she was telling him to calm down instead.

"Hey! How's she doing today?" asked Arya.

"She's great! Slept with me all night, it was so cute and then this morning she chased Leo up the cabinet. Such a hyper girl."

Then she saw Sadie follow behind Arya with her dogs.

"Hey Sadie," smiled Maya.

"Hey. How're you doing?" asked Sadie civilly.

"I'm good. Ready to put up these posters!" She laughed awkwardly.

Arya noticed that Sadie seemed more at ease than she did yesterday and less intimidated. She reached out for some posters of Coco, and Maya happily gave some to her. As long as Sadie stayed calm and civil, nothing bad would happen.

Chapter 7

All three girls were having a good time wandering around town putting up posters. The dogs were also getting along too, all yapping away at each other. Candy and Floss were fascinated with Coco, as if they had never seen a tiny puppy before. They would sniff her for a while and lift her ears with their noses.

The girls had put up nearly all their posters, so they decided to rest at a park so the dogs could be free. They bounded after each other like they had been tied up for days.

"Are you guys looking forward to your holiday?" asked Maya.

"YES! It is literally the only thing I've looked forward to this year. So much excitement, so little time!" rambled Arya excitedly.

"Me too, I can't wait to have so much fun with my best friend. Getting to spend all our time together. Just you and me and no one else," Sadie said to Arya.

Maya tilted her head and narrowed her eyes at what she said. Arya saw this and laughed awkwardly to avoid any tension building up.

"We can't forget our families too," laughed Arya, nervously.

"Yeah...you can't forget about them," replied Maya, curtly.

Sadie responded with polite laughter, but she wasn't joking. She wanted Maya to read between the lines and understand what she really meant. With no Maya or anyone else getting in between, Sadie would finally have Arya to herself.

Arya hadn't missed this trick either and it annoyed her greatly. She couldn't believe that Sadie was still being this petty. She just couldn't catch a break. Why did Sadie have to make everything awkward and make a big deal out of things? Especially in front of others. It was unnecessary. But Arya wasn't going to make a scene or mention it to her. She wanted to start the holiday on a high, especially with it being only a few days away.

"Alrighty!" she said, starting to usher them all along. "I think we should go start packing, we literally have the smallest amount of time left. And you know how your Mom is with repacking your stuff. She has to do things her way, so let's go! I'll talk to you later, Maya!"

They hugged and Maya said bye to Sadie, who brushed her goodbye off. Maya sighed, grabbed Coco and went home and Arya walked guiltily beside Sadie, trying to build up the courage to say something.

"Hey, Sades?" Arya started gingerly, "I don't think there was any need to say that. She knows we're best friends...it's not something you have to rub in, and it seemed unnecessary. Also, it's rude..."

And with that, she had opened the tin of worms. Arya just hoped it wouldn't backfire. It had to be said, especially after seeing the jealousy suddenly crop up in Sadie's personality in the last couple of days. Arya was fed up with it. Also, Arya knew that Maya was trying her best to brush off Sadie's digs but how long could Maya keep up with that?

Arya looked at Sadie and observed how her expression changed from bubbly to strained. Looking like she was thinking very intently about something. But Arya didn't understand what there was to think about, she was either rude or she wasn't. She watched Sadie open her mouth as if she were about to say something, but then she quickly closed it. This was repeated a few more times and Arya wondered whether she was trying to find the right thing to reply with.

Sadie sighed. "Sorry, I don't understand what you mean?"
Arya paused and replied. "Really? You really don't hear how you talk to her?"

"I honestly don't know what you're on about." laughed Sadie.

"You just...you just seem really petty with her. Whether you realise that or not, it's not okay. Not everything is a competition, and you don't even say bye to her properly...You seemed like friends last year, so what happened?"

Sadie rolled her eyes and simply said, "We were never friends. I was just being nice."

Wow, Arya thought.

She couldn't believe how immature Sadie was being. Her frustration with all this had reached boiling point, but Arya knew it was a losing battle, and no amount of arguing would get through to Sadie right now. All Arya wanted was for a real answer but knew that if she persisted for one it would annoy Sadie more and make things worse. She wasn't in the mood to deal with any more of Sadie's attitude.

Again, the thought of the holiday sprung to mind. She had to make sure nothing ruined it, and no drama was lingering in the air. It was their first getaway together since they were ten and it would be the last for a while. It had to be great.

Surprisingly, in all these years that they had been best friends, she never saw this side of Sadie and she just didn't know where it was coming from.

Sadie bumped Arya.

"Turn that frown upside down and get excited!" she chimed. "I've just got to drop the girls off back to Arthur's and then we'll go back to mine, okay?"

Arya left her intense thoughts aside and nodded. "Uh huh."

Arya watched Candy and Floss walk on each side of Bailey. They were all getting along nicely, despite Bailey being different and wondered why she couldn't have that with Sadie and Maya. Why couldn't they get along? She loved them both and wanted them to be nice to each other at least.

As they walked, the silence deafened Arya. Sadie was too busy looking at her phone to notice anything. Completely oblivious to the awkward tension that was rising in the air. It could be cut with a blunt knife. Eventually they reached Arthur's house and Sadie dropped off the girls, then skipped back down the path.

"Right!" she said cheerily. "Are you ready to start packing? I know I am!"

She grabbed Arya's hands and pulled her along and jabbered excitedly about what she was taking. What new clothes she bought and what books she be reading. Arya, however, was still deep in thought. Now wondering whether Sadie actually spoke to friends other than her. The thought bugged her like the sound of a buzzing mosquito that you couldn't find. She thought that it would be best to ask Rose about it. If anyone knew whether Sadie had more friends, it would be her. Arya then took a deep breath and cleared her mind for a bit. She needed to look forward to this, otherwise, she'll ruin it for herself.

"Are you going to buy any Minnie Mouse ears?" asked Sadie.

"Duh. Who goes to Disney World and doesn't buy ears?"

"I'm going to post every day to show people how much fun we're having together!" expressed Sadie, excitedly.

Arya paused. "Why do you need to show people that?"

"Oh. Just because... I don't know." Sadie pulled an expression Arya had never seen before. "Make them feel a little jealous?"

Arya's jaw tightened. This was another side of Sadie Arya just didn't recognise. Not only was she acting jealous herself, but she also wanted to make others feel jealous too. It didn't make sense.

Not long after this, they arrived at Sadie's house. Both her parents were back and there was thumping music coming from inside. Arya knew they were both having a good time. She always thought that they were adorable together. Whenever she had a down day, spending just ten minutes with them would lift your spirits entirely. Sadie opened the door and raced upstairs. Before Arya could follow, she let Bailey out into the garden. Arya approached Rose quickly.

"Hey! I wanted to ask you something."

"Shoot!" said Rose. "I love a good question."

"Umm...does Sadie talk to anyone else? Like does she have other friends?"

Rose looked taken back, as if it wasn't a question she had ever heard.

"Oh. Err...y'know I don't think I've ever seen Sadie spend time with anyone other than you. She wouldn't really tell me anyway. She's been quite secluded recently. Why do you ask?"

"Just wondering. No reason."

Her fears were confirmed. Sadie didn't seem to have any other friends, which made this whole situation worse. And Arya didn't know how to proceed. Friendships shouldn't be complicated. But it looked like theirs was turning out to be. Suddenly feeling like she had the world on her shoulders, Arya slowly walked upstairs, figuring out what to do next. She found Sadie in the spare room looking into a suitcase, with a huge pile of clothes next to it. And the sight of the room made her completely forget her worries within a second. The floor was covered with clothes and of course, books. More than the eye could see.

"Woah, you can't take all of this!" laughed Arya.

"Oh, damn. I didn't think you'd notice!"

"Here, I'll help you pick out the clothes you should really take," offered Arya.

The travesty of Sadie's packing lifted the mood instantly. Arya was no longer thinking about complicated friendships, Sadie was no longer

74

thinking about Maya and the tension had dissipated. They spent the next thirty minutes planning Sadie's outfits for the days and nights and a few extras for just in case. They had fun, Sadie pretended to catwalk and strut in a fashion show, just like the old days when it was just them two and the world was their oyster.

After deliberating how much stuff she should actually take, they finally started to pack everything in the suitcase. They tried to be as clever as possible about it – rolling clothes into shoes for example – but Sadie knew her Mom would repack. After they finished, they left for Arya's, so they could start helping her. As they were walking to her house, Sadie looked over at Arya's wrists.

"Did you forget to wear your bracelet?"

Arya looked down, her gut wrenching.

"Oh sorry! It slipped through my mind this morning. I just wanted to come by and see you."

Sadie smiled. She looked at her own bracelet and then grabbed Arya's hand and started skipping.

Arya laughed. "What are you doing?!"

"Come on, let's skip to yours!" giggled Sadie.

Arya gave in and skipped with Sadie. She let Bailey off his leash so he could be a little free, both humming to a song that brought back nostalgia. Blessing her with a warm feeling like sitting next to a burning wood fire, with the summer breeze wisping past them. Sadie wished it would always be like this, wishing the summer would never end and they would never grow old. She knew if she tried hard enough, this summer could just be about them two. She just needed to get rid of Maya, who had become an unexpected bump in her plan.

Finally, they stopped outside Arya's bright, sunflower-coloured door.

Arya sighed happily. "That was fun!!"

She opened the door and Bailey bolted into the house, booming down the hallway, into the garden where he found Kiaan, and began barking with happiness. The girls went up to Arya's room and saw her bed with clothes sprawled all over it.

Arya gasped. "What. The. Hell."

This was her idea of torture. She hated a messy room. Especially when it was hers.

"What's going on?!" she continued to gasp.
Aashi came rushing in, carrying a bunch of clothes with her.

"Sorry! Sorry! I was trying to pack the suitcases, and I guess I thought I could pack your clothes, but clearly, I can't!" She laughed nervously.

"We came back to sort my stuff! You didn't need to do anything." Clearly relieved, Aashi dropped the clothes and plonked on the bed, breathing a sigh of relief.

"Oh, I'm glad someone's happy with her actions. Now I have to clear all this mess off the floor!" joked Arya, trying to push her Mom off the bed.

But Aashi was having none of it and started tickling Arya, before dragging her on the bed. Both in a fit of giggles. Sadie watched with admiration, watching how blissfully easy it was for them to act like kids with one another. She loved the bond they had. Wishing with all her might that she could have an adoring relationship with her Mom, but it never felt sincere from her side when she tried. It always felt uncomfortable.

"Have you packed Sadie or is Rose going to try for you and fail as I did?"

"Me and Arya started but knew there was no point. So, we just put all my stuff together and Mom will do it herself, you know how she is. She has to have everything packed perfectly so it can all fit in."

"Rose likes to make sure no space is wasted!"

Sadie rolled her eyes. "Tell me about it."

Sadie sat down on the bed, wedged herself in between Arya and Aashi and sighed.

"I wish we were there now. I cannot wait more days. I just need to be there right now and let my stress fade away." Aashi raised one eyebrow.

"What do you have to be stressed about little one?"

"Oh...nothing," Sadie shrugged, trying to play it off. "It's just a saying."

Arya wondered whether she was telling the truth or not and whether that 'stress' was Maya. Either way she wasn't going to ask her. She didn't want any drama. Instead, Arya got up and walked up the staircase into her painting room, the one room where all her worries fade away. She felt at peace here and free from drama. It was her serenity.

Arya glanced over her artwork that she proudly displayed on her paint-splattered walls, smiling as she reminisced the days when she painted them. Her most beloved painting was a towering, magnificent tree that had each quarter of it corresponding to each season: spring, summer, autumn, and winter.

The painting began with spring. Where the air was light and free, the cherry blossoms blooming on the branches, the tiny shrubs looked full, and the birds were aflutter in a painted breeze. Then came summer, with the dazzling sun, crisp green leaves, clear skies, and the hint of a summer vacation plastered across the bottom. Autumn came billowing in and the leaves were painted with fiery oranges, scorching reds, and mellow yellows. The sky was warm and painted on the grass was a bonfire made to look like it was flickering away. She could almost hear the sound of the crackling fire.

Finally, the tree turned bare as winter blustered in. The snow had blanketed the ground and the heavy snow clouds filled the sky. The white was deafening and each snowflake that gently flowed down was intricately painted, each a unique shape. It was a remarkable piece of work, it filled Arya with pride, she couldn't let anything happen to it. It had taken her the longest time to sketch, draw, paint, and everything in between. No harm was to come its way.

After admiring her work, she moved past to what she came up here to get. Her favourite sketchbook and pencil. She thought it would be nice to see the snowy rooftops of Hogsmeade sketched in her book, or Cinderella's castle painted magically with a backdrop of scattered fireworks in vibrant colours. Once she got it, she made her way downstairs to see her Mom and Sadie lying on the bed chatting away. As she reached the bottom step, they both looked up to see why she had gone up to her art room.

"Just went to get my sketchbook!" said Arya, holding it up. "I can't go somewhere magical and not take this along with me!"

She then set it down on her desk, where she wouldn't forget to pack it later. Starting to feel more excited, she now felt this electrifying rush course through her. A holiday with Sadie, maybe it was what they need to get their friendship back to calm waters. No jealousy or snide comments. A revival.

Chapter 8

The next couple of days quickly went by, but Sadie felt like the nights dragged on. She had found it so hard to sleep because she was afraid to have nightmares, but wished it was closer to the big day. Arya however, slept soundlessly. It was early Saturday morning, the birds had started singing, the dewdrops on the grass were still glistening and the sky was crisp.

Seeping through the light curtains was a blinding cold ray of sun that dazzled the broken pieces of glass that made up Sadie's chandelier. The light reflected across the walls and beautiful colours sparkled in every corner, making the room feel like a shiny chrysalis. Even though it was early in the morning, Sadie woke up full of energy. Despite having another nightmare that had left her in a cold sweat, she couldn't let it dampen her spirit. Because today was the day, they started their long-awaited holiday! It was finally the day the girls had been waiting for.

She fumbled out of her bed with so much excitement she almost fell onto the floor, bursting out into laughter because she felt giddy like a little kid running after an ice cream van. On the top of her to-do list was having a quick shower. She could hear her parents bustling around, shouting at each other from different rooms, whether they had passports, locks for the suitcases, money and the tickets for the plane. They had been up much longer than Sadie had been, which made them feel even more stressed. She stood there and embraced the hot water cascading down her. Revitalising and freeing her from the paranoid thoughts about Arya and Maya that kept her awake for nights on end. There could finally be two weeks without

Maya, even the mere thought of her, butting in between Sadie and Arya. It was what she looked forward to most.

"SADIE! HURRY UP!" shouted Rose.

Rose had interrupted her thoughts and Sadie rolled her eyes. She thought her Mom was such a stress head, they had ages yet and all she wanted was a nice shower. But then came the banging on the bathroom door.

"Sadie, we have to leave in an hour. If you wanted a longer shower you should have gotten up earlier!"

Sadie begrudgingly stopped her shower, quickly dried herself and ran to her room. Slamming the door as she went. Then she ransacked her wardrobe, trying to find an outfit to wear to the airport. She wondered whether she should go in a cute floral dress, her comfy but cute loungewear or the standard top and jeans. After deliberating what to dress in, with a little pressure from her Mom, she decided to go in the cute, floral dress.

"You ready bub?" called Noah. "We're going to head off and meet at Aashi's now."

Sadie giggled and ran downstairs, ready for a trip of a lifetime with her best friend. There was nothing more exciting!

Meanwhile, Arya was getting all of Bailey's things together: his toys, food, treats and everything else. He was going to be staying with Maya for the two weeks they were away. She knew that Maya would take good care of him and preferred to have him stay with her on their first long holiday. Besides, Bailey would be much happier with her than being in an unknown environment. Maya's parents were the first to suggest it and Arya thought it was perfect! It also gave time for Bailey and Coco to bond too.

Getting Bailey's things together was the last thing Arya needed to do before they set off. She was always on top of everything. Making sure she had everything she needed in her backpack, she added an extra snack, and she was ready to go. Aashi and Arya's Dad, Kunal, were loading the suitcases into the car and Kiaan was in his car seat, already falling asleep. He was trying so hard to stay awake, but every now and then you'd see his head bob up and down. Arya took pictures, as you do.

As she put her backpack on the floor, she heard a car pull up and saw it was Maya and her Dad. Maya bounced out of the car and jumped into Arya's arms.

"Ohh, I'm going to miss you so much! I can't believe you're leaving me!" cried Maya, pulling a sad face.

"It's only for two weeks! It'll fly by, especially with Bailey bear, he'll keep you on your toes! He and Coco will have fun chasing after Leo! You'll have the best time trying to break it up." Arya winked.

"Oh god, I am not looking forward to it, it'll be like bickering siblings… but I also can't wait to get endless Bailey hugs." smiled Maya.

Arya took Maya's hand, and they walked towards the house to get Bailey, who was curled up in a ball under the dining table. He could sense that they were going.

"Bailey bear, come here," called Arya.

But all she got for a reply was whining and huffing. Arya felt bad, so she crouched under the table with him and cuddled her fluffy bear. Maya joined too and they had a cuddle party. Bailey licked their faces feeling pleased with this. Arya knew that he would be fine after a day or two, and he'd forget all about her. They slowly coaxed him out, while Arya grabbed his bag, and they left the kitchen. As the girls walked out of the house together, Sadie and her parents arrived outside. The first thing Sadie saw from the car was Maya and Arya together, and her stomach turned.

"What the hell! What is she even doing here?" muttered Sadie, angrily.

For once, she was grateful for tinted windows at the back of the car because her face was seething. Feeling deeply frustrated at how Maya was always getting in her way. From the window, she observed the girls together, they were laughing, happy, holding hands. That picture burned in her mind. She felt enraged and her hands balled up into fists. It aggravated Sadie so much, she unbuckled her seatbelt with so much force, it snapped back, clipping her face slightly. But she didn't seem to feel anything. She got out of the car and slammed the door.

Bailey jumped and his booming bark echoed down the street. Arya and Maya looked up and saw Sadie standing at the end of the drive.

Maya leaned into Arya and whispered, "Who made her angry? Or is that her resting bitch face?"
Arya knew what the face meant, but she lied to Maya.

"Oh, it's nothing. Probably because it's early and she isn't a morning person."

Rose and Noah also got out of the car and walked towards Aashi and Kunal, who were talking to Maya's Dad. They all chatted amongst themselves like teenagers at the back of a school bus. Their atmosphere was light and airy, but Sadie's was ominous and heavy as she sombrely walked over to Arya and Maya. Arya took a deep breath and put a happy face on.

"Morning Sades!" she beamed.

"Hey, Arya. I'm surprised to see Maya this early in the morning. Since she's not needed here." Sadie addressed Maya.

"Excuse me?" questioned Maya ferociously.

"I- err, meant that, well, you're not coming on this holiday, so I was just wondering why you were here. That's all..." backtracked Sadie.

Arya could tell Maya was greatly offended at that unnecessary comment and she didn't blame her. Saying someone wasn't needed, was like a slap in the face. But she knew Maya was more graceful and would always rise above it. She wasn't the sort of person to sink as low as Sadie just had.

"I'm here to pick up Bailey. He's staying with me while Ari is away," she answered.

Ari. Again, with that sickly sweet nickname.

"Oh. I didn't know he was staying with you." replied Sadie, with a surprised tone. "Well, I'm sure he'll have lots of fun with you. And... Arya will be having fun with me." she said as she looped her arm through Arya's.

84

This didn't go amiss to Maya. she knew exactly what game Sadie was playing, but she wouldn't rise above it, even though it made her mad. Arya could feel the heat rising from her friend. She prayed that Maya would ignore it. But if Sadie kept making digs at her, she knew Maya would snap eventually and Sadie would 100% play the victim. So, she needed to break the tension quickly before sparks ignited. As she was about to change the subject, Maya responded with a casual, yet light laugh, and then turned her back on Sadie and spoke to Arya without a second thought.

"OH! Can you get me a souvenir from Disney World? I'll pay you back, promise!"

"Um, you're not paying me for anything. You're getting a gift from me, so you'll just have to wait and see what I get you!" sang Arya.
The two girls giggled and smiled at each other.

Sadie stood there, frustrated that Maya wasn't even phased by what she said and now she started to feel awkward. She needed to include herself in the conversation and make Maya feel small.

"Please tell me you don't want the Minnie Mouse ears," she snarked. "Everyone gets them nowadays, so they're pretty basic now."

"Weren't you talking about them the other day? Seemed to me like you wanted one too." started Arya, feeling the heat rise in her.

Sadie looked at her with a furrowed brow, dumbfounded that Arya showed her up like that. Before she could react, Arya carried on.

"Besides, it's not a problem if Maya wants them because I want to get some too. We can be basic together." Arya smiled.

Sadie felt like someone slapped her. Her face burned. Arya was meant to be on her side, not Maya's. What was with Arya today, she thought. Feeling the intense urge to hold her tongue this time, she ended up just clearing her throat and then forcing out a laugh. Before the tensions between all three girls reached a pivotal point, Kunal walked towards them.

"Come on girls, time to get moving. Say your goodbyes and we'll head off."

"Ohh, I'm going to miss you, Arya. It's going to be a boring two weeks without you!" moaned Maya.

"I'll text you when I can, we can FaceTime too if we get a chance. Need to see Bailey bear at least once." said Arya, while ruffling his fur.

She kneeled down and hugged Bailey. "You be a good boy, okay? Don't be sassy! I love you very much."

She then gave him lots of kisses and cuddles. While Arya was cuddling Bailey, Sadie whispered to Maya, "Enjoy your time with the dog," with a sly smile on her face. Maya looked ready to hit her. But she held back, instead moving away from Sadie and shuffled closer to Arya. As she stood back up, Sadie quickly removed her nasty smile, like it was never there. Arya then gave Maya a big hug, swaying her from side to side. Maya was facing Sadie at this point and if looks could kill, she would have been burned up on the spot. Sadie's glaring eyes were deathly.

After their tender embrace, Arya let go and Maya walked towards her car with Bailey in tow. They decided that it was best if they left before, so Bailey wouldn't see Arya go. Maya instructed Bailey to sit in the back, made sure he was comfortable and got into the car herself. As soon as Maya clambered in, Sadie stepped beside Arya and took her hand, smiling across at Maya, staring right into her eyes.

The car left. Now that Maya was finally gone, Sadie felt immense relief and could now fully relax. She could relish in her accomplishment now, believing she had intimidated Maya, and hopefully this had sent a warning to her to stop interfering with their friendship. Sadie hoped Maya would now back off.

Looking back at Arya's face, Sadie's shoulders released their tension and the road ahead looked brighter. No longer would three be a crowd. It was just the two of them now and she couldn't be happier.

However, Arya felt a great mixture of emotions. There was anger and disappointment at Sadie for acting so petty towards Maya. But also, sadness that her two best friends couldn't get along, that they couldn't even be civil towards each other. Well, Maya could but Sadie seemed to just be too immature to act the same. Arya felt like she was stuck in the middle, with each arm being pulled on both sides. It was exhausting. All she wished for was for the two of them to get along, nothing more, nothing less. But Sadie seemed to want something very differently entirely.

Chapter 9

After a stressful airport trip, with both sets of parents having panicked over little things and trying to deal with Kiaan throwing a mini tantrum, they were finally in Orlando and their hotel room. They had a family suite, the parents had their own rooms, Kiaan had a small kids' room for himself, and the girls had a shared room on the opposite side of the suite. Their hotel was just a fifteen-minute drive from Disney World, and it was built so high that you could see all the parks from their windows.

Their anticipation was building up, ready to blow. All they wanted to do was go out, explore the parks and ride the roller coasters all day and night. But unfortunately for them their parents were too tired and just wanted to relax for the afternoon. Boring.

Although, they did decide that they would go to Islands of Adventure in the evening for dinner and have nighttime family fun instead, so there was something at least. When they reached their suite, everyone decided to take refuge in their rooms and have a nap. Kiaan had already passed out on his bed. The girls soon got bored, but couldn't do anything else, so they had no other option but to unpack their suitcases. Arya was eager to do this anyway; she liked being organised and efficient. She had already started unpacking by the time Sadie looked away from the impressive view.

"Really? Already?" questioned Sadie, one eyebrow raised.

"You're asking me that question like you haven't known me your whole life."

"True. But it's like the first day and we just got here," replied Sadie. "And it's all the more reason to be prepared and organised!"

Sadie rolled her eyes; this was one thing she didn't particularly like about Arya; her obsessive need to be organised. But she wasn't going to let it bother her. She loved Arya and she could love her quirks and annoying habits too. Sadie decided to collapse on her bed and admire Arya's way of ensuring her side of the room was a clean and tidy space.

She had started emptying her clothes first and sorted them into piles. Sadie noticed that Arya had split her clothes into day and evening wear. And by her glistening eyes and furrowed brow, Sadie could tell she was in full concentration mode and was thinking hard about something. Sadie didn't know why, but she was so mesmerised by Arya's facial expressions. How she could tell when Arya was transfixed on minor things. Sadie could see her talking under her breath and her nose wrinkling when she couldn't decide on something. Sadie breathed a happy sigh and thought: *there's nothing I wouldn't do for this girl.*

Once Arya had finished, she took a deep sigh, feeling instantly relaxed and she turned around to Sadie. She saw how intensely Sadie was looking at her.

"Why are you looking at me like that?" she laughed nervously.

"Oh. No reason. Was just watching you unpack. It's very interesting."

"Aren't you going to unpack?" asked Arya.

"Nope, I'm easy. I'll wear whatever I feel like," Sadie said, now staring up at the ceiling.

She then looked back at Arya and caught her fiddling with a ring on her finger. From a distance, it looked like a silver ring with an amethyst crystal in the middle. Sadie hadn't seen that before and it wasn't often that Arya wore rings, which is why she never bought her one. But this must be special for Arya to wear it and not the friendship bracelet that Sadie bought her, which was absent from her wrist. Again.

"What's that?" questioned Sadie.

"Hm?"

Arya then saw what Sadie was referring to, and her body went cold. She hadn't realised she had kept it on. She thought for a few seconds about what to reply. Should she make up a lie or tell the truth? After a few back-and-forth thoughts, she decided to try to tell the truth. She wasn't going to hide her friendship.

"Oh...it's just a ring." answered Arya, finally. Avoiding Sadie's eyes.

Sadie slowly moved off the bed and walked towards Arya. Her heart was beating in her chest, she could suddenly hear it in her ears, a deafening sound. Boom. Boom. Boom.

"From who?" Sadie politely asked with a cold, fake smile.

Arya could feel the hairs on her neck standing up. For some reason, she felt anxious and a bit worried. Arya then cleared her throat.

"From Maya. She made it for me...she's been making jewellery as a hobby...and gave this to me a couple of days ago."

She felt like she was whispering, like she did something wrong... but feeling like she was walking on eggshells was even worse. It was just a friendship.

Sadie suddenly felt hot like fire, her face burned, her fists clenched, and her breathing sounded unstable. She tried to compose herself. She couldn't lose her cool, not now. Not when it was just going to be her and Arya for two weeks. Sadie quickly turned away, trying really hard to fix her expression and plaster a fake smile on because she couldn't let her guard down now.

Hold up, she thought. Sadie had another idea... She wondered what if, instead of feigning a smile, she faked looking sad and hurt. She could make Arya feel bad and make her never want to wear that gift again, knowing how much it hurt Sadie. Would this be possible? Sadie thought it was. So, she dropped the fake smile and replaced it.

"Oh... that's nice." She began to pout. "I didn't realise someone *else* had given you a gift... Y'know after mine."

Sadie lowered her voice now and made it sound weak and hurt. Feigning a little tremble at the end, as then she turned around with a sullen look on her face.

"How come you're not wearing my bracelet? Don't you like it?" She forced her eyebrows to tense woefully and pursing her bottom lip out ever so slightly.

Arya felt a pang in her heart. She felt so bad for not remembering to take it off. She didn't think about how much it would hurt Sadie. She had disregarded her feelings entirely. Again.

"Of course, I do! Of course, I just didn't wear yours right now because it's so so special and I want to save it for special occasions! I brought it with me though, and I'm going to wear it every time we do something special. I promise. Here, I'll take this off now."

She clumsily started to take it off, trying to be quick so this could be over and done with. Once it was off, she put it in a little pocket in her suitcase, then looked up at Sadie with a shaky smile. Sadie's plan had worked. Arya had felt bad, and she now knew that Arya wouldn't wear that ring again. It was tarnished with this upsetting memory. Sadie was relieved and content.

She had won. But she still wasn't satisfied. She wanted that ring gone for good, but how could she do that? How can she make Arya get rid of it…or should she even rely on Arya to do that? Maybe she should sneakily steal it and throw it out the window at night when Arya was asleep. Then she could play it off and say that Arya misplaced it.

But she had to wait for the right time. It couldn't be done now because it would be too obvious. Arya would definitely be suspicious that she'd done it. So, Sadie decided to wait till next week and swipe it without Arya knowing.

Meanwhile, Arya stared down at the space where the ring had been, feeling sullen and down and hurt. She hadn't wanted to take it off, ever. She loved the ring and how it had made her feel. But she didn't want to keep on hurting Sadie, especially since they were away together. She wondered whether she should tell Maya what happened, but thought it was probably unnecessary. And it would probably just reinforce Maya's dislike of Sadie. Maya had been bluntly honest with
Arya the day before. She finally helped Arya to realise how needy Sadie was, especially when it came to her having other friends. How it just wasn't normal.

Maya also tried to make Arya realise that she needed to surround herself with better company, which was the opposite of how Sadie was coming across as if she wanted the whole world to disappear. Arya began to wonder where Sadie's neediness and possessiveness came from. It had started to become a recurring thought, and she questioned whether it was all her fault, whether she had done something wrong, something to cause it. Sadie had never showed these qualities before. Was it her friendship with Maya that triggered this or was it always in her? It had constantly been playing on her mind since mentioning Maya, and Arya wished she knew how to resolve it without hurting either friend.

Realising she had been quiet way too long now, Arya started to feel like Sadie's eyes were burning into her. Quickly glancing to the corner of her eye, she saw Sadie standing, there seemingly waiting for Arya to say something. Thoughts ran through her mind; she couldn't think of what to reply or what to say next, so she decided to distract both of them and do something.

"I was thinking, how about we check the hotel pool out?" she suggested. "I think our parents are pooped and Kiaan is napping, so we may as well explore it together."

"Ooh yes! That'll be fun," replied Sadie, eagerly, having immediately perked up at the thought of this. "I saw online that it has a hot tub and slides, so try and stop me from jumping in!"

Sadie then went searching for her swimsuit, rummaging through her suitcase, and throwing everything out onto the floor or scattering it on her bed. This made Arya wince, she hated mess, especially if she was staying in the same room. Sadie caught Arya covering her eyes and laughed.

"Oh sorry! I'll tidy it up after. You could help if you want." She smiled.

Arya forced a laugh.

She just wanted to get out of this room, out of this strange atmosphere and maybe she'd feel better. Sadie finally found her swimsuit and hurried to the bathroom. By the time the girls were both changed, Arya had managed to force herself to feel a little lighter. She did really want to enjoy their time together, to have fun and to not have a care in the world.

They quickly told their parents where they were going, and then excitedly made their way down.

As they drew closer to the swimming area the smell of chlorine filled their noses, the sounds of children playing surrounded them and their anticipation hit its breaking point. When they opened the door, they were overcome with the sounds of laughter, joyous screaming, and the buzz of excitement. Children splashing in the water, people flying past on the ocean blue, swirling slides and adults relaxing in the hot tubs. Sadie felt giddy and was eager to go on everything, she started pulling Arya along towards the waterslides and begged her to come along.

The girls had the best time; taking turns on floating lily pads, swinging off monkey ropes into the pool and racing down the slides. After a while, Arya went to relax in a hot tub and as soon as she stepped into the hot bubbling water she felt her shoulders melt. She leaned back and breathed in deeply and smiled. The incident in the hotel room had faded away, it was a memory of the past. Sadie was hungry so she had gone to grab some food from the bar. They had realised they hadn't eaten anything since the plane and were now completely ravenous!

As the hot, bubbly water swept over Arya, she noticed a boy with gorgeous bouncy, brown curls had decided to join her. He sat across from her, initially acting nonchalant and not looking at her, but scanning his surroundings. The atmosphere around them was loud, so there was no awkward silence, thankfully. But she did spot him cast a few glances her way. Not quite believing that he was looking at her, Arya felt like it had to be a mistake, but she also couldn't stop blushing. She gazed over at him and butterflies suddenly flurried in her stomach. His face glistened with that sun-kissed glow and his curls graced his forehead as if they were perfectly placed there. His eyes shimmered like emerald green oceans, but the one thing that made Arya swoon, was the cutest dimple residing in his right cheek.

Holy shit, Arya thought.

She couldn't stop looking at him, and every time he looked at her, she felt her cheeks go redder and redder. She started imagining what he sounded like, what his smile looked like and then it happened. He dazzled her with his smile, and that was it, she had melted into a puddle. Her stomach burst into more butterflies, thousands of them. And her heart warmed, as it does on a snowy winter day drinking hot chocolate. She started to make circles with her fingers in the bubbles around her, to make her look busy, but her face felt like it was on fire.

"Hey, my name's Eli," he said finally breaking the silence. "What's yours?"

Arya felt like she was going to be sick. A guy wanted to talk to her. A very hot guy, too. She couldn't compose herself, but she couldn't not say anything either. She shyly looked at him and could see his smile turning into a slight laugh as he was waiting for her to reply.

Do something! Arya thought loudly.

"Hi Arya! I'm Eli, nice to meet you," she fumbled out breathlessly, not realising she had messed up.

Eli laughed and blushed at the same time, while Arya facepalmed.

"Oh God... Sorry, I meant hi I'm Arya!" She shook her head feeling embarrassed.

She noticed Eli had looked down briefly, but his eyes remained focused on her, smiling like he was taking all of this meet-cute moment in, and it deepened his dimple even more. Arya couldn't seem to catch her breath. She was going to say something else, but he followed up instead.

"Are you on holiday too? I got here five days ago, but this is the first time I thought to slow down and relax a little. I'm glad I came to the hot tub at the right time," smiled Eli still looking directly into Arya's eyes. Her heart fluttered. She could hear her breath quicken, and she was surprised at how quickly this stranger had made her feel like this.

"Yeah, I am. I just got here today. But our parents are too tired to do anything right now, so we thought of coming here for a bit," replied Arya.

"Oh, are you with someone else? Boyfriend...sister...?" questioned Eli.

Arya knew what he wanted to know easily. "Oh, my best friend. She's just getting food. Both of our families have gone on holiday together."

She could see the tiny smile he had on his face reappear and he weirdly made her feel so happy. She didn't even know this guy, but she wanted to.

"Have you been enjoying it so far?" asked Arya.

"This is my happy place. I feel like I'm ten again and no one can judge because everyone is feeling the exact same."

"It's my first time here, so I'm open to doing anything!" said Arya.

"Oh, I'll tell you all the best things to do!" he said excitedly, then started listing things for her to experience.

He suggested each and every thing she had to do in the most exhilarating theme parks. What time was the best for shorter queues, and when and where to see the best nighttime light shows. Every trick and tip he had he relayed it to her, on and-on-and Arya took all this information in like it was the last thing she would hear. They didn't even realise the bubbles had stopped, they were just taking in each other's voices, laughing and vibing with each other's positive energy. Arya felt like she could stay here for hours listening to him, to his angelic voice, they ended up being so lost in their conversation, it could be nighttime, and they wouldn't have realised. Then she had an impromptu thought.

"So, where are you vacationing from?"

"I'm from Arizona, but I'm moving for college soon. To some coastal town with a goofy name like Cloudgham Cape…I bet you've never even heard of it."

Arya had to stop an incoming gasp. She internally screamed with delight.

"Know of it? That's where I'm from! That's so weird! I can't believe you're moving there."

"No way! I'll be there in a couple of weeks. This is my holiday before the big move. Y'know I might need a tour guide when I get there." He winked at her.

Arya blushed. "Of course! That would be so much fun. I'll take you around the best sites."

Just as Arya was about to ask him how they should keep in touch, she heard an "ahem".

Arya looked around and saw Sadie standing there with a tray of burgers and fries, looking sour-faced, like she had been standing there taking in everything they were saying.

"I got us food. You wanna eat?" Sadie pointedly asked Arya.

"Thanks! Yeah sure. Oh, Eli, this is my best friend, Sadie. And this is Eli! We just started talking and he's actually moving to our city! How cool is that?" Arya mentioned it to Sadie. Eli waved to her.

"Hey! Nice to meet you." He extended out his hand.

"Hello. What a happy coincidence," said Sadie, ignoring his hand. "We should eat our food before it gets cold." She motioned over towards the tables.

As Arya was getting out of the hot tub and wrapping the towel around her, Sadie glared at Eli. She hoped it conveyed everything she couldn't say out loud; *back off*.

He looked taken back and confused, but just as he looked about to say something

Arya said, "Maybe we'll see each other around?"

"Uh…yeah, maybe," he replied.

Sadie's and Eli's eyes were locked together. She took Arya's arm and steered her towards the table, the furthest from Eli, and she sat down with a sigh.

"I wasn't even gone long, and you already found someone else," whispered Sadie, with a strained laugh.

"Hey, he was cute, and he started talking to me first," replied Arya.

"You don't even know him," said Sadie, her body rigid.

"Who cares? I'm on holiday! Besides, he's moving to our city soon, so maybe we'll see each other again." said Arya, hopefully.

Sadie rolled her eyes. Here we go again. Another failed crush.

"You're not hoping for you guys to get close, are you? You literally just met," Sadie sternly pointed out.

"Well no. But who knows, maybe we'll become friends or something," replied Arya.

"Okay…" whispered Sadie.

She looked over to the hot tub and saw Eli still relaxing in there, but he was staring at her, only for a brief second and then he got up and walked away. A weird feeling grew in her. She hoped they wouldn't see him again.

Chapter 10

After the girls finished eating their burgers, they started to make their way back to the suite. As they were walking, Arya was lost in her mind, which was suddenly occupied with the thought of Eli. How their conversation flowed effortlessly and how at ease they felt in each other's company. She daydreamed of his lips, how the dimple on his cheek deepened the more he smiled and how the curls that were perfectly placed on his head bounced as he laughed. She was entranced by him. Yearning to hear his voice again, wanting it to sing in her ears as he spoke about anything. Even the way he talked about trivial things drew her in.

Arya started smiling, reliving their conversation. Her cheeks deepened in colour as she blushed, with only thoughts of him swirling around in her mind. Her heart had really been stolen by his charm. In the short amount of time that they spent together, she felt like they had known each other for longer, and all Arya wanted was to be in his company again. Her head was so high above the clouds, she felt the sun. Hoping that they would see each other again.

As the light was growing in Arya, Sadie was cowering in the darkness. Bitterness taking over her impressionable mind. Having watched Arya from the corner of her eye, she knew exactly what she was thinking about: that sickly sweet, puppy-eyed boy. She believed the universe was working against her, not being able to believe he was moving to their city. Sadie felt like she couldn't seem to catch a break. She couldn't understand why everyone seemed to be getting in the way between her and Arya. It was driving her mad. This holiday was just meant for them, no one else. Sadie had to make sure Arya knew this. She had to make sure no one would break their bubble; the bubble she had spent years perfecting.

Arya's voice suddenly rang through Sadie's mind, breaking the silence.

"Eli said he's going to Universal Studios tonight too. Imagine if we bumped into him," laughed Arya, hopefully.

Sadie looked at Arya and noticed how rosy her cheeks were and how they glowed with a certain happiness she had never seen before. Then her eyes moved to Arya's and saw how brightly they glistened. Sadie didn't care. Sadie hated this. It wasn't right, and it was ridiculous to spend time with some boy Arya had just met. Thinking about all the plans that she meticulously made, no one was allowed to ruin that, not for a stranger. No matter how happy he had made Arya.

"But we have plans, Arya, remember? I made a journal for our entire holiday. I thought you were excited for it all," replied Sadie with a dull tone.

"I know, I know. I am excited! I just thought it might be nice for someone to show us around, who knows more about the park than us."

Arya's argument fell flat. She wasn't selling it to Sadie. These next two weeks were meant to be blissful, enjoying time together. She became increasingly frustrated at Arya's ignorance and selfishness. How Arya was so blinded that she couldn't see how important this was for them. Sadie was struggling to hold her tongue; she knew any minute that she was about to hit the roof. It wasn't much longer until they were back in their room, until they were in a place where she could really let Arya know how she felt. And she wouldn't hold back.

After her agonising walk, they finally reached the suite, walking in silently. Sadie marched straight to their room and tightly clamped her hands around her wet towel.

"Umn Sades?" said Arya. "You've gone quiet."
Sadie's knuckles had grown white as she tightened her grip. She slowly turned to look Arya directly in her eyes

"Arya, no offence… But you just met that boy," started Sadie, boring her eyes into Arya's.

"Bu-"

"And this is a family holiday, as I've said a thousand times. Where we're going to spend time together as a family and as best friends," continued Sadie.

"Yeah, b-"

"And it's the first one together in a really long time. So, I would appreciate it if you didn't go off and spend time with some random boy that just happens to be moving to the same city." Her voice grew louder. "It may be fun for you, but it won't be fun for me. We don't need a guide showing us around. These parks are meant to give you a sense of magic and wonder. Exploring it ourselves is the best way to experience it. You've known him for five minutes. He could be a creep for all you know. Why don't you pay attention to those who have been there longer!"

Her chest was heaving as if she just caught her last breath, and her hands were balled into fists. If looks could kill, Arya would have been burnt up on the spot. But it felt like a load had been lifted off her shoulders. Sadie hadn't quite realised the amount of tension that had built up. How much strain it had put on her body.

She had to make Arya see some sense, whether it was about Eli...or Maya. Now, all Sadie could do was glare at Arya and wait for a response.

Arya's mouth was ajar, looking quite shocked at the sudden outburst. It had caught her completely off guard. After a few long pauses, she had taken in everything Sadie said. She looked at Sadie's eyes and noticed they were shining like she was about to cry and that sent a pang of hurt straight into her heart.   Arya felt awful. She closed her mouth and finally swallowed, even though her mouth was dry. She started to feel uncomfortable, wringing her hands together, thinking of how she should reply. And after hearing Sadie's side of the story, Arya realised Sadie was right and she was in the wrong.

How could she have thought that spending time with a guy she just met was more important than her best friend? Arya realised her priorities had become askew and they needed to be corrected, and Sadie was her priority. No matter how much Sadie had acted recently with Maya and her,

Arya realised she needed to work on herself too. And that meant not putting a guy she just met before her best friend.

"You're right. You're absolutely right... I-I don't know what I was thinking. I got so wrapped up in thinking about Eli that I lost sight of who I truly care about. I'm so sorry for even thinking about it. Of course, I don't want to ruin the holiday by doing that. Family time is important. You're important."

After taking a brief breath, Arya carried on.

"I came here to spend time with you and to make lots of memories. I don't want them to be tarnished with arguments or to revolve around a guy. So, forget I ever mentioned it and let's make this trip unforgettable, okay?"

Sadie stood still for a moment, glaring at Arya. The anger and frustration that was bellowing inside ready to burst out of her, had slowly diminished. Her burning tears dried up after seeing the anguish written on Arya's face, believing she was truly sorry. Sadie couldn't bear to leave Arya sad and broken, it felt like she was in hell. So, she took a deep breath in and out and let the fiery heat leave her body, like a flame of a match blown out by a changing wind.

An awkward silence ripped through the room. Both girls had their eyes on the ground, shifting their bodies side to side, unsure of where to go next. The sound of their beating hearts echoed throughout the silence and their arms begged for each other's warm embrace. But Sadie didn't want to make the first move, she always had too. But suddenly, to her surprise, Arya raced towards her and threw her arms around her and brought Sadie into the tightest squeeze. This hug felt like it lasted years and Sadie didn't want it to end.

Finally, they both let go and turned to look at each other's faces. Eyes surveying all over and smiles broadening, knowing that they were okay again. After exchanging silent apologies, they left it as that. Then they started getting ready for the evening. Sadie French braided Arya's hair, Arya picked out Sadie's clothes and the joy was breathed back into both of them.

A rapt knock on the door startled them and broke the little bubble they were in.

"Hey girls," said Aashi, slowly opening the door. "Are you ready? We're heading out soonish. The queues should have winded down now. So, y'know what that means...roller coaster mayhem!" Her voice got louder in the wake of her excitement. And her face was lit up with a joyous glow, it made Arya's heart soar.

"Yes! We're ready! This is going to be the best night ever!" Arya hastily replied. With Sadie jumping in the background, her face etched with an ever-growing grin.

"We'll be outside when you're ready. Kiaan is too hyper to sit too long, so be quick!"

Arya turned and galloped to Sadie. "ARE YOU READY?!"

Sadie grabbed her hands and they both started bouncing on the spot and spinning around in circles, shrieking incoherent words to each other.

"Okay, let's go!"

And they raced towards the door, both trying to get out at the same time, stuck in the doorframe. Their parents were laughing, watching them, and the girls were in hysterics trying to squeeze through. After bursting through the door with all their might, both families finally set off.

Never had the adults become more like their childhood selves. They were all buzzing with excitement, dreaming of the exhilaration they were about to experience. In the minivan, everyone was babbling away in their own worlds, waiting for a glimpse of their wonderland. And as the theme park entered their eyeline, everyone gasped and fell silent.

The lights of the park signs beamed into the inky, black surroundings and the sound of a thousand screaming voices echoed through the air. It gave the girls goosebumps and filled them with anticipation. They were itching to get onto a ride, any ride, it didn't matter. As they reached the entrance, they saw families leaving the park and adults entering. It was time for the big kids to take over now and you could tell they were going to enjoy this adventure. After they breezed through the ticket station and entered the park, their ears filled with the cheery theme park music and the sound of roller coasters zooming past. The breeze felt electric, and the girls were overcome with adrenaline.

Before they were about to bolt off towards The Incredible Hulk ride, Noah piped up with his fatherly figure voice.

"Now girls. We know how excited you are about this, and we know we won't be able to keep up with you. So, we decided to let you have this night to yourselves," he started.

The girls gasped, but before they could reply Noah carried on.

"But you must check in with us at least once an hour. Am I clear?" He raised his eyebrow.

The girls nodded frantically, so eager to run off to all the rides.

"I want verbal confirmation, please."

"Oh my god. Yes, Dad. We promise we'll check in, once an hour, every hour, on the dot," teased Sadie.

"Atta girl. Okay, here's some money for when you need food. Have a great night and we'll see you later!" roared Noah as he was ushering everyone off.

The girls raced to their most anticipated ride: The Incredible Hulk. Its garish and luminous green exterior screaming at them to take up the challenge of riding its gigantic body. The girls tilted their heads up in awe at its magnificent size.

"Woah"

"Yeah, woah. That's what we're going on?" Arya wavered for a moment.

"Yep. That's the ride you're so desperate to go on."

"It didn't look that big in the pictures..." whimpered Arya.

"Pfft. Are you too scared now?"

"No way! Let's go!"

109

They raced to the entrance of the queue, but since there weren't that many people waiting in line, they pretty much raced to the front within ten minutes.

"I couldn't even build myself up for this ride. I definitely thought we'd be waiting for at least thirty minutes!" moaned Arya.

"I bet once you go on this, you'll love every minute, and you'll want to go on it again and again. For sure." reassured Sadie. Nodding her head ferociously, as if she was also reassuring herself.

As they got closer, Sadie's stomach started to churn, and her heart thumped in her chest.

"Oh my god, oh my god. I can't believe I'm going on this for my first one. So stupid, can't do it. Nope." babbled Sadie.

"No, no, no! You can do this, Sades. We'll hold hands and face it together!"

They were then ushered on to the ride, they buckled themselves in and Sadie grabbed onto Arya's hand.

"Ouch! Not too tight. Don't stress, it'll be super fun!" shouted Arya, over the whirring of the mechanics.

Sadie gulped and closed her eyes. She barely heard the guy telling everyone to enjoy the ride because of the deafening ringing in her ears. And when she opened her eyes, they had started moving and were slowly approaching the dark tunnel. Lights started to flicker, the surrounding sounds started to boom, and people started to scream and shout with

110

anticipation. She started to feel the ride beginning to quicken and she knew something was about to happen, but she didn't know when. Then, all of a sudden, she was being hurtled through the tunnel, her hair was plastered to the back of the seat, and all Sadie could hear was the sound of echoing screams from herself and all around her. The roller coaster twisted, turned, dropped and took them on an exhilarating ride. And when it was over, she felt like her body had melted into the seat and she had no feelings left in her body. Sadie was just a puddle now.

"OH MY GOD! That was awesome!!" cried Arya.

But Sadie couldn't find her voice to reply. When the carriage got back to the platform and they were released from the ride, it took her a good few seconds to get back on her feet. She wobbled a bit, but Arya had her back, and they walked out together. With Arya bouncing with adrenaline beside her, Sadie felt sick to her stomach, and she needed to desperately sit down.

"Oh, come on Sades, it wasn't that bad! Surely you had some fun?" questioned Arya. "There's a bunch of other rides to go on too! You can't fail me now."

Sadie gulped and took a deep breath.

"I know, I know. I just need to catch my breath and steady myself, I'll be okay."

Arya patted Sadie's back. Then she leaned in and egged on Sadie. "Are you going to be too chicken to go on the Harry Potter ride?"

Sadie whipped her head up. "Are you kidding? I could NEVER miss out on that."

"Then get up! We got to head there now. I heard the ride is awesome at night."

Arya pulled Sadie up and they hugged. Sadie felt the warmth and calmness seep back into her as Arya rubbed her back. And now she was ready to take on any roller coaster without any fear.

Their next stop was Harry Potter World because they were very certain that they could spend the rest of the evening there. They almost dashed there out of pure excitement.   Dodging through the swarming crowds that were walking the opposite way and ignoring the tempting aromas of the delicacies and sweet treats the park had to offer. They wanted to save their stomachs for all things magical. Whether it was the chocolate frogs, Bertie Botts Every Flavoured Beans, Butterbeer, Pumpkin Pasties, anything Harry Potter related, they wanted to try it all.

As they approached the area, they could hear the familiar music bless their ears and a warm hug of nostalgia embracing them. Sadie caught her breath, and she felt tears welling up in her eyes. She was in awe. This was her childhood, right in front of her, and she felt like the luckiest girl in the world. And then, when she couldn't contain her emotions anymore, she let her tears fall gracefully from her eyes. And slowly but surely, they fell drop by drop onto her warm cheeks.

"Aww Sades. You're so cute!" hugged Arya.

They embraced for a while as they took in their view. Their eyes swept from the snowy rooftops of the buildings to the lights dazzling in the castle. Sadie had never felt so nervous and excited to experience something. Was it going to be everything she ever hoped for? Would it be more? Or would it disappoint her? She didn't know what was going to happen, but she was so eager to find out.

Then Sadie felt the weight of Arya in her arms, the feeling of home enveloping her and breathed in a sigh of contentment. She pondered on a thought that right there and then at this moment she was in, she didn't care whether it lived up to her expectations or not. She had everything she ever wanted right there in her arms. Her best friend. In the place she felt herself, where she could escape her sorrows and experience magic like no other. And she wasn't prepared to let anything ruin it. She didn't want to be anywhere else or with anyone else.

They took a picture to commemorate the memory of them having entered the magical world and took a step inside.

Chapter 11

Every day was better than the last. They indulged in too much fast food, drank too many creamy and rich milkshakes and went on so many roller coasters that they lost count! Travelling from theme park to theme park, throughout most of their holiday. Truly living up to Sadie's 'theme park crawling' idea. Although, they did go to a few water parks too, which were a refreshing treat from the unbearable queues in the scorching heat. The same amount of fun but a little less hot.

And when they were fed up with the constant adrenaline rush, they sunbathed and relaxed by the swimming pool. While they chilled there, it was Arya's time for sketching. She took inspiration from the photos taken of all the places she had been on this holiday and took her time drawing them. She had a way of making the pictures glow, even though it was just a pencil drawing on paper. But the real magic happened in her painting room. When she had the chance to paint at home, it would feel like she was back in Orlando all over again. That was her magic.

On this day however, the girls were relaxing in their rooms from a long day out. They both went on their phones to catch up with what was going on at home. Sadie had been busy posting as many pictures as she could which all included Arya in some aspect. Whether it was of the two of them smiling, eating food, sunbathing by the pool or in front of a gigantic, enthralling roller coaster. Every post of Sadie's was of the two of them and for everyone else other than Sadie, it had become boring.

Whereas Arya had more artistic-looking pictures, something to capture the beauty and magic she was surrounded by. And of course, with the occasional post of her and Sadie. At this point in time though, Arya was busy texting Maya.

Have you looked at his socials yet?

Yes! I did, he's a college boy! You didn't tell me that. And he loves animals too, your kinda man. I'm so jealous haha.

Haha, nothing is happening yet! Y'know he's moving to our city? I can't wait to be able to spend proper time with him. I've only been able to steal 20 minutes here and there.

I can't believe you're meeting in secret. I don't think it's right...

But I'm meeting him when she's busy and not with me .

I mean tbh, I still wouldn't do that. You promised her you wouldn't. She'd be upset if she found out.

I know I did... But I don't know, there's something about him that I can't get enough of. And it's not the most awful thing in the world... Anyway, I'll text you later.

Then Arya put her phone away. Maya was right. It was wrong to meet Eli, especially when she promised not to. She *was* being a bad friend this time. But she couldn't help it, she didn't mean to meet him at first, but every time Arya was walking around the hotel, grabbing her breakfast or by the pool, Eli happened to be there too. It was like fate was bringing them together and Arya didn't feel like ignoring it. She felt like they were meant to meet. There was also something about him, a pull he had, that just kept bringing her back for more. To spend time with him and hear his voice again, which she could have listened to for hours on end. But they only managed to get the smallest amount of time together, and the only way they could meet, without Sadie knowing, was in secret.

Arya didn't enjoy doing it like this, but she wanted to get to know him a bit before he moved there. There was no harm in becoming friends, even if she did hope for something more. But today was the last time she would see him, because he was leaving tomorrow. Today was her last chance, and she didn't want to miss this opportunity.

"When shall we get ready? I'm in such a cba mood right now," questioned Arya.

"Might go for a shower now, feel kinda yucky. I have to make sure I look my best for tonight. We're *finally* going to Magic Kingdom, so I want to look all sparkly," said Sadie as she got up.

She stretched and moved around to her wardrobe to figure out what she wanted to wear. As she was pulling back each hanger, trying to find her clothes, Arya quickly messaged Eli.

Hey, fancy meeting up in 10 minutes?

116

Usual place?

Sure thing, see you there!

Arya silently squealed with excitement. She couldn't wait to see him again, but she needed to go at the right time. As soon as Sadie went into the bathroom, it was her time to rush off. But Sadie was taking her time picking out her outfit today and Arya was desperate to go and meet him.

"Why don't you just pick something after you shower?" asked Arya with a strained laugh.

"Eh, I need to know whether I should shave my legs or not."

"Shave them anyway, not a big deal!"

"True, but still. I want to pick one before I go. What's the rush?"

"No rush," Arya answered abruptly.

Sadie wondered why Arya seemed to be in a hurry this time. Normally she would help her decide, but this time seemed different. Shrugging her shoulders, Sadie carried on browsing and didn't think too much about it. It wasn't really bothering her that much. Finally, she decided on her outfit: a sequined, mermaid coloured, halter neck top and her Disney shorts. The pockets had character patches and the button on her shorts was the Mickey Mouse logo. It was adorable and the perfect outfit for tonight.

Sadie suddenly heard a weird noise, so she turned around and saw Arya fidgeting her leg. Staring at Arya, she raised an eyebrow and watched what she was doing. She saw that Arya kept checking her phone and quietly sighing. She couldn't begin to imagine why Arya was acting like that. But Sadie grabbed her clothes and went to the bathroom instead.

"See you in a bit!" called Sadie as she closed the door.

This was Arya's chance to run, and she didn't waste any time. As soon as she heard the bathroom door click, she grabbed her key card and escaped. But as she stepped out of the room, Sadie came back out of the bathroom to grab her phone for music. Glancing around the room, she noticed Arya had disappeared and she wondered where she went. Thinking that she had probably gone to see her parents, she carried on into the bathroom, now equipped with her shower music.

Arya ran to the sofas at the end of the long corridor; this was where they had been meeting up. By chance luck, he was on the floor above, so this was the perfect spot, not too far for Eli and close enough for Arya to retreat back to her suite secretly. It felt like the universe was working overtime for Arya.

She was now waiting eagerly on the sofa. The day was so bright and warm, the sun shone through the ceiling to floor windows, and the view was just magnificent. The light that graced the hotel, lit up the entire corridor and created a summery ambience. Arya could feel herself sink into the sofa, which was toasty warm from the sunlight. It hugged her body as she closed her eyes and let the warmth of the sunlight kiss her eyelids and caress her face. Inhaling and exhaling, she felt relaxed.

"You look so peaceful right now," came a voice.

This made her jump. "Oh!" she recognised that voice and opened her eyes quickly.

"Aw, you're sweet," she whispered.
She moved further down the sofa.

"I wish we had longer to spend together and didn't have to meet in secret," moaned Eli sitting down.

"Yeah...I know. Not too long though, you're moving next week, right? And I'll be home after that!" cheered Arya, trying to lift the mood.

"What is your friend's deal? Would she not like you meeting me, or?"

"She's cool, just a bit needy is all," shrugged Arya.

"Well, she can't stop me from seeing you when we will be living in the same place."

"Yeah, I know..."

They spent the rest of the time talking about all the things they were going to do when they were together at home. Moving closer and closer together to the point, where they were sitting side by side, shoulder to shoulder and their hands were entwined with each other.

Little did they know that they had been talking for half an hour, and unbeknownst to the new lovebirds, Sadie was glaring at them from just outside their hotel room door. Her hands gripping the doorframe so hard her fingers were shaking and had gone pale. Her nostrils flared and her head felt like it was going to tear open. She was livid.

After all the talk that Arya had spouted about realising putting a boy above her best friend was the worst, she carried on doing it anyway. It made Sadie feel rage like never before. All she could think about now was this betrayal, how wrong it was that not only did Arya break her promise, but she did it right in front of her. Arya had lied. Rage was now building inside Sadie. Feeling like Arya had stabbed her in the back and had clearly felt no remorse or guilt. Especially while she was too busy snuggling up to him.

So much for her saying I was more important. Thought Sadie bitterly. She began calculating in her mind about how she to confront Arya about this. But she realised she wouldn't. Not yet.

Take a picture. Came a voice from the back of her head.

Not wondering where the voice came from, she didn't stop to question it, instead she obliged. Quickly grabbing her phone, she took a picture of the couple and went back to glaring at them. Now she had evidence, which she was going to use at the right time. Where it would hurt Arya the most. Sadie believed a lesson needed to be learned. Who was more important? Arya's best friend or some boy she just met? Arya's best friend or Maya. A girl that sprang out of nowhere. Sadie loathed her more than anything else.

And like a quick flash of lightning, Maya's face flashed before her eyes. She never imagined that some random school girl would take away her best friend, would try to replace her.   No matter how hard she tried to reassure herself; Sadie couldn't stop the sinking feeling that Arya was slipping away from her. Finding other connections that she couldn't provide, finding solace with new people. It ached her heart. All she could think about was how after all these years they had together, seventeen glorious years, their friendship now didn't mean that much to Arya.

In one summer, everything had changed. Sadie felt less confident that she could keep Arya to herself. It was one thing trying to keep her from Maya, but a boy... How could she compete with that? Nothing was going right; nothing was going her way.

Sadie closed her eyes slowly. Her breath was still shaky, her body still seethed with anger, but her mind now filled with sadness. She felt numb. She felt defeated. Still thinking about Maya, Sadie remembered the ring she gifted to Arya. That she was meant to steal it and throw it away, just like Arya had clearly thrown away their friendship. There wasn't a more perfect time to do this either. So, Sadie begrudgingly retreated inside, slamming the door as she went.

The door slamming made Arya jump. She quickly realised where she was and wondered how long it had been. She darted to her phone to check what time it was.

"Shit! It's been thirty minutes. I need to go!"

"Oh no, please stay a little longer!" begged Eli.

"I can't, she'll wonder where I've gone too. I need to think of an excuse..."

"Um…"

"I'll figure something out. I have to go now, have a safe flight tomorrow and hopefully, I'll see you next week!" Arya then grabbed Eli for a hug.

They stayed there for a few long seconds swaying back and forth. When they broke apart, they smiled at each other and Arya ran off. When she approached the door, she let her smile linger on her face and entered. She saw her parents chilling on the sofa eating some fruit and glanced at Kiaan colouring in his book.

"Look Arya, I got my signature book ready for when we go to Magic Kingdom!" jumped Kiaan, waving his Disney book in the air.

Arya grabbed Kiaan and spun him around and around, laughing and singing. They were both so happy, and the air felt light and pure. As she put Kiaan down, she sat next to him and looked at what he was colouring. It was a picture of Pooh Bear and Piglet.

"They're best friends, just like you and Sadie!" chirped Kiaan.

Arya glanced at it and wondered who Pooh Bear would be and who would be Piglet. Just as she was getting lost in her own world, their bedroom door opened. She turned around and saw Sadie dressed in her cute clothes and Arya beamed at her. Sadie beamed back and went to sit on the sofa next to her.

"So, are you going to get ready now? We'll be leaving soon, right?" asked Sadie, looking at her Dad for confirmation.

Instead, Kunal answered. "Yeah, we should get going soon, especially if we want to see a parade so Kiaan can get his autographs. Hey buddy?" tickling Kiaan.

"Yes!!! Can we go now! Please!" begged Kiaan, jumping all over the room.

They were all ready to go except Arya.

"Come on Arya, get ready soon. Otherwise, Kiaan will never let you rest," called her Mom.

Arya stood up and retreated to her room. She felt relieved that no one had noticed she was gone for a while. Her last meeting with Eli was a success, and now she wouldn't have to worry about sneaking off anymore. As she was basking in her personal achievement, Sadie stepped into the room. Hands in her pockets, holding the ring she had stolen, with a forceful grip.

"Where did you go?" she asked.

Arya stopped short and gulped. She turned around and analysed Sadie's face. It looked normal, glowing in fact, or was it sweat? She thought that Sadie couldn't possibly know anything.

"Oh. Just went for a walk...to get some fresh air," Arya mumbled looking off into the distance.

The voice came back and asked a question in Sadie's mind: *When did Arya start lying to you? Best friends don't lie to each other. You need to tell her off.*

"Not now!" she retorted back to the voice in her mind.

"Huh?" questioned Arya.

"Oh sorry, nothing."

Sadie didn't know where that voice came from, but it wasn't wrong. No matter how much she wanted to expose Arya, she couldn't, not yet anyway. Sadie was waiting for the right time when Arya couldn't escape or lie. Instead, she just smiled at her and walked out of their room to sit down next to her parents.

Arya dashed into the bathroom and quickly got ready, feeling lucky that Sadie believed her. Once she was dressed and everyone else had packed what they needed, they set off for another magical evening.

The anticipation was vibrant, and everyone felt like they were going to the best place in the world. As they were making their way there in the minivan, they were chatting away to each other, except one was louder than the rest.

"...I'm going to see Pooh Bear, and Piglet and Tigger and Mickey and Goofy and Woody and Buzz and Rapunzel and Stitch and Lilo and Elsa and Anna," Kiaan yelled. He wouldn't stop listing every character he had to meet, and yelling was the only way he could communicate his excitement. Every time someone would complain, he would yell louder because he needed to be heard.

"We get it! You're going to see everyone! Shhh," Arya jokingly outburst.

He stopped shouting for a small moment. But then the silence was interrupted with an explosion of noise, with everyone now talking over each other. But the conversation halted as the theme park came into view, with

124

loud chatters turning into hushed whispers. As they parked up, they quickly and quietly unloaded and marched to the entrance. As if they were saving their voices for inside.

Once they entered, the family huddled into a group and took a group selfie. Kiaan was too small, so Rose picked him up and they all had the cheesiest grins on their faces. They each had a beautiful, sun kissed glow painted on them, eyes that glistened with glee and hearts jumping for joy. This was the one park where they wanted to stick together as a big joint family.

They raced to the roller coasters, wanting to tackle the queues before they explored the rest of the park. The parents were smart enough that they had bought fast track tickets, so the queues were shorter than most. Over and over, they went on each ride, not giving up until they felt sick.

They conquered Splash and Space Mountain, defeated Zurg and thundered into the sky on a railway. When it was time for a break, they munched and nibbled on delectable treats that couldn't be savoured for more than five minutes, they were that scrumptious. They had let their noses decide where to get their treats from and they had no regrets. Once they were filled to the brim, they wandered off for a walk.

They watched everyone interacting with the characters. Kiaan had dragged his parents along to every character he saw for their autograph and a picture, and they all loved him. He was in his element, and he was enjoying every single moment of it. Arya had documented almost every move of his, taking videos and pictures. But he didn't want to be in any pictures with just Arya, because she wasn't as exciting as Buzz Lightyear was.

However, as the parades started, they settled down and sat on the curb with front row seats, so Kiaan got the best views. Everyone could tell how eager he was when he started crying seeing all his favourite characters come out to play and dance. He ran up to Pooh Bear when he marched over, and they both started dancing. It was the sweetest picture that anyone could imagine. Kiaan even got an autograph afterwards, and the look on his face was priceless. His cheeks were red with excitement and gratitude for his favourite character to have blessed him like this. Arya's heart fluttered with delight, seeing how happy her baby brother was, and nothing could ruin this moment.

Then she remembered she wanted to buy some Minnie Mouse ears for her and Maya, so she grabbed her Mom and went to the nearest shop, leaving Sadie with her parents watching the parade in amazement. Thinking that Sadie wouldn't notice.

When they entered the gift shop, they were bombarded with so many souvenirs they couldn't decide where to start. There were plushies exploding from every corner of the shop, ranges of clothing for every Disney film and character, and every knickknack in existence. Just as Arya was about to ask for assistance, her Mom finally found the Minnie Mouse ears shelf and called her over.

"I don't know how you're going to choose, there's so many. Do you even know what kind she wants?" she asked.

"Ahh, I don't know. There's loads... I'm sure she'd be happy with any. But I want to get the perfect ones," replied Arya, eyes gazing at the choices in front of her.

The first pair Arya looked at was covered in rainbow sequins and the ones next to it were pastel colour themed, they were gorgeous, but she wasn't feeling either of them. She surveyed the shelf and saw so many options: gold ears, blue ears, superhero ones, pink glittery ones, every Princess themed and of course, the original ears. Arya was stuck for choice, umming and erring at each one. Dancing on tiptoes trying to decide on what pair she wanted, because she also wanted the same one as Maya. They wanted to match.

After deliberating for what seemed like hours to her Mom, Arya finally decided on a mermaid theme. It was two-toned with an ocean blue that faded into an emerald green and deep shimmering purple. And the bow on top was a soft red. It was beautiful and she fell in love as soon as she laid her eyes on it. They were both at the very back of the shelf, as if it were meant to be. Arya knew at that moment, she had to snatch them up before anyone else could. She quickly grabbed them and raced to her Mom, who was busy looking at a snow globe.

"You're not going to get another snow globe, are you?" laughed Arya.

"And what if I am?" replied Aashi sassily.

"You already got one from the last park. What are you going to do with them all?"

"I'm going to display them! Also, this is just for Kiaan. It lights up! It can be his new night light. I think he'll love it," she replied, beaming.

"That's cute! Let's get it then. I've also decided on our ears."

Aashi glanced at the ears. "I only see two. Aren't you going to get one for Sadie?"

"Oh no, she doesn't want one. When we were talking about them before we left, she said they were tacky, so y'know. No point in getting her one," shrugged Arya.

"Hmm...but what if she gets upset?"

"Mom...we're on holiday together, what's better than that? I'm not going to get her something to commemorate this holiday when we have actual memories of it instead," explained Arya.

"Okay, okay. But don't come crying to me if it all goes wrong." Arya groaned and rolled her eyes.

They queued up to buy their items and Aashi quickly grabbed some popcorn too.

"Hey, I'm on holiday, gonna get me some snacks."

As soon as they were done, they went back to join the group, who were all still watching the parade in awe, having not moved a muscle. Sadie turned to look at Arya, smiling all the way.

"Hey, where did you go?" She cocked her head to the side like a quizzical puppy.

128

"Oh, just went to the souvenir shop with Momma." smiled Arya.

"Ooh cool. You didn't miss anything exciting. The next parade is going to start soon though."

Arya was glad Sadie hadn't questioned what they got from there. That could be another day's conversation. But for today, it was all about keeping the magic in the air.

However, while she was gone Sadie had had the perfect chance to get rid of the ring that was burning a hole in her pocket, weighing her down. While no one was looking, she had thrown it into the street and before she could have a second thought, a character had stepped on it and walked away with it. The ring was now stuck on Eeyore's shoe. And that was it, it was gone forever. Sadie felt relieved and Arya came back not realising what had just happened.

After that they went for their dinner in an enchanting restaurant. Kiaan was happily munching away, his cheeks filled with food like a chipmunk, looking in all directions for a glimpse of the different characters flitting around the tables. By the time they finished their meal the next parade was beginning: The Disney Electrical Parade.

It was a magical experience because it happened at night, where the sky was an inky black blanket, but just like magic the lights of the floats suddenly illuminated the darkness, like a glimmer of hope, exploding into showers of a thousand lights parading down the streets. It was an extravagant and awe-inspiring experience that brought a buzz to the crowd.

There was music blaring, and everyone was moving their feet and dancing. It was like one big party, and they were all invited. They grooved to the beat and watched the lights twinkle as the floats glide past them.

But the parade was nothing compared to the fireworks that beautifully ended the night. Both the families made their way to Cinderella's Castle, where they had an amazing view. The girls stood side by side holding hands. As the show was starting, it felt like they had been transported into a world of their own. Where they were the only people there in front of the castle, witnessing the beauty before them. Through the explosions of colour that rang through their bodies, echoing in their ears and shining in their eyes, they were surrounded by the enchanting magic.

In all directions they were faced and engulfed into an array of colours. Magnificent and majestic colours that had the power to describe every emotion that ever existed. It was breathtaking. Arya had goosebumps, feeling like she couldn't catch her breath. She had never seen anything so amazing in her life. She couldn't stop her eyes darting in every direction of the fireworks, trying to take all of it in. Not wanting to miss a single one.

Sadie normally wasn't a fan of fireworks, but for once she let that negativity wash over her and enjoyed this experience. And she was glad she did.

Sadie stole a look at Arya, she studied her face and as she wandered her eyes onto Arya's, she gasped. All she could see was the light of the fireworks gorgeously reflecting in Arya's heavenly, brown eyes. It just never stopped, seconds upon seconds, minutes upon minutes, there was a constant display of brilliant colours manifesting many shapes on Arya's face. She had become an artwork that Sadie couldn't take her eyes off of. It was precious and wasn't to be touched by anyone else. No matter how long she looked at her and into her eyes, it felt like there was never enough time to absorb every emotion etched onto Arya's face.

The crinkle under her eyes from where she was smiling, the laugh lines in her cheeks, the fluttering of her hair in the summer breeze, or even the flicker of her eyelashes every time her eyes moved to capture the fireworks before her. There was never enough time. Butterflies bloomed in Sadie's stomach. The ethereal glow of Arya's face had now transfixed Sadie, and she couldn't help but melt. Especially at the smile that had stolen her heart. She never saw Arya this happy before and she wanted to be the only person that could witness this paradise of hers.

She gently squeezed Arya's hand. Arya squeezed back. Then Sadie leaned in and whispered,

"Together forever, right?"

"Forever."

Chapter 12

After a few more exhilarating and tiresome days, it was finally time to go home. Arya was excited to leave because she wanted to see Bailey. She missed her lovable bear so much. Maya had been sending her daily pictures of them cuddling or even the puppy Coco climbing all over him. Maya's Mom finally agreed to keep Coco, and she had settled in so easily she had become part of the family. Arya was so excited to see them again. She hadn't played with a puppy since Bailey, so she knew she would be visiting Maya first thing. And of course, she needed to get Bailey, too.

Sadie on the other hand, was the least excited to go home. She knew when they would get home, Maya would be all over Arya. Whether she wanted it or not. Would she be pushed out? Would Maya weave her way in between them to the point where Arya and Sadie aren't best friends anymore? She couldn't risk it. She didn't want to witness it. Throughout the last night, Sadie had been thinking of a way to avoid going home. She knew it would prove difficult, but nothing was too extreme for her. Anything to spend more time with Arya.

Tossing and turning all night had made Sadie restless. Her thoughts of how to steal extra time with Arya went from telling everyone that the flight was cancelled to making a scene on the plane which she realised was stupid. Now becoming increasingly frustrated, she had turned on her side to look at Arya sleeping. Her hair was all over her face, lips slightly ajar and the gentle sound of her breathing swept over Sadie. At that moment she knew she needed more alone time with Arya, and nothing would stop her from getting it.

A thought had come to her mind. Leaving her passport behind was an idea she could do. Their flight was the last one on that day so if they didn't notice her passport was gone until they got to the airport, they would miss their flight. Meaning she'd at least get another day with Arya. There was no way she could extend it longer, she realised that, so doing this was the only way she could at least get more time. But was that all worth it? She thought so.

On the afternoon of their return flight, Sadie started to think of how to initiate her plan. Would she need to distract her parents or sneakily steal it while they weren't looking? She wasn't sure. While she was slowly packing her bag, she became lost in her thoughts. They had all become entangled, wondering whether this was the right thing to do.

But the voice boomed in her mind: *This is definitely the right thing to do. Another day with just us two, that's all you want. Stop overthinking it.*

She listened to it as it echoed in her mind repeatedly. Allowing it to take over her decisions as if she had no mind of her own. And once the voice had made its bed, Sadie had no choice but to listen to it. Besides, she actually agreed with it, knowing it was the right thing to do, and she knew Arya would be grateful that they got the extra day together. This was all Sadie could think about. A sneaky smile then crept upon her face, eager to start her plan.

While Sadie had been busy in her mind, Arya had been bustling around packing her suitcase and making sure she hadn't missed a single thing. After she was confident, she had everything, she made her way back to their room. Arya noticed that Sadie seemed unusually quiet and was absent-mindedly packing her bag, not taking any notice of what she was packing away.

"You're not stealing that remote, are you?" laughed Arya.

But there was no response from Sadie, who continued to pack it. So, Arya grabbed a pillow from her bed and threw it at Sadie.

"HEY!" shouted Arya, playfully as the pillow hit Sadie's face.

"What the hell?!" yelled Sadie, taken back.

She swiftly threw the pillow back at Arya and began a pillow fight. Sadie climbed on her bed and whacked all the pillows at Arya who fell back laughing, gasping for breath.

"Okay, okay! Stop it!" fought back Arya.

"You started it!" replied Sadie.

"Only because you weren't paying attention! You were so focused you ended up packing the remote!"

"Huh?" questioned Sadie, head cocked to the side.

Arya walked over to Sadie's bag and pulled it out. Holding it up with a dumb smile on her face.

"Oh."

"What's up with you?" asked Arya.

"Nothing."

"I'm your best friend. You can't lie to me!" stated Arya.

"Are you?"

"Am I what?" questioned Arya, taken back.

"Are you my best friend?"

"Wh- why would you ask that? Of course, I am!" exclaimed Arya defiantly.

Sadie pulled a face like a toddler being told 'no'.

"What? Spit it out" said Arya, becoming frustrated.

"Nothing! Just you seem to be getting closer to Maya...and I feel like I'm getting pushed aside," admitted Sadie.

Arya's face straightened and turned serious. She had been expecting this, but not now.

"Am I not allowed other friends?" asked Arya, sternly.

"Well....no, I didn't say that. Bu-"

"But what? Why are you being like this? Every time I'm with her or talk to someone that is our age that isn't you, you become angry and controlling."

"That's harsh. And I am not controlling!" shouted Sadie.

"Yes, you are! You won't let me spend time with any other people in peace. You have this big face on when I do, and you make me feel bad! You don't get to decide whether I can have other friends or not!"

But before Sadie could reply, her parents came into the room.

"Hey, is everything alright? We heard raised voices..." questioned Rose.

135

"Everything is fine," replied Arya with a strained smile, while walking out the room.

Rose approached Sadie while her Dad stood at the door.

"She said fine. We all know what that means," stated Noah, matter-of-factly.

Rose tutted and ignored what he said.

"Is there anything you want to tell me bub?" she asked soothingly.

"No, it's nothing. Just a stupid fight. It's okay," mumbled Sadie, with her head looking down. Rose looked at Noah and he shrugged his shoulders.

"Ah, friend's fight! It's not the end of the world. This is the first time you've been together all day, every day for two weeks. You're probably just stepping on each other's toes," explained Noah.

"Yeah, it's nothing to worry about. But maybe once we're home, you should have some time apart?" finished Rose.

The thought of having time apart made Sadie's stomach turn. She didn't want that and wouldn't allow that to happen. She had to resolve this issue, and she knew for definite that she had to delay them coming home. Even if it was only for one more day.

Meanwhile, Arya had stormed into her parent's room, who were busy trying to make Kiaan take a nap.

"Look, you're going to be really tired if you don't have a nap now."

"But you're not taking a nap!" argued Kiaan.

"I don't need to. I'm not a baby."

"I'm not a baby!!" cried Kiaan.

Aashi pushed Kunal. "Don't agitate him, stupid."

Kunal just laughed, picked him up, and dropped him on the bed. "Naptime!!"

Within five minutes of Kiaan trying to fight the nap off, he was suddenly fast asleep. Kunal laughed and shook his head.

"Kids, eh? Can't live with them, certainly couldn't live without them!"

Aashi laughed and threw clothes at him. They suddenly noticed Arya was pacing back and forth by the door.

"What's up buttercup?" asked Kunal with a cheesy grin.

"Sadie is really getting to me..." Aashi rounded up next to Kunal.

"A problem with Sadie? That doesn't sound good. Was it about the ears?" she quickly asked.

"What ears?" questioned Kunal, confused.

"I did warn her about the ears."

"But what ears? Why would you give someone ears?" They both started talking over each other.

"It wasn't to do with the stupid ears!!" shouted Arya. The outburst made her parents jump.

"Sorry, sorry!" Her Mom said, holding Arya's shoulders. "What was it about then?"

Arya's thoughts were just bellowing over each other, screaming from all directions. Screaming contradicting thoughts at each other, it was a fight between right and wrong thoughts, and they were becoming too much to bear. She needed to let it out.

"She's controlling. She's obsessive. She doesn't let me have other friends! She makes me feel bad about it, and it's like I'm torn between being best friends with her and best friends with Maya. Why can't she just leave me alone?!" exploded Arya with a frustrated outburst.

Aashi and Kunal looked at each other and both sat Arya down on the bed. They both tucked her hair behind her ear and rubbed her back. This was something they had always done since Arya was little, to calm her down. And it always worked. Arya could feel her shoulders loosen, her jaw unclenched, and her fists relax.

"I'm sorry," she said, with a defeated sigh.

"What are you saying sorry for?" asked Kunal.

"For that rant. You probably think I'm being a drama queen."

"Nope. Not at all, you're entitled to your feelings, and you're allowed to express them. Never apologise for your feelings, especially to us," said Kunal, kissing her head.

"Why are you frustrated with Sadie? Because you think she won't allow you to have other friends? I've never noticed this from her," questioned Aashi.

"I don't think. I *know* she won't let me have other friends. You haven't noticed because it hasn't been a problem until this summer. When me and Maya got closer."

"Ah. Okay. Well, have you talked to her about it?" asked Kunal.

"Uh, yeah. That's why I stormed over here? Because we fought?"

Aashi gave a stupid look to Kunal behind Arya's head and rolled her eyes. He responded with a dumb shrug.

Normally, conversations like these went over his head. Not fully understanding the mind of his seventeen-year-old daughter. So, her Mom always took the reins, but this time he seemed to know what to say.

"Look, this is just part of growing up. Sometimes you move on from your old friends and find new ones, and there's nothing wrong with that. If you have true friends then they'll accept that and move forward with you," started Kunal. "But if they become jealous and hold you back, then they're not true friends. True friends will always be there for you and let you grow," finished Aashi.

Arya pondered over this thought. Was Sadie a true friend if she was going to make her feel guilty for having other friends? Was she truly holding her back? She didn't want to think that about Sadie, they had been best friends for so long. Surely, she wasn't being unsupportive of new friendships. Or was she?

Arya's parents watched her, as she tried to work it all out in her mind. So much to untangle. So much she wasn't sure of anymore.

"Maybe you've just spent too much time with each other, and you need a break?" suggested Kunal.

"Yeah. Yeah, maybe that would be a good idea. When we get home, I'll have a little space from her, there's no harm in that," nodded Arya.

Suddenly, she felt a lot better. Space was all she needed to repair their bond. Aashi stroked her head again and brought her into a hug. Arya thought she would say something cute but was completely wrong.

"Have you packed your stuff, Arya?" whispered Aashi.

"God, yes Mom! All packed!"

While Arya was busy unwinding with her parents, Sadie was in her room alone, sitting on the bed, trying to figure out how to begin her plan. She needed to get a hold of her passport, which was the essential part. They were set to head off in just over an hour's time. She just had to keep an eye on the passports, so it was easier to take hers with little time for people to notice. Her parents were busy packing last minute things, and she knew Arya was with her parents, so she had time for herself.

Feeling sleepy, she decided to close her eyes for a bit, now she was finished with her packing. Her mind was circling with the thoughts of Arya and Maya. And this quickly manifested into a nightmare.

It started with Maya and Arya laughing at Sadie, but she had no idea why. She was trying to grab Arya and bring her to her side, away from Maya. But Arya wasn't cooperating with her, she kept snatching her arm away from Sadie's grasp and ran away with Maya. Sadie started chasing her, but no matter how fast she ran she couldn't catch up. She felt like the air around her was becoming dense and cold, and within a moment's grasp, it became harder to breathe.

"Sadie."

She turned around and saw a figure emerging through the rain. It was Arya, but it didn't look like the Arya she knew. This one had a menacing look, unfamiliar to the face it masked. She was holding their friendship bracelet, which she then dropped. As it hit the ground with a thud, it broke into a million pieces.

Sadie jolted upright in her bed, gasping for air. Her head felt clammy, and she quickly regained the environment she was in. She looked around and realised where the sound of the thud came from. It was Arya who had just dropped her suitcase on the floor. They both looked at each other.

"Do you know where my ring is?" she asked.

"What ring?" replied Sadie.

"The one Maya made for me."

Sadie gulped. 'No. Why would I know about that?"

"I don't know. Thought you might have taken it."

"Well, I haven't. I don't care about a stupid ring," shot back Sadie.

Arya looked at her with contempt. But decided not to take it any further. The ring was probably somewhere in her suitcase.

"We're leaving in thirty minutes," is all she said before she walked out of the room, her suitcase in tow.

Again, Sadie was left with her thoughts in the dark.

What would she say about the ring?

What did her dream mean?

Was their friendship in deep trouble?

She knew now more than ever she needed to make amends with Arya, before it was too late. Sadie quickly marched out of the room with a purpose and slipped into her parent's room. They had gone down to the reception to enquire about something, so this was her chance. There on the bed were their passports, it wouldn't be hard for Sadie to steal hers and leave it behind, because hers was in a passport holder.

All she had to do was take the passport out, and leave the holder, as long as her Dad didn't check them before they left, she could get away with it.

From the corner of her eye, she could see someone approaching the room. She had nowhere to hide her passport, so she stuck in the back of her shorts and put her top over it. And as soon as she has a chance to retreat to her room, she'd stash it somewhere. Then she realised the person approaching her room was her Dad, and she panicked.

"You all ready?" he asked.

"Yep. Just checking my passport is in here." she replied, holding her passport holder up.

"I've cross-checked them all, and they're all there. So, we're set to go!"

Sadie smiled and then quickly scurried back to her room. It was empty, so now was the time. But suddenly Arya walked in and grabbed something from her bedside table. Sadie had no choice but to quickly drop her passport in the drawer of her side dresser and slammed it shut. Arya gave her a quizzical look but then walked off. Just as Sadie was about to put it somewhere else, her Mom walked in and pulled her out.

"Let's goo! We need to do some last-minute things at the reception."

Everyone was busy getting their things together, but Sadie was lost somewhere else, her mind on her passport. Could she really get away with it? She watched her Dad holding all of theirs and a nervous flutter in the pit of her stomach erupted. She needed this to work. She wished her Dad would stop checking and to her surprise, he did. There was no third or fourth check of the passports. Clearly, he was satisfied that he had them all and they all left the room, one by one.

The parents were chatting as they walked down the corridor, Kiaan was slowly dragging his tiny suitcase along, moping that it was time to go home, and the girls were at the back not saying a word. It was like they were back in their bubble, but this time it was dull and empty. They couldn't hear anything else other than the deafening silence between them.   The tension was too great to even attempt to reconcile, and Sadie was tired of trying to defend herself. She decided to keep quiet, drop her head and carry on walking, not making a sound. Avoiding Arya at all costs, for now anyway.

While Sadie was wallowing in her own self-pity, Arya on the other hand, quickly started to think of something positive to mask the silence she was in. Thinking about how she will be reunited with Bailey and Maya soon and looking forward to meeting Eli again. Her thoughts raced from being able to hug Eli, to jumping on Maya and even kissing Bailey all over. Oh, how she missed her Bailey bear. Slowly but surely, she felt a smile grow on her face, thinking of Bailey literally warmed her heart and left her head feeling lighter. Her clouded mind cleared. Arya was so excited to go home.

After what felt like a millennium to Sadie, they finally reached their minivan. Arya got in from one side, and Sadie got in from the other, both moving in complete silence. While they were waiting in the van and the parents loaded the luggage into the back, Arya texted Maya for a bit.

Me and Sadie had a fight…

Oh no. What happened?

I'll tell you when I'm back, too long to text. But it feels pretty awkward now.

Arya put her phone down and sighed. She relaxed in her seat and closed her eyes for a few seconds. She was glad that Kiaan was sitting in between them, it filled the empty space that had been created and would mask the tension that was building up. For once, she wouldn't have to be next to Sadie, and out of the whole trip this was when she needed space the most. Sure, it wasn't a long drive to the airport, but space is space, and she was glad to get it.

Sadie twiddled her thumbs, wondering who Arya had texted. Was she saying something bad about her? Did she tell someone they argued? Was she texting Eli or Maya or someone else that she had no idea about? She wasn't sure, but she needed to get her mind off it. So, she grabbed her headphones from her bag and put on some music. If there was anything that could distract her and lift her spirits, it was music. Without a doubt.

She let the music fill her ears and she breathed in deeply and sighed. Things will work out, they always do, she has nothing to worry about. She averted her eyes away from the window for a second as she saw the adults getting in, she saw her Dad say something to her holding the passports up, but she didn't pay attention.

Sadie just nodded in response and looked back out the window, observing another family that had arrived at the hotel, they also happened to have two girls with them. They were jumping around and looking as happy as she and Arya were when they first came. Sadie fell into doom and gloom watching them, wishing things would have ended differently, but maybe she had a shot at redemption when they had this extra day.

The engine of the minivan purred and came to life, she looked back at Arya and then at the window, wondering about how she can use this time to make it up to Arya, again. Should she use her words, or are her actions better? One thing was for sure, she wasn't going to waste this chance to fix things between them. She needed it more than anything, and for her nightmare to not come true her life depended on it.

Chapter 13

The journey to the airport wasn't a long one, but the tension in the backseat felt like it lasted years. Despite the persistence of her favourite musician trying to lift Sadie's mood, she couldn't help but feel the cold shoulder she was receiving. It made her feel unsettled. And even though Kiaan was between them, it felt like there was a gap bigger than a gorge separating them. She wished she was smart enough to have more control of her feelings, but she always let them get the better of her. However, she was so determined not to let Arya be taken away from her, especially by someone she only spent a summer with. Only Sadie could be her best friend, no one else could. Sadie thought whether seventeen years of friendship meant anything to anyone, anymore.

Arya had spent her time staring out the window, taking in the golden sunshine for the last time, since autumn was soon approaching back home, and she knew the sun wouldn't glow like this. She always felt so happy when she was basking in its glorious light, and she especially hated the cold. More than anything she wanted to move to California where she could feel free, dream big and soak in all the sunshine that she wanted.

Which was one of the reasons why she wanted to go to college there, and she hoped she'd make it. Her application was almost ready to send in October. She just wanted to get rid of it already. It was constantly giving her stress. Hours had been spent talking to Maya about it, because they were applying for the same college. They both had spent so much time writing their applications, helping each other perfect it and proofreading till their brains were fried. Maya also helped Arya put her portfolio together, which was more helpful than Sadie had been.

Arya glanced over at Sadie and wondered whether she had finished her applications yet. They barely talked about colleges, Sadie also procrastinated with her applications, saying she'd do it later. But later never came. Sadie also tried to avoid the conversation as much as she could; she didn't like change. Arya could predict how Sadie would react to finding out that she and Maya were hoping to get into the same college. Arya knew it would reaffirm in Sadie's mind that Arya was kicking her out and didn't regard her as a best friend anymore.

Arya felt annoyed and frustrated. She hated how Sadie made her feel guilty for being friends with Maya. And how she thought that Arya was replacing her when she wasn't. How could her best friend think these bad things about her? She couldn't replace Sadie, and she never wanted to, she just wanted other friends as well. Thinking about how this drama will continue for the rest of the summer, Arya rolled her eyes looking at Sadie and turned back to the window. She was looking forward to the space she would be getting more than anything.

When they arrived at the airport, everyone grabbed their luggage out of the minivan and made their way into the airport. Arya was holding Kiaan's hand and Sadie was still listening to her music. While their parents were trying to find where to check in, Arya looked at Sadie who seemed to be in a world entirely of her own. She tentatively walked over and called out to Sadie. She didn't hear and Arya didn't want to talk to Sadie more than she needed to right now, so she gave up calling her name and tapped on her shoulder instead.

Sadie swivelled round. She noticed that it was Arya who was trying to get her attention, and it sent a jolt in her stomach. Were they about to talk again and make things up? She slowly took her headphones out with promise.

"Yeah?" she asked. "Sorry, I had my headphones in."

"I realised. You should probably take them out while we're in the airport. Just so you can pay attention," replied Arya.

A voice in Sadie's mind boomed. *Was that it? That's what she was going to say? Is she not even going to say sorry for snapping at you? She shouldn't be telling you what to do. Fight back, Sadie!*

The voice was right, she wasn't going to stand there and let Arya tell her what to do. She wasn't a child. And her tone of voice irritated Sadie even more, since she wasn't even going to apologise for her outburst.

"Excuse me?" questioned Sadie, one eyebrow raised.

"Just take your headphones out and pay attention, that's all. Otherwise, you'll get lost and then blame everyone else," reiterated Arya.

Fight back!

Sadie thought Arya had some nerve treating her like a child. She had now reached her breaking point and felt like snapping back, and this time she wouldn't care how it would upset Arya.

"I'm not a child Arya, in case you didn't realise. I can also multitask, unlike you."

149

Arya paused, feeling confused at what Sadie meant.

"Explain," was all she could say.

"You can't even keep two friends without kicking one to the curb like a stranger as soon as you've met someone else!" snapped Sadie childishly, eyes like daggers.
Arya looked baffled, too, taken back at Sadie's immature, albeit dumb dig. Which was once again aimed at her friend's choices. She'd had enough for one day.

"Oh, why don't you just grow up, Sadie? Play a different tune for once. I can't be bothered to deal with you. I'm so done. Come back to me when you've learnt how to be a good friend," huffed Arya, and she stormed off back to the parents.

"That's rich coming from you. Why don't you learn to be a good friend!" called Sadie.

Arya paid no heed to this remark. She tuned out Sadie's voice completely.

Now Sadie was seething with anger watching her best friend walk away. Pure hatred was brewing inside her. But as quickly as her anger increased, she quickly snapped out of it and realised what she just said. She felt sick for snapping at Arya, especially with a dumb remark. Sadie felt so frustrated with herself and immediately regretted everything. Quickly turning away from everyone, she let her tears fall silently, having been unable to hold them back. Biting down on her lip so she wouldn't make a sound.

Every time she wanted to mend things with Arya, she ended up making it worse. It was like she had no control of what she was going to say. Not thinking before she opened her mouth. And now, Sadie just felt like running out and not coming back. Splashes of warm teardrops fell onto her hot cheeks and down her face. And no matter how hard she tried to stop, her eyes kept brewing tears, but she had to let them fall out before re-joining the group. Because Sadie didn't want everyone knowing she had cried, especially Arya. There would be too many questions that she didn't want to answer, and she didn't want to annoy Arya anymore.

After a while trying to compose herself, Sadie heard her parents calling her over. She sighed and hastily wiped her tears away with her sleeve. She painted a smile on her face and walked over. As soon as Sadie reached them, Arya moved away and stood by Aashi. Sadie looked at her crestfallen, feeling heartbroken. Rose noticed this and moved closer to her. She lifted Sadie's head up and smiled at her. Sadie reluctantly smiled back and her Mom stroked her head. Sadie was in such an awful mood now, the only thing that could cheer her up was knowing she was about to get more time here, with Arya. Whether or not they were talking, at least it would just be them.

As the group stood in the queue to check in their bags, Sadie's stomach started turning. This was when her plan would come to fruition. She hoped she wouldn't get in trouble for it and that it would all be worth it. Her parents were next, so she walked with them and her hands started to quiver. The man at the desk asked for the passports and as her Dad reached for them, Sadie eyed them intensely, glaring at her holder. Noah handed them over to the man and he checked them all.

Everything was fine. They were all there.

Confusion clouded her mind. That can't be right, thought Sadie. What happened to her passport? It wasn't supposed to be there, what had happened?

She was shaking her head expecting this to all be her imagination. As soon as Noah got them back, she snatched them from him.

"Hey!" he said.

She hurriedly slipped to her passport holder and ripped it open. And there it was. Her passport. As clear as day.

"Wha-" she stammered.

"Excuse me, may I have them back? No need to snatch your passport, we all know you hate your picture," laughed Noah.

"How is my passport here?" asked Sadie, without thinking. "I mean…"

"Oh, Arya told me she thought you left something behind in the drawer as we were leaving. So, I went back and found this. And it's a good thing I went back to check! I did tell you in the van," he answered. "I have no idea how it got there, though. I checked them a million times," said Noah.

His voice now trailing off as Sadie thought back to when they were waiting outside the hotel in the van. And she remembered briefly that her

Dad had shown her the passports, but she hadn't taken any notice. Sadie then looked at Arya, who was glaring at her. She knew something. She knew what Sadie had tried to do, Sadie was sure of it. She then handed the passports back defeatedly.

Her plan was ruined. All gone, by a dumb mistake of hers. Her world started crumbling around her, and she felt like she had fallen through the floor, like the tiles had swallowed her up. Falling into the darkness, just like her attempts to make things better.

Suddenly, she was brought back to reality, by Arya's clear but fierce voice.

"Why did you leave your passport?"

"I- I didn't mean to," stammered Sadie, with sweat starting to form on her head.

Arya scanned Sadie's face, and knew she was lying.

"Yes, you did. And I will find out why."

Sadie felt threatened. She gulped and moved away. Their friendship had now reached a level that it had never felt before, ice cold.

She knew there was no point in trying to make amends now, it was a lost cause and quite frankly, she had given up for today. No matter what she did, it always made things worse, and she was tired of looking like the bad guy.

So, she decided to keep her distance from Arya. Put her headphones back in, follow the crowd and keep quiet. But Sadie couldn't stop looking at her. She watched Arya walk, with a stiff step and a slight slouch. That was her walk when she was upset, and Sadie's heart dropped even further. It couldn't get any lower now. And she knew it was all her fault. She made Arya feel like this. With a heavy sigh, Sadie looked at the ground and carried on walking.

The journey wasn't as bad as Sadie thought it would be though. Since it was an overnight flight, everyone decided to sleep, and Arya was the first to doze off. It seemed like she was eager to be in a state where she wouldn't need to converse with anyone, especially Sadie. This was probably because they still had to sit by one another, as if they had changed seats, it would have been even more obvious to their parents that something was really wrong. So, as soon as they sat down, Arya put on her headphones and sleeping mask on and that was the last peep out of her during the flight.

After a couple hours had gone by, the plane was no longer filled with the buzz of people chatting or children fussing. It had steadily gotten quieter and quieter. The plane grew darker as the lights dimmed.

And all Sadie could feel was the gentle hum of the plane and the occasional snore of a sleeping passenger. She should have felt content in that moment, but she was suffering through an inner turmoil. She gazed longingly at Arya with a sad expression on her face. Wishing she would wake up and talk to her, but she didn't, and she wouldn't. She then noticed Arya's hair had now fallen carelessly over her face. Sadie debated in her mind, whether to move it off her face or not.

She went for it, slowly moving her hand over to her, but suddenly the voice rang through her mind, sharp and clear.

What are you doing? Why are you caring for her when she trashed our friendship and brushed it to the side?

This made Sadie stop and hesitate as she pondered over this thought. It was right, for the most of it. But this was her best friend, and she loved Arya very much. Sadie couldn't stop caring for her any more than she could start hating books. It was engraved in her heart and soul. She pushed away the thought and that voice to the back of her mind and slowly reached out to Arya's face. Gently, she caressed her hair in between her fingertips before sweeping it away. And then quickly retreated her hand, just in case Arya woke up. After that, Sadie looked out the window.

Scattered below her, was an array of lights ablaze and shining at her. It seemed like a swarm of a thousand fireflies were flickering below. It was a beautiful and magnificent sight. It drew her in with such an intense force, her eyes now dazzling with the view below. Gradually feeling a warmth growing in her heart, she sensed that the lights were telling her it would be okay.

And after Sadie felt like she had absorbed every inch of the comforting light, she sat back and relaxed in her seat. A calm and serene smile slowly grew on her emotionally exhausted face.

Then it was two in the morning, the flight was over, and she was back at home and in her bed. She felt shattered. Only now she couldn't sleep. She thought that maybe after Arya had time to sleep on the plane, that when they arrived home, she would at least talk to her. But no, that wasn't the case.

The car journey was filled with silence and awkwardness. And when it came to saying goodbye to Arya and her family, Arya didn't even look at Sadie. Her parents went in the house first and she picked her brother out of the car, grabbed her suitcase and wheeled it to the front door.

Then it closed shut with a dull thud that echoed in Sadie's ears. She just wanted to go home. To go to sleep and wake up to another day, but to no avail. She was still wide awake, her thoughts swimming around her. The guilt was catching in her throat, and she immensely tried to block out the voice that made her question everything.

But she wasn't the only one having a sleepless night, because a couple streets away sitting on her bed, was Arya. She hadn't gone to sleep yet. She hadn't even changed out of her clothes. The silence of the outside world was compelling, but the silence in her mind was overbearingly loud. She was so tired, her body was exhausted, but she couldn't rest. She didn't particularly like sitting in the dark, but she too was emotionally drained to move, and felt like she didn't deserve the light.

She felt like she had been chewed up and spat back out by Sadie. Like she was constantly in a state of battle with her friends, and she wondered when it became like this and why Sadie couldn't see what she was doing to her. Arya thought about everything Sadie had said in the hotel room before they left and back in the airport. It was like a slap in the face and the mark was still there, imprinted on Arya.

Then all of a sudden, she couldn't take it anymore and she burst into tears. Uncontrollable tears streamed down her face. Dropping into her lap, tear after tear, after tear. She didn't try to stop them or wipe them away, because she had no energy to move, and she didn't care. The stage of hyperventilating shortly took over and with every staggered breath she took, the voice of Sadie burned in her mind:

"*Are you my best friend?*"

"*Pay attention to those who have been there longer!*"

"*Y'know, you can't even keep two friends without kicking one to the curb like a stranger as soon as you've met someone else!*"

"*Why don't you learn to be a good friend!*"

Over and over these thoughts boomed in her mind, and each time more tears welled up in her eyes. Her grip on her bed became harder and she felt weaker with every uncontrollable sob. Her body started quivering as if she was losing her grip. She started shaking her head, trying to shake the thoughts out of her mind, trying to reassure herself that Sadie was wrong and that she was a good friend, a good person.

Turning her head up to the ceiling, she slowly closed her eyes and the last of her tears seeped out. Her breath quivered as it drew in and she found herself slowly collapsing onto her bed. Fingers tingling and the feeling of numbness slowly taking over her body, coupled with the heavy weight of guilt and confusion sitting on her chest. And then finally, she curled up into a ball of sadness, with tears forming again and cried herself to sleep.

157

Chapter 14

It was the next morning and Arya finally rolled out of bed, feeling groggy and lethargic, unable to recollect when she managed to fall asleep. All she knew was that her eyes were sore and heavy. If it weren't for the sunlight that had been blinding her eye through a tiny slit in the curtains, she might have stayed in bed all day. Right now, all she wanted and felt she deserved was the darkness. The easy option was to turn away from the window, but the light was still illuminating her room.

Having no other choice, she was forced to leave the comfort of her bed and move her stiff body, to encase herself in the darkness once more. She slowly walked to her curtains, grabbing it with a strong force and was about to yank it shut. However, as she lifted it up, she saw her saving grace outside. It was Maya and her Bailey bear. Suddenly, the darkness jumped out of her with a click of her fingers. Now full of cheer and delight, she felt the sunshine on her and raced downstairs. As she headed to the front door, her parents were peacefully eating their breakfast on the dining table, when they heard a ruckus named Arya, dashing down the stairs.

"What's with all the hubbub? Why is she still wearing the same clothes?" asked Kunal.

"Beats me. I'm surprised she's even awake," shrugged Aashi.

Arya wrenched open the door and Bailey came bounding in and jumped on her. Both falling to the floor, followed by an attack of his tongue, licking every inch of her face. He had definitely missed her. Arya couldn't stop laughing, trying with all her might to get him to stop licking her.

"Oh, I've missed you too!! How have you been, boy? Did you miss me?" said Arya, ruffling his fur and giving him all the kisses.

When he calmed down, Arya brought him in for the biggest cuddle she's ever had. And right there and then, she knew she was finally home. Through all of Bailey's fur, she could see Maya grinning like a Cheshire cat and laughing at Bailey.

Arya couldn't stop grinning either, seeing her two favourite things after a night of sadness. It certainly felt like a dream come true. She got up and Bailey soon ran to her parents, and Arya ran to Maya. They spun around as they hugged, locking in a tight embrace, anyone would have thought they were apart for months! Finally, they both let go and started bouncing with happiness, like two toddlers.

"Oh, I missed you!" sang Maya.

"I missed you too! So glad I'm back home!"

"I was going to call you and tell you I was coming, but I wanted to surprise you!" said Maya.

"It was honestly such a nice surprise. I'm so glad you came," smiled Arya, equally talking in rushed terms. "Do you want to come in?"

"Yes! We need to catch up!"

Both girls walked harmoniously to Arya's room, with Arya now having a spring in her step, chatting away in sync.

"Oh, now she walks," chuckled Kunal.

When they both entered the bedroom, Arya collapsed on to her bed, spreading out like an angel.

"Tired, are we?" laughed Maya.

"Beyond tired," sighed Arya

"You do actually look beat. Did you get back really late?"

"We got back after midnight, can't remember the time. But it wasn't the time that made me tired," hinted Arya.

"What is it then?" asked Maya as she sat beside Arya, pushing her arm to give her space.

Arya pondered over whether to tell her what happened. She already knew that Maya had her issues with Sadie, and she didn't want to make them worse. But then again, if she didn't talk about it, it was going to eat her up. And that would be the worst thing to happen. Talking always heals things. So, she decided to open up. After what felt like thirty minutes of talking nonstop about what happened in their hotel room, the airport, the passport and the ride home, Arya finally stopped and caught her breath. Her shoulders felt they had been ironed out, and she felt a great relief. She caught a glance of Maya, whose mouth was wide open.

"How is she not tired of whining about the same story over and over? Who cares if you have other friends. Does she expect you to only ever be friends with her?" moaned Maya, rolling her eyes.

All Arya could do was shrug her shoulders defeatedly.

"And what was with the passport? Why was she shocked it was there?" questioned Maya.

"I don't know. I found that really weird. I'm pretty sure it was her passport that she put back in the hotel drawer. It's like she meant to leave her passport behind," said Arya.

Maya carried on thinking. "What if she wanted to leave her passport so you couldn't fly home?"

Arya shook her head.

"No, that's dumb. She wouldn't do that; besides she would get into serious trouble if she did. It must be something else."

"I don't know. Sounds like something she would do," shrugged Maya.

This left Arya in thought. She needed to be honest with herself and did think that at first, but surely it was a stupid idea. She sighed and looked up at the ceiling. Her eyes wandered over to a picture of them on the wall. She wished they could be as happy as they once were when that memory was captured. When did it all go wrong, she thought.

"I'm actually nervous to tell her about Eli, whenever that'll happen. He's already moved here, and I want to see him again. Do I tell her that we're friends? Because we will be meeting up frequently, and I can't hide

161

that forever. Hiding it at the hotel was one thing, but not when we'll all be living in the same city," worried Arya.

Maya remained quiet and Arya understood why completely. She knew that Maya thought it wasn't right that Arya had seen him secretly and could already predict that Sadie wouldn't react well to it at all. But there was nothing anyone could do about it.

Arya couldn't stunt her growth just for Sadie's sake, it wasn't fair on her, and no one should have control over someone else's life. Sadie would just have to deal with it and accept that Arya was now expanding her relationships, beyond just the two of them.

"Are you going to see him soon?" asked Maya, finally breaking through the silence.

"Yeah, seeing him tomorrow. I really can't wait," she replied, butterflies blooming in her stomach.

They smiled at each other, but Arya still found herself thinking about Sadie. Why couldn't she share this excitement with her? Wasn't that what friends do? She and Maya gossiped for a little while, and then Arya suddenly remembered. After spending five minutes searching through her luggage, she finally came upon tissue paper that held Maya's brand-new Minnie Mouse ears. She took them out and gave the gift to Maya.

"Oh my god. These are beautiful! Oh, wow, wow, wow. Thank you so much! I love them!"

"They were the last two of that colour and design, and I knew it was a sign," winked Arya.

She took the ears from Maya and gently placed them on her head, then leant back and admired the way it looked, holding her face like a proud Mom. Maya checked them out in the mirror and then grabbed Arya's from the wrapping and placed hers on her head too, and they both giggled.

The following half an hour was spent divulging everything that happened on Arya's holiday: what she did, where she went, what she ate and about Eli. Then Maya told Arya all about her daily antics with Bailey and Coco, how they both would follow each other around and wind Leo up. Coco hadn't given Bailey much of a chance to miss Arya. She hadn't left his side the entire time and they had become best friends. Arya felt super happy hearing it, because she was worried that Bailey would hate her for leaving him, but all's well that ends well.

They chatted to great lengths, played with Kiaan and Bailey in the garden under the golden sunshine, and by the time they were all tuckered out, it was nearly dinner time. Arya's parents asked Maya to stay for dinner. She had become an integral part of Arya's life now and they loved her. Their dinner was a traditional Indian curry of potatoes and aubergines with chapatis. You couldn't eat a more classic dinner. It was also their first Indian meal they'd had since before the holiday. And boy, did they really miss home cooked food. Aashi had made enough to feed the entire street and yet it was all scoffed down their throats, with not a morsel left.

Bellies full, everyone was heading into a food coma. Kunal had a nap on the sofa while Aashi put on her Indian soaps and got stuck into the new drama that day. Kiaan played with his beloved toys while Bailey watched him, and the girls went back upstairs. Despite having a terrible night and a difficult wake up, the rest of the day had turned into a nurturing day for Arya. She needed the love she was getting from her family and Maya, and she was starting to feel truly happy again.

When they reached Arya's room, Maya pointed out something that had always sparked her curiosity.

"I've been here a few times, and I've never actually been up there..." she said, pointing at the staircase.

"Oh! Wow, I can't believe I've never shown you. It's my painting room! It used to be an attic, but we never used it, and Mom came up with this idea. She was getting tired of seeing my artwork scattered around my room, this was when I was messy. So, she killed two birds with one stone and converted the empty space into my own creative freedom. Now the attic has a purpose, and my room has been clean ever since!" explained Arya.

Maya nodded, taking in Arya's long explanation. "Can I see it?"

"Of course!" jumped Arya.

Arya led the way up the intricate stairs, to the room that was aglow with the setting sun. Maya gasped as she walked in. Arya watched her as she scanned the room and saw all of Arya's different artwork hung up, the paint splatters smeared on the walls, the numerous drawings laid out on the table. She felt proud.

"Wow, this is so cool. I can't believe you have a room just for your art," Maya laughed in amazement.

"Me neither. It makes me so happy. It's cut off from the rest of the house, and with the basking sunlight I end up creating my best pieces of art here."

"What's your favourite artwork?" questioned Maya.

Arya turned Maya to look at her favourite painting, the one with the trees changing seasons. She clasped her hands together like she was a proud parent and beamed at the painting. She never stopped admiring how delicately the tree changes in the season, how the colours magically merged with each other, but each had their own spotlight. She felt it was mesmerising. Maya was about to reach out to touch it, but Arya stopped her.

"Oh no, please don't touch it. I'm super protective over it and I don't let anyone touch it. Sorry!" admitted Arya.

"Oh sorry! No, that's okay. I get it, you're really proud of it and you don't want anything to ruin it," Maya said understandingly.

Arya smiled, then sighed, turning round in circles.

"I've really missed this space. I go in here to let steam off in my paintings, but also just to escape the world. It's heaven."

"I can imagine! I wish I was creative," sulked Maya.

"You've just got to find your calling!"

"That's so cheesy. But I get it. Maybe one day," said Maya.

Arya showed Maya other pieces of her work and her ideas of what to work on next. They sat on the floor with her paintings scattered around them and Arya encouraged Maya to have a go at one herself. Maya had painted a sunflower, big and yellow, inviting and comforting, with a single bumblebee perched on the flower. Maya felt shy, explaining that it was her favourite flower. Arya smiled and said she loved it and then hung it up on the wall. They both stepped back and admired it. Arya had now shared her favourite place, which previously only Sadie had seen, meaning her friendship with Maya was now solid.

The sky outside grew darker and darker as the night came. Streetlights turned on and the noise of the outside world and chattering birds started to wind down. They were tidying Arya's paintings up before heading back to her room. She briefly glanced outside and had a feeling that someone was staring at her from across the street. Arya moved closer to the window and turned the light off to see if she could have a better view. But then Maya interrupted her investigation.

"Let's go watch a movie! I'm really in the mood for one."
Arya, however, barely heard her as she stared out the window.

"Arya? Helloo?" Maya asked again, tapping her on the shoulder.

"Huh?" asked Arya, snapping out of the moment.
Maya peeped over her shoulder. "What are you looking at?"

"Oh. Nothing, just thought I saw someone looking up here. Must be my mind playing tricks on me."

The girls then went back into her room and started to choose a movie to watch, getting their snacks ready and settling down for the evening. But little did Arya know that someone had been watching her and had been for a couple of hours.

Across from Arya's house, was a bench hidden amongst the towering street trees. It was usually covered with tiny blue flowers that fell off the branches, but not this evening. Sitting very still, with a stiff back, and blue petals floating down onto her head and lap, was Sadie. She had wandered to Arya's house on a walk and saw that Maya was there through the bedroom window. This upset her greatly, not even a day had gone by since they came back, and she had already invited Maya around. Again, she felt like she had been pushed out, she never felt good enough.

However, she decided not to do anything, not to verbally react to Arya or make a scene. Instead, she just waited and waited. Waiting for when Maya left, she was curious to see how long she'd be spending with Arya, what they were doing, and she wanted to be there when she left.

She was about to give up waiting, and started to head off home, but then she saw something that made her sick. It burned her body as if she had just gotten branded like a cow. There was a light on in Arya's art room. It meant only one thing, that she had shown Maya her space and her art. That was meant to be a special place that only special people could see. Sadie moaned. Even Arya's parents don't go in there and it angered Sadie so much that Arya had let Maya in.

She doesn't deserve it!" shouted Sadie, disturbing a couple of birds. "That was mine and Arya's special place. How could she let someone else in?"

Her eyes started welling up and angry tears began to stream down her face. She looked at her hands that were now clenched.

"How could she do this to me?"

Within a split second, she decided to call Arya. She whipped her phone out and pressed her name. It rang and rang. There was no answer. She carried on ringing, but no one answered. She let out a frustrated cry. What should she do? Turn back home and try again with Arya the next day? No, she decided to stay on the bench and wait for when they came out. After what felt like a couple hours, she heard a movement from across the street. She looked up with a cold and tired expression on her face and saw Maya leaving Arya's house. Watching them hug and part ways.

Then Sadie eyed Maya walking alone down the street and before she knew it, she was following her from a distance. Her hood up and her footsteps slow and quiet. The air had a sudden chill that wisped around Sadie's face, clutching at her hair. Maya had knelt to the floor to tie her shoelaces that came undone, and Sadie wanted to approach her. But she wasn't sure how. Then she briefly glanced at her feet and noticed a thick log.

The voice boomed the voice in her mind.

Grab it. Hit her with it. Get rid of her.

She silently reached down to grab the log. Her steady and numb hand grabbed it with full force. It was brittle, cold and felt like a heavy weight. Slowly, she stood back up and made her way gravely to Maya, who seemed to have been struggling with her laces. Sadie's pulse started to echo in her ears with each step she took closer to Maya. Her steps sounded like explosions in her head and her breath turned ragged. Was she really going to do this? Was she really that desperate?

She had almost reached Maya's back. Her arm swung up and she was ready to send it crashing down on her head. But a porch light from across the street came blazing on and Maya had shot up, just as Sadie had run behind a tree. Maya looked around and then carried on walking, unbeknownst to what could have happened.

Behind the tree, was Sadie hiding and profusely sweating, with her heart now feeling it was about to jump out her chest. Her hand was still gripping the log and when she realised it, she dropped it, as if it had scorched her skin. She couldn't believe what had come over her and what she was about to do. She became frantic and threw up. Then with a heavy heart she collapsed to the floor and rested against the tree, putting her head between her legs. Uncontrollable tears streamed down her face and utter disgust ran through her mind. Feeling sick to her stomach that she was about to do something so barbaric. What was she thinking?

After she composed herself, Sadie finally decided to make her way home. She was certain that Maya was long gone and back home, so it was her time to leave too. She shakily picked herself up from the hard, cold ground, swaying slightly and suddenly started sprinting home. It was as if she was trying to outrun the voice living in her head that was so cruel and filled with hatred.

With each frantic footstep she took, it felt like she had a block of lead in her shoes, weighing her down. Sadie kept running and running, until she couldn't bear picking her feet up anymore. And ended up tripping over them, crashing down to the floor outside her house. Steadying herself on her hands and feet, she sombrely stood up and retreated to her house. Quietly she opened the door to her house, and snuck her way in. Her parents were reading in their corner and had called out to her.

"Hey bub, where have you been?"

"Out. I'm going to bed. Please don't disturb me."

"Oh...okay. Well goodnight, love you!" chimed her parents in sync.

Sadie didn't feel like saying it back, she felt empty, and love had no place in her body right now. As soon as she entered her room, she stripped off her clothes and ran straight into the bathroom, feeling the urge to scrub every inch of her body and to rub off the guilt and stench of evil she felt inside.

She ended up spending thirty minutes in the shower, until her body was red raw from the intense scrubbing and the increase in temperature that she kept turning up. It became hotter and hotter and before she knew it, it started to burn her skin. She couldn't take it anymore; the scorching sensation was too much for her to handle. Feeling like she was going to pass out, she switched to ice cold water that numbed her skin.

Once she felt like she was clean, she put on fresh pjs and clambered into bed. She wanted to forget what happened, push it out of her mind. But every few minutes, she had flashes of what happened that night. From the moment she realised Arya had let Maya in her art room, *their special place*, to feeling so much anger, she wanted to hurt Maya. In that fleeting moment, Sadie had wanted to hit Maya's head with a log so hard that she died. For a second, she wanted to kill someone. It didn't make sense; it didn't feel like her. Sadie felt so disgusted and disappointed in herself. Who knows what would have happened to Maya if she went through with it?

Sadie felt like she was going to throw up again. Quickly, she grabbed a pillow and covered her face, so all she could see was total blackness and muffle her cries.

Slowly but surely, she fell asleep...But then the nightmare happened. She was alone again. Walking towards the edge of a bridge that overlooked a small spring. There was tumultuous water thundering down. She shivered looking at it and the air that wafted over to her was as cold as ice. She didn't want to fall in there. The feeling of isolation started kicking in, but then she heard a whisper.

"Sadie."

Sadie started moving towards where the whisper came from. But she stopped short. It was Maya. A menacing look crept upon her face, a creepy smile spread, and a maniacal laugh escaped her lips.

"What? Did you really think Arya would be here? She's not your friend anymore and she never will be. She's my friend, my best friend."

"No, no, I'm not listening!" shouted Sadie, frantically shaking her head. "This can't be true. We're best friends! Why would she leave me?"

"You're possessive. You're needy. You're controlling. And she's had enough. She doesn't need you and she doesn't want you."

"Shut up!" roared Sadie.

Anger was seething in her and all she could see was red. She moved so fast that Maya didn't see her coming. She stood there on the edge of the bridge and continued laughing. Not realising that Sadie was fast approaching, full force, ready to push her. In an instant, their bodies collided.

Sadie woke up in a fright. Her head was clammy, her top stuck to her back and the sickness in her stomach came back with a fight. She couldn't understand why she kept having these nightmares, what did they mean? Why were they so dark? Not being able to come to find an answer, she slammed back onto the bed and laid there till the sun came up. Eyes open, breathing staggered and not a tired bone in her body.

As the day dawned, and the birds chirped their morning call, she knew what the resolution was. She had to give Arya space. Even if it was for a couple of days, or even weeks. And maybe these intense nightmares would go away, maybe she could fix their friendship and maybe Arya wouldn't feel the need to leave Sadie.

She had to try.

Chapter 15

It was weird how one day could start so terribly, but the next day could start in the best way. This is exactly how Arya felt.

Instead of her alarm ringing in her ears like a foghorn, it graced them like a morning bird call. She opened her eyes, saw the sun brightly shining in her room, and she effortlessly rose from her pillow. Her phone had pinged from the side dresser, and she grabbed it with anticipation, because she knew who it would be from. As her eyes scanned the text, her smile broadened, thinking about how magical she hoped her day would go.

I can't wait to see you!

Eli.

Her eyes lingered on the message, knowing that in a few hours she would be seeing him again. Never had a simple text like that made her smile like a child on Christmas morning. She hastily replied and jumped out of bed, ready for what the day might bring. Running into the bathroom, she quickly brushed her teeth, had a steaming hot shower and met her first obstacle. What was she going to wear? Every outfit she took out of her cupboard was thrown (delicately) on her bed with dissatisfaction. She couldn't figure out what vibe she was going for.

Beginning to feel too worked up over something simple, Arya relaxed and took a step back. Taking a brisk walk around her room and up the stairs, she was welcomed by the warm glow in her favourite room and instantly knew what she wanted to wear. Knowing the sun would stay high in the sky throughout the day, she decided on wearing her favourite dress, a white, flowy dress. That was adorned with her favourite flower, the simplistic but delicate daisy. There wasn't a more perfect time to wear her favourite things. After all she wanted to look and feel her best. To accompany her cute outfit, she picked out her daisy earrings and necklace to match. She caught a glance of herself in the mirror.

"Too much daisy? Or... not enough?" she said to her reflection as she grabbed her daisy ring. She smiled at herself for five seconds. Then frowned.

"That's too much," she said as she placed her ring back on her desk.

Although, as she put her ring down, she thought about Maya's ring that she lost. She never misplaces things, so she couldn't understand where it could have gone. Then she noticed the grey plush bag sitting in her trinket plate. Emptying the contents in her palm, she knew her outfit would feel complete wearing her "daisy chain" friendship bracelet from Sadie. After putting it on, she stared longingly at the bracelet that adorned her wrist. Arya sighed but carried on.

Twirling her hair around her fingers and completing the final touches, she was now ready. Arya set off with the springiest step as she skipped down her street. After a few steps she realised this was her first date in a long time and suddenly began to feel quite nervous.

Normally she would talk to Sadie whenever she felt like this, but this time she couldn't. Not after Sadie's relentless arguments, when Arya had tried so hard to make her feel better. Besides if Arya were to ask Sadie how to keep calm during a date with a guy she wasn't meant to have seen during their holiday, it wouldn't go down well. It was the last thing Arya wanted to do. All she hoped for was that Sadie's sudden possessiveness would disappear, and their friendship could turn back into what it once was.

Arya sighed.

She missed Sadie, but it had only been a couple of days since their argument. Arya still needed more space. She hadn't replied to Sadie's calls the previous night, and Sadie hadn't followed up either. In a few days maybe they'd patch up, and things will be okay again. She could only hope.

As she was arriving at the park where she was meeting Eli, she felt as if the sun shined a little brighter on her. Her smile grew as she saw his silhouette under the tree, waiting for her. Butterflies grew in her stomach and her already flushed cheeks became even more red. She was just a few steps away from him, when he turned his head around and he saw her. He quickly jumped up with excitement donning a cheeky grin on his face and he bounded to her, like an excited puppy. Arya noticed he had a small bouquet of flowers in his hand. She sighed happily and smiled.

"Hey!" he said eagerly.

"Hey Eli," giggled Arya shyly, her face now glowing with happiness.

After they spent a few seconds swaying side to side with glee, lost in each other's eyes, Eli snapped back to reality. Finally realising he was still holding the bouquet, he gingerly handed it to Arya. It was made of daisies, bundles of blue hydrangeas, a few sprigs of violet asters and heavenly yellow yarrows dotted around.

"I made this myself. The garden in the house I moved to has the sweetest-smelling flowers and they reminded me of you," he explained shyly. "And surprisingly, they match your dress too! Maybe it was meant to be."

Arya blushed. "Oh wow, this is so lovely. Thank you."

Slightly swooning, she couldn't wait to put these in her room. She wanted to see them every morning and be forever reminded of him. Arya gently accepted the flowers and tentatively brushed them with her fingertips. The flowers had the most beautiful fragrance, that instantly calmed her nerves. She looked up at Eli and noticed he was longingly staring at her, with glistening eyes and a warm smile. Arya saw the right dimple in his cheek appear and it made her blush even more, as if that was even possible. A shy laugh unexpectedly escaped her lips.

They then started walking around the park. Through the cherrywood trees, passing clusters of daisies that were scattered in the lush grass and along the riverbank. Letting the gentle rush of water flow through their ears, and their conversations flowed just as naturally. They talked about their favourite things, their interests and what they had planned for the rest of the summer. As soon as Eli knew he was moving here, he had become desperate to see the sites of the coastal city. He had always lived inland, so this was a new experience for him.

Although, he also knew of places that Arya hadn't visited, so they agreed he'd show her around areas she hadn't heard of before. Like the Alvord desert, which wasn't too far from where they lived. He told her about the desert and how if she ever wanted to go, he would take her, and they could camp under the stars. This made her squeal with excitement. After their stimulating conversation, they parked themselves on a patch of empty grass under a lone apple tree. Arya looked up at the tree and wondered why it was the only apple tree around.

"A bird most likely dropped an apple seed here years ago, and now a beautiful apple tree has grown." he whispered.

"How did you know I was thinking about the tree?" asked Arya.

"You had this look about you and I just figured it out." he replied, smiling coyly.

Arya was amazed at how he could know that. Was she that predictable, even this early on into whatever this was between them? Or was he just a good reader? She was unsure. It made her wonder whether Eli was a deep mind.

"What do you think it represents?" she asked.

Eli scrutinised her face for a moment, then looked at the tree and thought for a while. A minute went past, and he finally answered.

"I think it means something beautiful can emerge anywhere. Even in a place where it's not meant to be. Even when against all odds, it will grow into something you didn't expect it too. From the tiniest action of dropping a seed, to even introducing yourself to someone new..." he replied with a soft demeanour.

She knew what he was referring to.

"That's so cliche. But I like it," replied Arya, playfully pushing him.

Eli laughed and took her hand and circled his fingers in her palm. This soothing motion sent chills up her spine. But in a good way. Arya then laid down on the grass and looked up at the calm sky. Eli followed suit after, and they both laid under the apple tree. Holding hands and enjoying each other's company. Even the silence was comfortable. It felt natural. Arya began thinking about whether they would become a couple, how she would introduce him to her parents and all the wonderful dates they would go on. Her mind started running a mile a minute, thinking about her future with this guy she had fallen head over heels with. Would they be together? Was she moving too quickly?

She tuned in to her body and really felt his hand in hers, how each finger was intertwined in hers. He felt strangely like home. He made her smile, he made her laugh, and he made her feel comfortable. What more could she want?

"I was thinking...that I still need my tour guide if you're still interested?" asked Eli coolly.

"Of course, I'll take you to all my favourite places!"

"I'd really like that," smiled Eli.

They sat in silence for a few minutes, taking in their quiet harmonies

"I never asked, but did you move here with your family?" wondered Arya.

"I moved in with a couple of friends from my high school that are going to the same college. We didn't feel like staying in dorms or being separated," explained Eli.

"Oh, are you guys close?" asked Arya.

"As close as can be! You should come round one day, they'd love to meet you," said Eli.

After getting ice cream by the river, Eli then walked Arya back home. They hugged and she walked to her front door, head in the clouds. As she was going in, they both waved to each other, until the moment the door shut. Arya then quickly peeked through the window to see what he was doing. All she could see was a huge smile on his face as he walked away. It was like she had slid into a whirlwind romance!

Everything was happening so fast, but it just felt right. Everything about him made her feel quaint and tranquil, she was on cloud nine. Hoping she could stay there with no brewing storm on the horizon.

Arya quietly squealed and slid down the front door until she was on the floor. She thought about him, and there was nothing in the world that could stop the biggest smile from forming on her face. She flopped her head onto her lap in bewilderment that she found someone so amazing. How had this feeling sprung up so fast? She felt like she was in a movie, having a prime-time romance. And then quietly giggled to herself. After a few moments, she heard a familiar tippy tap of paws on the floor approaching.

She looked up and saw Bailey with his head cocked to the side looking at her, and then she looked further up and saw her Mom doing the same.

Arya burst out laughing. "I can't even tell the difference between you guys."

"Well, at least I'm cute and cuddly like Bailey bear!" cooed Aashi. Giving Bailey a scratch behind the ear that made his tail wag happily. "Why are you on the floor anyway? And why are you looking so happy and radiant? Oh, and where did you get those lovely flowers from?" asked Aashi, one eyebrow raised.

"Oh, umn...the answer to all your questions is that I may have met a boy..." admitted Arya, ready for a telling off.
But surprisingly Aashi's face lit up.

"Oh my god! Really? My Arya with a boy? Miss 'too shy to order her own McDonald's?'" laughed Aashi.

She picked up Arya by the hands and asked her to spill the beans. They chatted for a while, while making dinner. Arya could always talk to her Mom about anything, whether it was about boys, or about boring things that no one else would be interested in. They had that special relationship; it was like they were really best friends instead of mother and daughter. And her Mom was just as excited as she was about Eli. Wanting to know absolutely everything about how they met. At first, she disapproved of how Arya would sneak off and meet him, but there was nothing she could do about it, so she let it slide. Then she asked a question that Arya was unable to answer.

180

"Did Sadie know?"

Arya paused, and the cheery feeling she had slowly washed out of her. She knew her Mom would be disappointed that she had done all of this without letting anyone know. Knowing that her motherly voice would take over and say it was irresponsible of her. And Arya agreed with that, because it was, but she hadn't thought properly as she was too head over heels.

Arya felt bad about the whole situation, especially for breaking her promise to Sadie. Then her heart had a slight twang, thinking about Sadie and how she missed her already. Arya knew they needed to patch things up, but believed it wasn't her fault they had an argument in the first place. Instead of having this inner fight, she decided to ask her Mom for advice.

"What do I do about Sadie?" asked Arya, quietly.

Aashi paused. "Oh...do you feel like you've had the space you needed from her?"

"I'm not sure. Maybe?"

"If you're unsure, then maybe you're not ready. But then again, she is your best friend. And maybe she's just going through a tough time, and she needs you too."

"But then she shouldn't be creating arguments with me and making me feel bad all the time," huffed Arya.

Her Mom sighed.

"Listen," she said in a stern but sincere way. "Sometimes people can't control their feelings or reactions to things that upset them. Have you ever thought that maybe she was really upset and could be feeling left out?

You can't tell her how to feel...you need to talk to her and let things out in the open. Otherwise, they'll play on both of your minds, and it'll make the problem bigger than it actually is. Clearly, it's bothering her."

Arya took in all the words her Mom told her and it made her wonder if she was being selfish. Selfish in only thinking about how she was feeling from Sadie's outburst and not thinking about why Sadie had the outburst. Arya thought about how it was very possible that Sadie was feeling left out, and perhaps it was up to her to reassure her best friend and clear things up once and for all. Maybe Arya needed to make Sadie understand that she loved her way too much to ever push her out.

After realising she had been in the wrong just as much as Sadie was, maybe even more so, Arya quickly hugged her Mom for opening her mind and ran upstairs, ready to call Sadie.

She ran into her room and flopped onto her bed. Pulling her phone out of her bag, she looked at it. Her phone screen was of her and Sadie, looking happy, looking like best friends. Arya was the one that needed to be a good best friend now, because clearly, she had failed in that area. This wasn't going to be an easy call for Arya though, she really hated conflict. She took a few deep breaths to psych herself up. After she was ready, she called Sadie. But there was no answer. It rang out, every time Arya called her. Confused, Arya sent a text.

Hey Sades...call me please.

She then decided to call her phone just one more time. To her surprise it was now switched off. Arya was confused as to why Sadie had now turned her phone off. Did she not want to talk to Arya? Or did her phone coincidentally die? Arya didn't blame Sadie if she didn't want to talk to her though.

A couple streets away Sadie was sitting on her bed in the dark under her blanket, reading a book, with a tiny clip that emitted light attached to it. She only ever read like this when she was in a sombre mood, which was pretty much every day recently. She had been so engrossed in her books that she hadn't realised someone had been trying to call her. Her mind had been somewhere else. She had a way of being completely sucked into any book she was reading; she could totally immerse herself in the world that was described, and she was happier there.

While she had been in this world of her own, she heard a nagging sound, like a buzzing and she had tried hard to ignore it. But it was persistent. It frustratingly pulled her out of her imagination and brought her back to reality. Her head snapped up and looked at her phone. Her eyes looked tired but deranged at the same time. She had stress lines in her furrowed brow and her hands had been clamped around her book so hard that there were now nail marks in the pages. The name of the caller was burning on her phone. Flashing in her tired eyes. But she didn't answer. She didn't want to.

Sadie thought maybe she should make Arya feel like she had made her feel; left out, alone in the woods, isolated and lonely. She let it ring and ring until she was done with it and turned it off. Then off she went back into her world, reading through the night, content in her imagination.

Arya, meanwhile, went to sleep crestfallen. Hopes of reconciliation that would have to wait for another time.

Chapter 16

Arya woke up with a start. It was early morning and all she could think about was Sadie. She grabbed her phone from the side dresser, hoping there was some notification from her, but there was nothing. No calls and no texts. It seemed like she was getting the silent treatment this time, but maybe she deserved it. Arya sighed. Feeling defeated she laid back on the pillow, pondering over her thoughts. Should she just let Sadie be, have her own time and wait for her to reach out? Or should she go over and resolve the conflict they were currently in? Arya decided on the latter.

As she got out of bed, she thought about creating one of her thoughtful 'Sadie care packages', something she put together whenever Sadie needed cheering up. She would collate Sadie's favourite things in her favourite wicker basket and gift her with it. It always cheered Sadie up. What worked the most was food. Sadie loved food, any type and she loved trying new things. So, that's what Arya's task was, to find something Sadie hadn't tried yet. She just needed to figure out what that was, and whether she had it in the house.

Arya always had a stash of Sadie's favourite snacks, though she didn't know. She knew that an assortment of her favourite sweet treats would soften Sadie's heart a little, and that's all she needed. All Arya wanted was to make her smile and feel like herself again. To reassure Sadie that she loved her with all her heart, and always would, no matter what happened.

And the cherry on the top would be a piece of art made by Arya. Because, more than anything, Sadie loved thoughtful and handmade gifts, especially from Arya.

This time she decided to paint something for Sadie. Yesterday, her Mom had sent her pictures of the holiday that she had taken. And Arya came across one of her and Sadie with their backs turned towards the camera, watching the fireworks at Magic Kingdom.

There was something about this picture that caught Arya's breath. She wasn't sure whether it was the sky that had been illuminated with captivating, colourful fireworks or the way the girls were standing together at that moment. It looked so intimate, so closed off from the rest of the crowds, just the two of them holding hands and enjoying the view. It really spoke to Arya, and she decided she would paint that moment with her watercolours.

She had woken up during the night and was unable to fall back to sleep and she knew this would have been the perfect time to get creative. So, she quietly walked up to her stairs and entered her creative space and sketched out that picture. Including every aspect of it, from the shape of the fireworks and the finer details of the castle to the wisps of hair that were blowing in the summer breeze. She decided to draw only the two of them on the canvas and no other people because it would always be her and Sadie against the world.

Once she was done, she started painting the background, with her inky blue watercolours. After that she flicked in drops of black watercolour and blended it into the blue, so it merged and created the midnight sky. But

186

she couldn't do anymore, as it needed to dry, otherwise it would create one blotchy mess. Instead, she had another go at getting some sleep and hoped to finish it in the morning.

With another fresh start to the summer day, Arya went back into the room to see how the painting had dried, and she was impressed. It really did look like a night sky. She stood proudly by her easel, and started dotting the stars with her white paint, and creating her fireworks with an array of colours. As she let that dry, she quickly painted her and Sadie. Arya was very quick with her art but never made a mistake. Having perfected her creativity. After an hour, she was finished, and it looked beautiful. She was overjoyed to have created such a lovely painting of her best friend. Arya just hoped Sadie loved it as much as she did.

While she let it dry under the morning sun, Arya rambled downstairs to the cupboard where Sadie's favourite snacks were kept. They were stored behind the potatoes and other root vegetables, it had to be kept secret from prying eyes…and by prying eyes, she meant her baby brother. He would never think to look for treats there.

She was about to leave the kitchen when she saw a pack of barfi, an Indian sweet delicacy. It was a condensed, milk-based dessert, that was almost like a very thick slab of biscuit. But it was a sweet treat you would eat in moderation, too much would make anyone feel sick. They were normally coloured white, but over many years, many different variations and flavours had been created. And Arya's favourite type was chocolate barfi. It was the same as normal barfi, but with an added layer of dark chocolate on top, it was delicious. And this particular pack was indeed the chocolate version, so Arya stole a few pieces and wrapped them in tissue to give them to Sadie. It was something she hadn't tried yet and was eager to since she heard so much about it from Arya.

Once Arya was satisfied with all her sweet treats, that would probably ache Sadie's teeth, she made her way upstairs to find the precious wicker basket. What was special about it was that it looked exactly like Sadie's basket she had perched on her bike when she was a little girl.

Unfortunately, when they were eight years old, her bike was stolen at the park and Sadie never saw it again. This broke her heart. She was so attached to her bike, and they never found the same one again. Nor did Sadie want a different one, because she would know it wasn't the same. She never forgot about it either. So, one day when Arya had grown to love crafting, she made an exact replica of Sadie's beloved basket and gifted it to her on their birthday.

It was a soft, yellow wicker, with a silk white inner lining inside the basket. On the outside, it was decorated with fluffy white clouds and a brilliant rainbow that stretched from one side to the other. It was the epitome of happiness that Sadie desired in her life. When Arya surprised her with it, Sadie burst into tears, truly overwhelmed with happiness and the love Arya had for her. She managed to sneak it away at the start of the summer, just in case she needed it. Like she knew something would go wrong.

Once Arya took the basket out of its carefully wrapped tissue paper, she started creating her care package. On her bed, she laid out the drying canvas she painted and admired it once more. Hoping that Sadie would see the beauty of it, and the meaning behind it. That no matter where they were, whether in a crowd of bustling people, or perched on their favourite bench, it was always them against the world. They were best friends for life, and nothing could ever change that.

After the canvas had dried, Arya smiled in contentment and placed it at the very back of the basket, standing up. She then laid a Harry Potter colouring book, something that Sadie would love to fill and then a few pamper pieces, such as soothing feet masks, golden eye masks, an exfoliant face scrub and floral scrunchies. She hoped it would help Sadie feel taken care of and loved. Then to finish Arya added in the snacks and a bunch of flamboyant flowers on the other side. The final touch was the heart confetti Sadie had gotten with Taylor Swift merchandise that Arya sneakily stole for moments like these.

Once Arya was happy with how everything was laid out, she quickly changed and dashed out of the house, feeling the warm summer embrace of the sun. A positive feeling flourished in her body; she could feel in her bones that things would work out. Project 'Make Sadie Smile' was off to a good start. She just needed to try her best and maybe not bring up anything to do with Maya or Eli till things were okay between them.

That needed to be brought up last, because Sadie needed to feel important and wanted for once since she hadn't felt loved for a while. Sadie needed to be put first because Arya couldn't bear knowing she felt like she was last in Arya's life because she wasn't. Despite the numerous guilt trips Sadie had sent Arya on recently, she just couldn't let Sadie feel any less important. That wasn't how best friends should treat each other. It wasn't in Arya's blood to let people down and she had always tried her hardest to please everyone. She had been bitten by the people pleaser bug and felt it was her duty to keep everyone happy even if it put her last.

Arya started to power walk with determination, down her street and around the corner to Sadie's. It was breezy, but the bright sun was shining down on her, keeping her warm. Arya felt like it was a sign that things would work out and friendships would renew. Her walk was quiet too, there weren't that many people around, considering it was still the summer break. But she liked the quiet, she relished in it.

Finally, she reached Sadie's house. There were no cars on the drive so she guessed Rose and Noah were out and Sadie must be alone. This made her feel at ease because now she could talk to Sadie freely and they could let everything out and release their tensions without prying ears. Arya slowly walked to the door, building up the courage for what would be a tough conversation and finally rang the doorbell.

She waited.

There was no answer, so she tried again. Still no answer. She wondered where Sadie would be. As she was just about to walk off, the door opened. In that split second where her head was turned away from the door as it creaked open, her heart jumped into her throat. Because she knew Sadie

190

would be at the foot of the door when she turned her head back. But to her surprise it wasn't Sadie, but Rose.

"Hey, love!" chirped Rose. "How are you doing?"

"Hey Rose, I'm okay..."

Arya stood there awkwardly. Rose knew something was wrong. "Are you looking for Sadie?" she asked.

"Ahem...yeah. I want to talk to her." replied Arya.

"She's not at home right now. Maybe you could call her? She'll pick up if you did."

Arya nodded slightly, knowing that Sadie wouldn't, because she hadn't yesterday.

She said goodbye to Rose, turned around and started walking aimlessly down the street. Not knowing where she was going but wondering where Sadie was. She knew Sadie didn't spend time with anyone else. Maybe she went for a drive, though she could never drive without Arya in the car. Maybe she didn't need Arya anymore. Or maybe Sadie was just at her piano lesson, Arya thought. So, she quickly dashed to Arthur's house, but she saw no car and heard no barks. He wasn't home, and Sadie wasn't there. Arya was deep in thought now. She felt uneasy. Where could Sadie be?

Arya's day had turned from hopeful reconciliation to a search party. Travelling from place to place in search of her best friend. She started at Red Lake Park, peaked through the trees, scanned the lake and climbed over the small hills, but she couldn't find a whisper of Sadie there. She wandered over to Sadie's favourite book shop, where there was a rustic bench under an archway of wine-coloured flowers. They had claimed this bench as theirs. But the bookshop and bench were empty. They were also near the towering hills that clambered down to the coast. Arya walked with purpose up them and walked across the coastline, but still nothing. Not even a peak of Sadie and it had now been hours. She called and texted her too, but there was no answer. Arya felt down and drained. She decided to go home and try again tomorrow.

Little did she know that Sadie had another place that she went to, that Arya had no idea about. But Sadie only went there when she needed a break. This time it wasn't as relaxing, because she was facing a dilemma. She needed to remind herself that she was her own person. That she wasn't tied to only Arya. Their friendship didn't control her emotions, her feelings or her existence. And above all she needed to reset the balance in her so she wouldn't think about doing horrid things again. She almost didn't recognise herself anymore and this was why she decided to go.

There was a meadow just past their rustic bench, slightly up the hill circled by trees, which had given the perfect spot for a tranquil hideout. The meadow was alive with wildflowers that welcomed you with open arms as soon as you stepped into their home. There were red clovers, daisies, buttercups, dandelions and long wispy grass, where you could lie down and disappear. Each plant was scattered around the tiny meadow, creating an ambience that felt like an ethereal fairy garden. It had the ability to transport Sadie away from whatever turmoil she was facing, to her own enchanted forest. A world away from here.

It had been a couple of hours of lying hidden in the grass now, where she had allowed the rest of the world to go by. Her shoes were off, her hair tied up and her sunglasses cast to the side. The breeze wrapped around her bare feet, and fluttered her eyelashes, while she basked in the afternoon. Despite feeling tranquil, she still felt unsettled that she could no longer feel the warmth of the summer sun. But she tried to look past this and fall into a trance within this serene environment. Where the only sounds she heard was that gentle breeze wisping through the trees and the sound of the distant waves from the coast.

Everything else had been blocked out. But then a thought appeared in her mind and distracted her for a split second. She suddenly became aware of a piercing sound that abruptly brought her out of her trance. Looking around to find the source of the disturbance, she finally looked down and saw her phone ringing. However, as soon as she picked up her phone it stopped, and she realised how many missed calls she had. There were now ten missed calls, and they were all from Arya. She sighed. A brief cloud floated by and blocked the sunlight, just for a brief moment and covered Sadie in a cool shade. She begrudgingly opened her phone and called Arya back. It was answered almost immediately.

"Hello? Sadie? Are you okay?" came the voice Sadie deeply missed.

"Hey. Yeah, I'm fine. What's up?" replied Sadie.

"I just wanted to see you...if you wanted to see me?" whispered Arya.

Sadie could hear the pain and desperation in her voice. She had given her enough grief, for now. She couldn't bear to give her anymore.

"Sure. Shall I come over?"

"Oh, yeah. Yes please..." answered Arya.

"Okay, see you soon." Then Sadie hung up.

She closed her eyes, sat up straight and opened her chest to take in the deepest breath she had taken that day. As she slowly got up, she was blinded by the cool sunlight once again. She made her way back down the hill, along the busy high streets, but she didn't let it distract her. She had her destination, and she was hoping for happiness at the end of it. Thoughts were racing through her mind. What would the atmosphere be like? Would the conversation be awkward? Would they make up? Would they fight again? Would they hug? Because more than anything, Sadie missed the feel of Arya's embrace.

Soon enough she was outside Arya's door. Just as she was about to ring the bell, the door sprang open, and Arya leapt in Sadie's arms. She was surprised at this sudden embrace, but she adored it more than life itself. Sadie wrapped her arms back around Arya and they stayed like this, for what seemed like forever. She could feel Arya's rapid heartbeat and rushed breathing, and hers started to match. Then they pulled apart, even though Sadie wanted to hold on longer.

"Come in. I've got something for you." whispered Arya.

Sadie followed her, intrigued. Was this a guilt present? Her curiosity peaked.

As she came into the house, she heard the familiar sound of tippy taps on the floor and saw Bailey scamper towards her. Clearly having missed her presence. She hugged him and ruffled his fur, before following Arya to her room, with Bailey in tow. As soon as Sadie entered Arya's room, she was blinded by daylight that seemed to follow them around. This is what she used to enjoy most about the summer. Now, Sadie ached for the sun's warmth to radiate through her bones, but it seemed to be her enemy right now. Just blinding her, icing her out. Whereas Arya felt like she had been graced with the sun's loving embrace. It filled her with the hope of reconciliation and their friendship tightening. She looked at Sadie and saw her brilliant blue eyes glimmering in the sunlight as they followed her to where she was now sitting.

Arya perched herself on the bed, one leg underneath her and one moving back and forth, showing her nervousness. Sadie's eyes moved down to Arya's hands and noticed they were placed delicately around a wicker basket. A wicker basket Sadie knew all too well. A basket she only saw on desperate occasions, when all other attempts at bringing her happiness back had failed. Sadie just blinked a few times, trying to stop the tears from billowing over. She was about to say something, but Arya interjected.

"Before you say anything," she started, "This isn't a gift to win you over or anything. I just wanted to cheer you up...and tell you that I'm here for you. Always."

She then took a deep breath and carried on.

"I know I've been an absent friend and an even worse best friend recently. I haven't been there for you and, well there's nothing I can say that can make it better. But I can show you what you mean to me." She finished, her eyes glistening with brimming tears.

Then she pushed the basket gently towards Sadie.

Sadie sat down and gingerly touched the basket. She traced the clouds and the rainbow on the front with her fingers and rubbed the inner lining in her fingertips while taking short breaths. She loved it so much, the nostalgia that made this basket was now paired with love. Love for her best friend, who always knew what to do to bring a smile back to her broken soul. Her eyes glanced over the treats, the flowers and the home spa treatments. Then she saw a canvas perched at the very back. It must be the painting, Sadie thought. She pulled it out and observed it. It was a painting of the two of them watching the fireworks show on holiday. Sadie's eyes travelled over the night sky, illuminated with a thousand colours, to the tops of the castle and down to their interlocked hands. Her heart fluttered. She liked seeing their intimate moments.

"It's beautiful. It really is. Thank you," cried Sadie.

There was nothing else left to say between them. But they embraced as if they were long lost, sisters. They continued hugging and when they finally parted, they both had tears streaming down their faces. They knew instantly what each other was thinking and feeling, without saying a word. The rest of the day was filled with reconciliation, hugs and pamper sessions.

They felt re-energised and reunited. Sadie ended up spending the rest of the day at Arya's, they ordered a Chinese takeaway and made ice cream sundaes. Watched their favourite movies and talked about anything and everything. Letting out all the tension that had been building up between them. It was cathartic.

Suddenly, both girls had the same idea:

"Shall I stay over?!"

"Do you want to stay over?"

Their eyes widened with fascination that they thought the same thing and at their connection. It was a wonderful night, just the two of them. Hours went by playing Mario Kart, making sure they played every race until their fingers couldn't take the little buttons anymore. After they were gamed out, they made chocolate chip cookies and had cuddles with Bailey. It was such an indulgent night, but they didn't care. Because they got their love back and that's all that mattered.

However, in the midst of their fun, a buzz vibrated through the night. It was Arya's phone receiving a text. She had gone downstairs to grab some drinks, so Sadie was left in the room. Alone. But this notification hadn't gone amiss to her, who noticed the phone light up the dimmed room they had created, purely for cinematic effect. She was curious but knew she shouldn't look. They needed to trust each other; they had discussed that in great depth just earlier. But Sadie had a nagging feeling in her mind and opposing thoughts swimming through her brain.

Should she, or shouldn't she? Where was the trust she promised she'd give Arya? Where was this obsessiveness she promised herself, she'd let go of? She didn't want to break that trust with Arya this quickly, but she wasn't ready to share her with anyone else. She needed to know who was texting her so late, and why they couldn't leave her be for one day.

And with that last thought, a switch had flicked in her mind. Her head slowly turned towards the light emitting from the phone which had vibrated again. This person was clearly asking for Arya's attention. Sadie's interest went from curiosity to invasiveness. She had to know who it was. Quickly jumping to the other side of the bed, she grabbed the phone. As soon as she saw the name, a scowl crept up on her face. Her heart thudded in the deep chasm of her chest and her jaw started to clench.

It was Maya. With two texts. Asking Arya about how it went with Sadie.

Was there nothing kept between her and Arya anymore? Did the whole world have to know the problems they endured? Especially Maya, why did she have to know, Sadie thought. She started furiously pacing up and down the length of the bed, wondering what to do next. She needed more space to think, she felt suffocated.

The phone was placed back on the side table like it hadn't been touched, and she walked up the stairs to Arya's art room. She needed to breathe and needed to calculate her next steps. What could she do to finally separate Maya and Arya for good?

Thoughts racing, feet pacing, she gazed around the room, looking for some sort of epiphany, and then she found it. Her stare was fixated on something on the wall. Then as if an imaginary light bulb appeared above her head, she had an idea of what to do. Sure, it would break Arya's heart, but that was needed to ensure the friendship between her and Maya would be severed, for good. That's what Sadie hoped for. Pleased with her idea, she had to come up a plan. But for it to work, she needed to become "friends" with Maya, no matter how much that made her skin crawl she had to make it work. Just as she was about to imagine it, Arya called from downstairs.

"Sades? Where are you at?" she called.

"Oh! Coming!" replied Sadie. Then she casually walked down the stairs, as if there was nothing on her mind.

"What were you doing up there?" asked Arya, her eyebrow raised curiously.

"I thought I heard something weird outside...You get a better view from up there," lied Sadie.

"I swear the other day I saw someone just watching me through the upstairs window. But when I turned the light off to see, they were gone," said Arya. "It must have been my imagination…" she trailed off, deep in thought.

Sadie gulped. It was a good thing she had worn a black hoodie, something no one would ever think she would wear. She had blended into the night. She watched Arya deep in thought and she quickly changed the conversation.

"I was thinking...that with us getting back on track and promising each other to be better best friends. I was wondering if you would like it if I spent time with Maya? I mean, us three all together?" asked Sadie.

Arya looked taken back, she had not been expecting that at all. It completely blindsided her. It had shocked her, but she appreciated this idea. It showed that Sadie finally cared enough to befriend her friends too. Despite her feeling overjoyed at this, Arya also thought it was really weird for Sadie to suggest this. Especially since it was so sudden and completely out of the blue. Nonetheless, she was ecstatic and jumped at this opportunity. But decided to play it cool.

"Um, yeah that would be great. Amazing actually. It would mean a lot to me...but only if you're ready to. I'm not going to force you to do anything," replied Arya awkwardly.

"It would be my pleasure," smiled Sadie.
But it wasn't genuine, and Arya was too naive to see it. And she just smiled and nodded.

"Great! How about tomorrow? The three musketeers," chimed Sadie.

Arya couldn't control the pace of her heart beating. She was so happy. Her heart felt like it was fluttering and getting caught in her breath. She was delighted that her two best friends would be spending time together... Sadie and Maya. Arya got into bed and Sadie followed. Both smiling at each other, but for different reasons.

The three musketeers. I like that. Arya thought.

Chapter 17

The next day came around pretty quickly. Arya had a feeling like she was on top of the world, ready for whatever the day would bring. This was something she had been hoping for all summer, for her two best friends to spend time together and maybe be friends themselves. It was impossible to choose between the two of them, and she never wanted to be in the position of having to pick over the other. So, she prayed with all her heart that Sadie could accept Maya.

She lay in her bed, eyes wide open with a tender smile slowly appearing on her face. Her eyes peeked over to Sadie to see if she was awake, but Arya saw that her eyes were peacefully closed, and her breathing was shallow but harmonious. She continued to gaze at her, with a full heart, now that Sadie was becoming a bigger person and putting aside her jealousy for her sake. It meant even more because she hadn't forced Sadie to spend time with Maya either. This was completely her own idea and that's why it felt more genuine to Arya. They didn't have to become best friends themselves, but if she was able to be close to both without hard feelings and spitefulness, then that's a win.

However, Arya couldn't help but admit she felt slight suspicions about the situation, since it was so out of the blue. With sudden paranoid thoughts swirling in her mind: Was Sadie being truly genuine? Did she really want to put her jealousy aside for her sake? Is there an ulterior motive?

Each question boomed louder and louder, occupying her mind until there was no empty space left to think. To breathe. But she put her foot down, she had enough of thinking bad about Sadie without reason. Reminding herself that it was just the paranoia that had grown in her mind this summer. That it was all far-fetched and not worth the time wasted overthinking the worst. Sadie seemed like a changed person to Arya, she had to have full faith in her.

Sadie's eyes burned. She knew that Arya was looking at her, but she didn't dare move, not yet anyway. She wasn't asleep either, having woken up from a disturbed sleep a while before Arya had stirred awake. Her mind was filled with a debate: why did she suggest that they all spend a day together? What was her motive? Would she frame Maya for doing something horrible to Arya? Was she that cruel? These were the questions that plagued her mind. Continuously flying around. It was starting to hurt her head; the tension was building up yet again. But like clockwork, whenever she doubted her intentions, the voice boomed in the back of her mind.

This is your only chance to get rid of her. Don't be a coward.

She had no clue where it came from, but it had so much power over her. Sadie listened to it like it was gospel, like it was a matter of life and death. It was right though; she was tired of sharing her friendship. She was there first and these last seventeen years hadn't all been for nothing. Arya would always have only one best friend and that was her, only her. No matter what friends came their way, Sadie wouldn't let anyone else come between them, she'd bet her life on it. And that was what today was all about, making a move that she hoped would cause Arya to throw Maya away, like she was discarded trash. And then she hoped that would be the end of it.

Thoughts popped up here and there, wondering whether things would go right, but every time she doubted it, the voice in her mind would reassure her. Like it was soothing a baby, telling her everything would be okay. Once Sadie was settled, she decided it was time to now "wake up". Her eyes fluttered open as if she had just awoken from a deep slumber. The first thing she noticed was Arya on her stomach, staring at her with a creepy look on her face.

"What the hell Arya!" she shouted, throwing a pillow at her face.

Arya bellowed with laughter. "Why did you throw a pillow at me? I just thought the first thing you should see when you woke up was my beautiful face!"

Sadie's eyes sparkled. Arya was precious. Arya was hers.

The girls spent another hour in bed watching TV. It was a peaceful morning. When they couldn't ignore their hunger anymore, they went downstairs to have some breakfast. Arya made Sadie's favourite: blueberry pancakes, drizzled with maple syrup, so sweet and so yummy. Sadie always said that Arya made the best pancakes. But then again, Sadie thought anything made by Arya was the best, nothing could match it. When they were about to settle down to munch their breakfast, the familiar sound of Bailey's paws came dancing around the corner. He came in looking sleepy and took a big boy stretch and a gigantic yawn.

"Oh, look at this poor boy, such a hard life, isn't it?" cooed Arya.

Bailey barked happily. Arya giggled and threw him a blueberry, and he lapped it up as if he hadn't eaten in days. She got his breakfast ready, and they all sat down to eat. When Arya had finished, she gingerly placed her knife and fork on the plate, while she was thinking about how to ask Sadie about what she wanted to do today. What she wanted to do with her and Maya. Once she gathered up the courage to ask, she cleared her throat. Sadie looked up with her head cocked to the side. Arya just smiled sheepishly in response.

"So... What's the plan for today? I mean, what are we all going to do? Me, you and... Maya?" asked Arya, cautiously.

Sadie paused mid mouthful. She had known the question was going to come eventually, but she had to act like it didn't faze her. Quickly, she swallowed the mouthful without properly chewing it. It was dry, just like how her mouth had suddenly become. The thought hadn't come up about what they could do, and she needed to think of an idea sharpish. Suddenly she had a brain wave.

"We should do something that you love. We could go to the park, have a picnic and paint something there or..." said Sadie, trailing off.

Arya's heart warmed at the thought of this. "I love that! That's such a cute idea. I'll text Maya now and let her know."

Earlier that morning, as soon as Arya woke up, she told Maya about Sadie's wish for them all to spend time together. Initially, it took Maya by surprise, but she eventually warmed up to it after Arya explained how much it would mean to her. Once the plan was made, Sadie left to go back home and get ready. She walked home like she had the weight of the world on her shoulders.

Today was a big day to set everything in motion, and she couldn't let it go wrong. She couldn't let the voice down either. When she got home, she quickly changed and was running the plan through her mind as if she were rehearsing a play, when a knock hammered at her front door. It was Arya and most likely Maya. She went to the mirror, looked at herself and liked what she saw. The reflection smiled back at her too. She felt pretty. *Prettier* than Maya. It was very vain, of course, but Sadie believed it would favour her in the fight of who would Arya choose. She took a deep breath and calmly made her way downstairs. Each step filled with purpose; each step filled with determination.

Arya and Maya were chatting nonchalantly, with the sun beaming blissfully on them. And Bailey and Coco were behind them, yapping at each other. It was like a funny mirror image of the girls.

They then heard the door click and open in full swing and there in the shadow of the sun stood Sadie, with lots of make-up on, something she rarely does and poised as if she was better than the company she was about to keep. Arya looked perplexed. She hadn't seen Sadie look like that unless they were going somewhere nice, but she didn't mention anything. All she did was smile and gaze at Sadie, ready for her two best friends to rekindle their differences.

Sadie walked out of the house just as the clouds covered the sun and sent a small shiver down her spine. Still not having said anything to the other two, she closed the door behind her. Then she turned around and greeted them both, looking at Maya longer than she did at Arya. Was she trying to intimidate her or was trying to act friendly? Sadie didn't know, but she ran with it, thinking it was what the voice would want.

"So! Shall we go somewhere to buy food for our picnic?" suggested Sadie.

"Sounds like a great idea," smiled Maya. This small interaction brightened Arya's day.

The girls set off with the dogs leading the way. At first, it was quiet and kind of awkward. They didn't know what to talk about, not knowing how to even start a conversation. Arya was too busy being preoccupied with keeping the peace between them. Her focus was on breaking a conversation off if it got too heated and not starting an argument. Sadie watched Arya and knew she was overthinking something, so she decided to break the silence and keep up her act.

"How's Coco doing? Is she settling into her new home?" she asked. Arya looked at Maya from the side of her eye and saw she was surprised the question was directed at her.

"She's been great," Maya said. Arya saw her relax a little. "Settled in really well, but my cat is still a bit cautious around her. I'm sure they'll like each other soon."

Sadie smiled at her, barely listening, but working hard to maintain her demeanour. Maya was letting her guard down with her. And that's what she wanted. She needed to befriend Maya a little, engage in conversation, and not let any suspicion arise against her. Sadie racked her brain trying to think of more topics to bring up to lure Maya into a false pretence of friendship, when a brilliant idea struck her. Everyone loved animals, and people who love animals were always assumed to be nice, Sadie thought.

The only way to connect to Maya was to connect with Coco and hopefully, that would succeed. Besides, Sadie assumed that Maya was quite gullible and would lap it all up, just like a dog.

"Can I walk her? Like, take her lead?" asked Sadie quietly, looking forward instead of at Maya.

Maya looked up in surprise. "Oh…"

She looked at Arya, who shrugged her shoulders. Then to follow up, Arya gave her the "look" to reassure her that it was alright. Sadie could tell a lot was going on in Maya's mind right now. There was mistrust, anxiety for Coco's safety. But also, Sadie sensed she was getting through, that her ploy was leading somewhere. Just another little push and…

"I mean if you're okay with that. I love dogs and she's SO cute," emphasised Sadie, with a pleading look.

"Yeah, of course!" Maya said finally. "Just, I'm not sure if you'll be comfortable with walking a puppy. She's quite energetic."

This didn't sit well with Sadie. Was Maya was belittling her, saying she couldn't handle a tiny little dog? But she tried not to show her aggravation, it was just a dog, it would be easy she thought.

"I'll be able to handle it!" Sadie said, trying to hide her strained tone.

Sadie took the lead and held it in her hand as if it were something valuable. She didn't intend on doing anything wrong to Coco, she just needed to build Maya's trust since she loved her dog, and Sadie was sure it was a fast way to win her over. Besides Sadie did genuinely like dogs, and Coco really was cute, especially how she walked as if she were trying to go quicker than her tiny legs could take her.

Immediately after Sadie took the lead Coco tried to take off, pulling the lead with all her small mighty strength, just to run ahead of everyone else. At first, Sadie felt like she was losing control of her already, but before Maya was about to react, Sadie regained control. And Coco was brought back next to Bailey and calmed a little. A relieved smile gently grew on Sadie's face. Arya spotted this and nudged Maya to look, they both smiled and relaxed. Things were going okay, Arya thought that animals always resolved differences. She was really glad that Sadie took Coco.

"Shall we go to the cafe by the park? Grab some sandwiches, salads and drinks?" suggested Arya.

Sadie nodded in agreement.

"Sure. Although I'll need to properly check what I get, nut allergies are the worst," moaned Maya.

"I'm sure we can find you something!" smiled Sadie. She had just thought of a wicked idea.

The three of them walked to a small, rustic cafe next to Red Lake Park. It had a cabin feel to it and looked quite homely. As soon as you opened the door a warm breeze welcomed you in. The walls were built with rugged logs, the floor creaked with the sound of their footsteps and the entire place smelled like a bakery, but like Christmas at the same time. There were five tables in the middle, each with a tall candle that had vines adorning the base, which were placed on a red and white gingham cloth.

On one side of the cafe was a fridge filled with a variety of pasta salads, fruit and yoghurts, in all the flavours you could imagine: mango and passionfruit, strawberry and kiwi, blueberry and honey and so on. It was mouth-watering. On the other side of the cafe was a fridge full of sandwiches, freshly baked and rustic looking.

The smell of them drew Sadie closer and closer, she just had to have one. Arya also craved one of their sandwiches and chose their sundried tomato, mozzarella and spinach one, while Sadie took a while longer to decide. She was looking for something specific...something that she could use for another purpose. It took a while, and she almost gave up, because she thought they didn't have a flavour that had what she needed. But she eventually found one, a sandwich filled with provolone cheese and pesto, with pine nuts.

Perfect, the voice boomed.

The girls then lined up with their drinks and a fruit punnet. Arya eyed what Maya had chosen.

"What did you get?"

"I got a summer pasta salad! I love anything pasta," she exclaimed ravenously.

After they bought their food, they made their way over to Red Lake and found the perfect spot to sit under. A big cherrywood tree that had flowers in full bloom surrounding them. The air was light and calm, and the park was surprisingly quiet. Arya and Maya let their dogs off their leashes for a bit, still keeping a close eye out on them and laid out their own gingham blanket onto the soft grass.

The food was kept in Maya's black floral totem bag against the tree and the painting supplies were slowly being unpacked by a delighted Arya. Sadie observed Arya, making her feel overjoyed that something so small like this had made her so happy. Realising how much she had been slacking in the friend department recently, almost forgetting these little moments of gloriousness. But she couldn't let this happiness deter her from the plan, her mission. *I'm doing this for us, Arya. One day you'll understand*, thought Sadie.

Arya was singing in her head while she was setting up the painting stations. She had dreamed of a moment like this, not just for Sadie and Maya to mend their differences, but just with anyone. She had always fancied organising a painting date, but she never found anyone to do it with. But now, it was finally her turn.

Since she had planned for a day like this long ago, she had already stocked up on all the art materials and they were still in their packaging, ready for this day. The ripping of the clear plastic was so satisfying to Arya, as she tore it away from the small canvases and breathed in the smell of new materials.

Sadie had been eyeing her doing that.

"You're so weird!" she laughed.

Arya turned her head sharply, not realising she was being watched. She poised herself and replied.

"Don't disrupt my aura!" in an eccentric voice.

Sadie side hugged her, and they both sat there giggling to themselves. She felt like it was back to normal, just the two of them coming to the park on a Saturday morning just like they used to. She lived in those memories and never wanted to leave them. But then reality hit when Maya spoke. And Sadie's eyes shot open as fast as lightning struck.

"Aw, these small canvases are so cute. Where did you get them from?"

212

Sadie sighed, but no one heard her.

"This local arts and crafts shop in the city," Arya smiled.

Maya sat down next to her and helped squeeze out the paints onto the palettes. Alongside the primary colours, there were pastel pinks, sky blues, deep forest green, golds, whites and blacks.

"Did you buy the whole shop?!"

Arya sheepishly hid her face behind her hands. Although a tiny glimpse of her cheeks was still visible and were now blushing with the colour of freshly squirted pink paint on the palette. All the girls smiled and helped set everything up and they started chatting about what they wanted to paint. After finally deciding on their ideas, the girls got stuck in. They all became so focused and in tune with their paintings that they blocked out their surroundings. Arya being the most focused. Her brushstrokes touched the canvas so delicately, she always painted dreamscapes and heavenly art. It was amazing how with one brush she painted so many different textures, thought Sadie. It was genius and Arya was a real artist. She always felt so proud watching Arya paint and was always in awe of her work.

Sadie's eyes unglued from her painting and peaked over at Maya's work and saw she was beginning to paint a small chocolate blob. She snarkily laughed to herself, thinking how poor it looked. But as she continued looking, it magically turned into a little chocolate puppy, it was Coco. Maya then started taking inspiration from Arya and began using her brush to create different textures too and right now she was creating the look of Coco's fur. Within an instant, it began to look realistic and too good.

Sadie rolled her eyes.

Then she glanced up and noticed she couldn't see the real Coco anymore. She searched for Bailey and when she found him, she hoped Coco was shadowing him, but she wasn't there.

"Uh Maya, I can't see Coco..." uttered Sadie.

Arya and Maya both shot their heads up and began looking around frantically for any glimpse of a chocolate brown puppy, but they couldn't spot her. All they saw was Bailey lying down and they rushed over to him. But not Sadie, she stayed put. Knowing that this was the only chance she was going to get. Now was the time while the others were preoccupied. Shuffling over to the totem bag with the food, she opened her sandwich box and picked out all the pine nuts, they were small so she hoped Maya wouldn't notice them.

Next, she grabbed Maya's pasta box, carefully peeled off the sticker that kept the box closed and tipped the pine nuts into the pasta. After that, she carefully stuck the lid back onto the box and gave it a quick shake. Sweat had started to form on her forehead, she wiped her forehead, trying not to look like she had just done a dirty deed. But Sadie was desperate. She had no choice.

When she glanced around to make sure the others weren't in view of what she did, Sadie got up and started to look around for Coco herself.

She noticed that they hadn't checked the little bush Bailey was next to, maybe they thought it was too tight for anything to squeeze in. Regardless, Sadie decided to pry it open, and right in the middle of the tightly packed bush was a little chocolate blob that had been painted on the canvas.

"There you are, little one," whispered Sadie.

She picked her up gently and brought her into her chest and gave her a little kiss. Then she looked around for the girls and found them looking down by the lake.

"Hey!" shouted Sadie. The girls looked over at her, and then Sadie pointed to the sleepy Coco in her arms.

"Oh my god!" cried Maya and she dashed over frantically to Sadie. "Where did you find her?!"

"She was in that little bush next to Bailey. I guess he was lying there keeping an eye on her," suggested Sadie, slightly shrugging her shoulders.

She noticed Maya's tensed forehead relax slightly, her lips stopped trembling, and she breathed out deeply, relieved that Coco was found.

"Thank you so much Sadie," she said breathlessly. "I didn't even think to look there. I thought it looked too tight and small."

Now tears were brewing in her eyes. Sadie felt a pang in her chest. Was this empathy? Towards Maya? It didn't make sense. She tried to crush the feeling, whilst patting Maya's arm. She couldn't start actually liking Maya. It would ruin everything.

"Don't worry about it. I found her. You can relax now," reassured Sadie.

After that fiasco all three girls walked back to their blanket, with the dogs accompanying them, who would not leave their sight now. They continued with their paintings, Sadie happily painting away, Maya constantly glancing at Coco, and Arya totally lost in her own world again.

They painted for another hour, with the occasional conversation between them all and a break to play with the dogs. The sun was shining so bright that Maya took a break from her art and had a little sunbathe. Sadie decided to sunbathe as well, although it didn't feel as glorious as it used to, it just felt ice cold.

She wondered whether Maya was starting to warm up to her, especially after she found Coco. Because if she was, that's exactly what Sadie wanted. She and Maya opened their eyes at the same time and looked at each other, a smile passed between them. Sadie took a quick glance at Arya and noticed she was still painting passionately, her hand fluttering around as if it was dancing to a ballet sequence. The colours harmonised on the canvas, but of course they would, Sadie didn't expect anything different. She moved closer to get a better look at what Arya had created.

Her canvas was painted with the lake, as if she was sitting in between the waterline, both above and below the lake. Half of the canvas was the clear, glistening surface of the water, with sprouts of weeds and grass on the banks, trees in the upper background and a glimpse of the sun shining above. The second half of the canvas was what she imagined was below the surface. The sand and dirt blanketing the ground, rocks and pebbles scattered across the lakebed, small fish seemingly swimming all around and the light breaking through the water barrier. It was mesmerising. There was so much going on everywhere you looked. A fire burned in Sadie's stomach, which happened every time she was transfixed and taken away by Arya.

She looked at her work, which was okay at first. It was just a daisy, which was Arya's favourite flower. But the more she looked more at it, the more she hated it and wanted to destroy it. But she couldn't, she didn't want to ruin the atmosphere that had enveloped Arya. So, she took some deep breaths and tried to push it to the back of her mind that Maya was better than her at something. Then with the finest paintbrush, she could find, she wrote in a bright blue:

For Arya.

"I'm hungry!" said Maya, suddenly.

Sadie whipped her head around so fast, that it clicked her neck. But this was it.

She wondered what would happen when Maya had the nuts, she wondered whether she was going too far. But the voice in her head reassured her that she wasn't, and her troubles will end soon. And at that thought, she grabbed the food out of the bag and handed each meal to everyone. She gave Arya's first who took it graciously, she placed her own in between her lap and then gave Maya's last, making sure she looked at her while doing so. Maya took it happily; she looked ravenous and excited to finally eat.

217

Arya and Sadie happily tucked into their food, and Maya opened hers and gave it a mix. She then took a forkful of pasta with an assortment of luscious vegetables and began bringing it close to her mouth. Sadie watched like a hawk, her eyes dark and focused, having spotted a pine nut within the mix. She felt like everything had turned into slow motion. Watching the fork slowly approaching Maya's mouth, who was opening her mouth gradually, her heart thumped. But all of a sudden, the fork was whacked out of Maya's hand. And Sadie was thrown back to reality.

"What was that for?!" exclaimed Maya.

"You were about to eat a nut!" shouted Arya.

Maya looked at her confused.

"But there's no nuts in it. Look, it even says that on the box," she said, pointing at the clear 'No nuts' sign.

Arya then went to where all the food had fallen on the blanket and searched for that tiny pine nut, when she found it, she held it up to Maya.

"Here, I knew I hadn't gone crazy," said Arya, justifying her action. Maya checked the rest of her food and found a few more.

"That's weird. Where have they come from?" she questioned, looking at the others.

Arya just shook her head, not knowing how it got there, and Sadie shrugged her shoulders nonchalantly. They all decided not to dwell on it much longer, but Sadie was seething inside. Her frustration was evident on her face; another plan had failed. She was so angry, but she couldn't show

218

her emotion without looking guilty. So, she stuffed her face with the sandwich. Arya had given some food to Maya and told her to have some of the snacks too, so she wouldn't go hungry.

When they were finished eating Maya put their rubbish in the bag. Sadie watched her pick up the sandwich packet, look at the ingredients, then turn back to them.

"You had pine nuts in your sandwich," Maya said mutedly.

The air went quiet. All of a sudden it felt like the only people in the world were just those three girls. The atmosphere felt heavy around Sadie, but she just stared back, not knowing what to say or do. Like she was a deer caught in the headlights.

"So?" asked Arya.

"So, don't you think it's a bit weird that I find pine nuts in my food, even though it specified there would be no nuts? And she's the only one that had nuts. The exact nuts that were in my food..." Maya explained with a tone that was getting higher and higher.

"Surely, you're not saying that Sadie put them in there. Are you?" laughed Arya, clearly bewildered at this accusation.

"Well, how else could it have gotten there?" said Maya, defending herself.

"Oh wow, you're actually being serious," replied Arya, eyes wide open in shock.

Sadie just looked at both of them, she had no idea what to say, she didn't think this would happen so soon. Nervousness began to creep over, and she couldn't help but keep swallowing.

Arya carried on.

"It's clearly a mistake on the cafe's part. The food all came from there and they make everything fresh every day. It could have easily been mixed in without intention. It's ridiculous to accuse someone of doing something so wrong."

Maya looked at Sadie, who was looking back at her, without blinking and without looking away.

"Come on Sadie, you wouldn't do that would you?" asked Arya.

Sadie paused.

"Of course not! I can't believe you would think I would do that, that's so insensitive of you. You're acting crazy," said Sadie, pretending to sulk.

She watched Maya going through a clear thought process of doubt. She was calming down; the adrenaline of the situation was wearing away. Sadie saw her eyes clear.

"I'm sorry. I-I don't know what I was thinking. I take it back, I shouldn't have said that," said Maya, clearly still shaken but no longer angry.

Arya didn't know what to say or do, so she cleared her throat and suggested that maybe they go back to her house. They packed up their art supplies and blanket, called their dogs over and headed back. It was a silent walk to Arya's, with them all deep in thought. Arya was upset that Maya had

220

accused Sadie of something so dreadful. But they were both her friends, and she needed to diffuse the tension.

Despite the low mood that had enveloped the other two, Sadie was silently enjoying this. Taking in all the silence and relishing in her achievement. Hoping this would be the start of the distance between Maya and Arya. It was even better that Maya had straight away accused her, because she had insulted Arya's best friend, which wouldn't sit right with Arya. Sadie's inner thoughts told her that if Maya kept accusing her of things it would drive her away from Arya. Maybe this was the game she should play?

"Shall we have a pizza night?" suggested Arya, light-heartedly. "And watch movies or play on the Switch or something?"

"Sounds good to me!" said Sadie enthusiastically.
Maya cleared her throat slightly. "Yeah, sure."

She had a slight frown on her face and this made Arya sad. She rubbed her arm to let her know it was okay, and this seemed to lift Maya's mood slightly. But that tiny bit of affection didn't go unnoticed by Sadie, she didn't think Arya would start to melt already. A burning fire grew in the pit of her stomach. Rolling her eyes, she realised she needed to step up her game even more and had no choice but to carry on with her original idea, which was perfect now they were all going to Arya's.

They eventually made it back to Arya's home, where they let the dogs off their leads and into the garden to play. Arya took the bag full of rubbish off Maya and went to dump it all in the bin. As she was taking out each piece of empty food packets, she paused when she took Sadie's sandwich box out. She read the description. It did say that it contained pine nuts. Arya paused before throwing it away and then she grabbed Maya's pasta box that clearly said it contained no nuts.

She tapped her finger on the box rhythmically in deep thought, thinking about the nuts and wondering how they got there. They were the exact type that Sadie had; Sadie couldn't be that cruel to physically hurt someone. Could she? Arya had to block this thought out because she was certain that Sadie couldn't do something like that. Arya tried to reassure herself that it was a mistake, and that Maya had been mistaken. Throwing the box away she also tried to throw away the foreign thoughts plaguing her mind.

The rest of the evening went by smoothly after Arya tried hard to lift the tension. She encouraged everyone to play a few games of Mario Kart, and before you knew it, it felt like nothing had happened. They played until they all had won a race or Grand Prix. Arya and Maya had won more than Sadie however, which made her jealous. Unfortunately, she was quite the competitive type.

When Aashi came home from work and Kunal with Kiaan, they decided to order lots of food. Two large cheese pizzas and one with pepperoni, a side order of potato wedges and garlic bread. For dessert, they ordered individual cookie dough pots from a local dessert place.

They overindulged again. Everyone seemed to now be at peace with each other and Arya hoped it would remain that way. After they ate, all the girls went up to Arya's room and put some music on. Arya suddenly had the urge to paint her nails, since they had chipped, and she detested having chipped nails. Maya decided she wanted hers painted too, but Sadie wasn't bothered about hers. Arya and Maya chose what colours they wanted and started painting, while Sadie watched. Maya liked the colour she put on and asked Arya whether she could borrow it, which she happily allowed.

Now in a happier mood, Maya popped the nail polish bottle in her bag, with an eagle-eyed Sadie watching her. Sadie felt like she had won the lottery. Never had she come up with a devious idea so quickly, as she had just done. The nail polish bottle gave her an idea to accompany the next devious attempt at ruining their friendship. All she had to do now was wait for an open window.

When their nails were dry, they went up to Arya's art room to put up her canvas. She had a hard time placing it because there were too many pieces on her walls already and she was running out of space. She dawdled for a while, trying to figure out the best place to put her work. Finally, she decided to put it right next to her window, so she had inspiration whenever she looked outside. As she turned around fully pleased with her decision, she saw Maya admiring her favourite piece again. But she didn't notice the lingering eyes of Sadie transfixed on Maya from afar.

"You really like that painting, don't you?" laughed Arya.
Maya turned around with a warm smile on her face. "It's really beautiful, who couldn't love it!" she exclaimed. "I wish I could have it,"

"Its place is on the wall," Arya said in a singsong tone.

And then she and Maya walked back downstairs, hand in hand. This burned a raging fire in the depths of Sadie's stomach and like a switch, she flipped. The time was now and without a second thought, she grabbed the frame off the wall and ripped out the painting that had taken Maya's heart and began her next step. Laughter rang from below, which fuelled the scalding fire and Sadie was ready to do anything to tear that friendship to pieces. She hid the painting behind her back and started to descend downstairs.

With every step she took, her mind became clearer, and a second thought had its chance to worm its way in: should she really destroy this painting, Arya's favourite artwork, just to ruin a friendship?

This thought interrupted her mission and made her stop at the bottom of the staircase, pondering over what was right and what was wrong. However, before she divulged into her consciousness, the voice she so longed to shut out, crept into her mind again, blocking out all guilty thoughts.

There's no other way. It's for her own good. It has to be done.

The voice always had a higher power to influence her mind than her consciousness, it was too powerful to let any weakness in. Heeding to the voice, she left the staircase and followed through with her wicked plan. She noticed Maya wasn't in the room anymore and Arya was in her bathroom, so this was her only chance.

Quickly, she stumbled over to Maya's bag and stashed the painting under whatever else was in there. Then she carelessly opened the nail polish bottle and poured a fair amount of polish on the painting and then left the bottle open. If Maya hadn't taken this bottle in the first place, Sadie would have been stuck on how to frame her for ruining Arya's favourite painting. It looked like Maya was good for something, after all, Sadie thought cunningly.

Before she turned away, she had a quick glance at the painting she just destroyed. She gasped as she saw the thick colour beginning to swallow up the art, the paper turning limp from the wetness of the nail polish and the painting becoming tarnished with the bitterness of Sadie's heart. An unexpected pang of sadness struck her because she knew she ruined her best friend's work and most likely her heart.

As quickly as she could, she grabbed the bottle, regretting what she had just done. But it was too late. The painting was no longer graceful and awe-inspiring. It was now a mess. Just like Sadie's life had become. Suddenly, she heard footsteps coming toward the room. She dropped the bottle like it was a murder weapon and jumped onto the bed, far away from the bag.

Maya came back in and sat down. She noticed Sadie seemed out of breath, but didn't care as to why. Then Coco climbed on to her and was soon sleeping peacefully in Maya's hands. Sadie watched her body gently move up and down as she breathed, she couldn't look away because she had become instantly transfixed.

Looking at something so innocent, after doing something so deceitful... She needed to leave before the guilt washed over her and was painted on her face for all to see. However, thankfully Maya announced that

225

she was going to head home, little Coco needed to sleep in her bed and Maya had to get up early the next day.

It was a relief that Sadie didn't have to quickly dash off before her because it could have been seen as suspicious.

Sadie said goodbye to Maya and Arya walked her downstairs. As Maya walked out of the room, with her black totem bag slung around her shoulder, Sadie stared at the growing patch of wetness that she hoped Maya wouldn't notice till the next day. Her heart started beating so fast, that she could feel the pulse in her neck thumping away, and her head became tightly tensed. Sadie knew she couldn't take back what she did now, all she hoped for was that none of this was done in vain.

She stayed for a couple more hours because it was just them two again and she loved every minute that they spent together. She was dreading the next day when she knew her fateful action would eventually get back to Arya. But decided that she would be there for her through the revelation entirely. By coming to the house early in the morning in the pretence of wanting to spend an entire day with Arya.

So, whenever Maya would guiltily make her way to Arya's, Sadie would be there to be the shoulder to cry on.

Although she hadn't told Arya she was coming over because she didn't think Arya would mind, since they always spent their entire summers together. Sadie assumed it would be fine. And she had to be there for this to work, so Arya would see that Sadie was the better friend all along, who listens to her and never leaves her side and Maya was the ungrateful friend who couldn't leave things well alone.

Once Arya saw that Maya would be thrown out of her life for good, at least that's what Sadie hoped.

Chapter 18

The next day started as normal as any other day. Arya was busy with Bailey and Kiaan after forcing them on a long hike with her. After an hour she had to make a pitstop at the ice cream truck for her brother because he'd become stroppy from the walk and needed a pick me up, and Arya couldn't be bothered to deal with his mood anymore.

She had received a few texts from Sadie in the morning, asking how she was and that she wanted to come round to see her, but Arya replied saying she was spending time with Kiaan. Sadie hadn't replied to that. Oddly though, Maya hadn't replied to Arya either. She messaged her that morning to see how Maya was feeling after what happened yesterday. Maybe she was just busy, Arya thought.

It was the afternoon when the sun had risen to its peak, and both brother and sister were now perched on the top of the hills at the edge of the city. These hills had always been special to Arya. She felt at peace whenever she was here. It was a place of tranquillity. And there was a sense of enchantment especially on moist, damp days when clouds would form between the hills. If you were lucky and were high enough, you could witness this formation with your own eyes. It would feel like a blanket had formed over the city, and you were in another world, high above watching over everyone else.

While she was daydreaming about this phenomenon, Kiaan had been keeping busy protecting some chipmunks that had appeared out of nowhere and that Bailey had also spotted. He kept trying to bite them, but

Kiaan remained in protective mode, trying his hardest to shoo Bailey away, telling him not to eat 'Chip and Dale'.

As soon as Arya noticed she pulled Bailey back and gave him lots of attention to avoid his wandering eyes. They both then took in the beautiful sights together, as they have always done since he was a puppy. The bustling of the crowds trailing up and down streets, the flutter of butterflies dancing in the light breeze and the rush of the waves from the coast. Arya felt so lucky that she lived in a place that had everything.

While she was in her own world, her thoughts wandered to Eli. She hadn't seen him in a while and didn't want to wait any longer. So, she quickly texted to ask whether he was free later. He responded with the same amount of haste as if he had been anxiously waiting for Arya to ask. They made a plan to grab some milkshakes and go for a walk on the beach at sunset. It sounded romantic to Arya, and she began blushing at the thought of how this was now a date. Butterflies blossomed in her stomach.

It took the three of them a while to reach home since Kiaan's little legs couldn't hack the long walk. But when they finally reached their street, Kiaan suddenly had a spring in his step and started to run home. Arya laughed and watched him now skip along the street happily as if he hadn't just had a tantrum and cried. As she got closer, Arya saw a shadow by their front door. Someone was standing outside their house. Trying to keep up with Kiaan, she quickened her pace.

He finally reached the end of the front drive when he shouted, "Hey, Sadie!" in his bubbly voice.

As Arya walked closer, she saw that it was indeed Sadie. Arya rounded off onto her drive.

"Uhhh, hey Sades. What are you doing here?" she asked, head cocked to one side in confusion.

"I thought I'd come round to see you!" replied Sadie, smiling sweetly.

"But I told you I'd be spending time with Kiaan today and I've got plans later too…" Arya trailed off.

Sadie's face turned sourish. "Aren't you happy to see me?"

"Sadie, I saw you yesterday and the day before that. I told you this morning that I would be busy," replied Arya, sternly. She was starting to feel slightly annoyed now.

Hadn't anything changed?

Sadie paused. Arya had called her by her full name, Sadie, instead of her nickname. She didn't do that, ever.

"Right. I'll just go then…" Sadie began to sulk away.

Arya had to try hard not to roll her eyes. She hated it when Sadie gave her the guilt treatment. They had been through this, hadn't they? She was allowed to have a life outside of her.

"Can you hurry up, guys? I need to go pee!" said Kiaan, jumping up and down.

"Ah, sorry!" called Arya as she quickly went to open the door to let them in.

When she turned around, she saw Sadie walking slowly away, kicking a stone on the floor and looking like she had just gotten told off by her Mom. Arya sighed.

"You can come in for a bit, but I am busy later, so you can't stay too long."

"Yeah, yeah, I'll leave after. Just thought it would be nice to spend time together. Uh, more time together!" Sadie laughed awkwardly.

Arya fake laughed and sighed again. She didn't understand why Sadie was so adamant to spend time with her. They literally spend all their time together for the last couple of days. Wasn't she sick of it now? They walked in and Arya went to the fridge to grab a bottle of orange juice. She watched Sadie intently, who whose eyes kept glancing anxiously at the front door. Arya wasn't sure why. Did Sadie want to go home already? Before Arya could ask her what she was staring at, Sadie had whipped her head around to look at Arya. Arya's eyes widened at her expression. It seemed like a forced, creepy smile. She was unsure how to describe it.

"Ha...are you okay Sadie?" she asked.

Sadie sighed. There it was again. *Sadie.* Why wasn't she using her nickname for her?

"Yeah! All good," she replied, her fake smile straining at the edges. "Just happy to be here, with you."

Arya wanted to scream. It all felt so forced and sickly.

231

Sadie carried on.

"I was thinking about going through our photos from the holiday so I can start on my scrapbooking! What do you think?"

Arya was momentarily surprised out of her confused suspicion. This was actually nice idea. She still felt something was going on, however.

"Yeah, that sounds fun. I kept a few things too, like my ticket to Disney World, a sweet wrapper that had a character on it and stuff like that. You could use that in your scrapbook."

"I love that! We probably have lots of photos to look through, we should get started!" said Sadie, enthusiastically.

But she was met with an unenthusiastic response from Arya. Which she wasn't expecting.

"Not today though, Sadie. I already have plans, and I want to spend time with Kiaan this afternoon. Which I have already mentioned..." Arya trailed off.

Sadie felt like someone had shot an arrow straight into her heart. What did she have to do to retain Arya's love and attention? Why couldn't Arya always be there for her? She would drop everything for her anytime, so why couldn't Arya do the same?

"Right. I didn't realise how boring I must be for you not wanting to spend time with me," sulked Sadie.

Arya rolled her eyes but made no attempt to hide it this time.

"Oh, stop it, Sadie," Arya pleaded exasperatedly. She threw her hands up in the air in frustration. "This has nothing to do with how exciting

232

or boring you are. Why do you make everything about yourself? The world doesn't revolve around you. I have other friends that I want to spend time with too. Why don't you get that?"

Sadie stood back in anguish, her jaw dropped.

"I didn't realise I gave you so much grief! Sorry for wanting to spend my summer with my best friend! Obviously, you don't enjoy our time together anymore!" Sadie shouted, her body was now shaking.

"Are you serious?!" Now Arya was shouting too. "You are so petty. You always make me feel so guilty about everything! How is that friendship? It's toxic Sadie. You don't get to tell me when I can and can't spend time with you. You don't get to tell who I can spend time with either. You don't own my life, so please stop acting like it!"

Sadie gasped.

"How can you call me toxic? Our friendship toxic? All I ever do is be there for you, I'm always there for you, I always want to be with you! You're the toxic one, you're the one that puts people over me all the time, whether it's your dog, family or even Maya! I would never do that to you. So, who's the toxic one now?!"

Arya's eyes seethed with anger.

"His name is *Bailey*! And how are you calling me toxic? Do you even hear yourself, Sadie? I'm so sick and-" she shouted but was interrupted by a hammering on her front door. Arya took a deep breath, wiped her face and started pacing towards the door, leaving Sadie breathless and shaken.

It was Maya with a crestfallen look on her face. She was also holding something crumpled up that stank of what she thought was nail polish. Arya looked at whatever it was confused.

"Maya? What's up? What's that? It stinks!" she asked plugging her nose.

"Um... I don't know how this happened, I-I don't know where it came from…" mumbled Maya quietly, trying to hold in her tears. She then opened up whatever was in her hands and showed it to Arya.

A broken gasp escaped from her lips. She took the nail polish-stained paper that once was a thing of beauty and held it with such carefulness. Turning it over gingerly, as if the back would be something different, but it wasn't. Her artwork was gone. Destroyed. It would never be seen again. It broke her and she started crying. Maya went to hold her hand, but Arya stepped back.

Sadie had been watching intently and now was the pivotal moment. It was time to shove Maya out of their lives for good. Sadie swooped in like an eagle, a saving grace and embraced Arya, without moving her glare from Maya's crestfallen face.

"Arya," cried Maya. "I'm sorry! I don't know how it got in my bag. I went home, and my bag was wet, and I found the nail polish bottle I borrowed from you, it was open, and it had spilt everywhere. But I had no idea your painting was in there! Please believe me!"

"Oh, come on, do you really think she's going to believe you?" retorted Sadie, from Arya's shoulder.

"Wha-" gasped Maya. "I'm telling the truth!"

Arya lifted her head from Sadie's shoulder. Her face was puffy from crying, that painting meant so much to her.

"I told you...I told you not to touch it, it's special to me. I told you," she cried.

"But I didn't touch it!"

"Then how did it get in your bag?" asked Sadie.

"That's what I don't know!"

Arya had walked to the kitchen table and sat on the chair, feeling like the air in her had deflated. She touched the painting, hoping it would come back to life, to what it was. But it laid there crumpled. She was distraught, not only was she devastated about her painting, but what was happening to her friendships?

On one side, her best friend of seventeen years was becoming so obsessive over her, of their friendship, to the point that it was now ruining it. And on the other hand, her new best friend went behind her back and took something she was told not to, and now it was destroyed. Her friendships were just falling apart, and she didn't know what to do.

Maya started to walk towards Arya, but Sadie blocked her way and crouched by her instead. Maya backed away, then Sadie saw a change come over her face. Her eyes widened. She pointed at Sadie.

"She did it!" cried Maya.

Both Arya and Sadie shot their heads up.

"What?" asked Arya bewilderedly.

"S-Sadie did it. She put the painting in my bag. Who else would have done it?"

Arya looked shocked. Sadie looked surprised, but inside she was smiling. Maya did just what she wanted. Before the smile crept upon her face, she reacted.

"How dare you accuse me of that! Why would I do that?" she replied and then turned to Arya. "I wouldn't do that to you. You know I wouldn't. Why would I purposely destroy something that you love? I could never do that. It's not in me," she whispered. "She's the one who kept eyeing up your painting, wishing she could take it. Remember?"

Maya tried to interrupt, but Sadie carried on.

"Why else would it be in her bag? When would I have even had a chance to go near her bag? Conveniently, she's accusing me, just like she accused me of trying to poison her!"

This thought struck in Arya's mind like lightning. Sadie was right. Maya had accused her of two things now. What else was she ready to accuse her of? Arya decided that enough was enough. Sadie was possessive, but she wasn't cruel or a pathological liar. Sadie was also right. How could she have done that? She wouldn't hurt her.

Finally, Arya cleared her throat.

236

"Okay, I've heard enough. Maya, you need to stop accusing Sadie of things. First, you accuse her of purposely putting nuts in your lunch and now you're accusing her of putting my art in your bag, opening up nail polish and destroying it? No way would she be that calculated and cruel. That's not Sadie."

Tears began to fall from Maya's eyes. Her voice broke.

"Bu-but, I really didn't do it, I swear. It was Sadie...it has to be her!" she pleaded. Then she appeared to piece something together. "Before I left yesterday, she seemed out of breath for no reason! Maybe she rushed upstairs to get it and then dump it in my bag!"

"That's ridiculous Maya," said Arya quietly.

"I can't believe you're accusing me of doing this. I'm her BEST friend, I would never hurt her. It shows what kind of friend you are. I think you should go now," ordered Sadie.

Maya looked at Arya, chest heaving with heavy breaths, hands balled up in fists. "Please, Arya," she said.

Arya sighed. "I think it's best if you go. After I told you not to touch it...yo-you still did. And it's ruined. I just need you to go now, please," whispered Arya defeatedly.

Maya slowly looked from Arya's sad face to Sadie's. Sadie could hardly hide her satisfaction, but she did her best and glared sternly at Maya, who quietly said, "I'm sorry," and left.

The door closed with a click that echoed. And then they were both left in total silence, in the dark now the sun had been covered by the clouds.

In Sadie's mind she celebrated, triumphant, feeling spectacular that she had finally got rid of the one person that had disrupted Sadie's world. And she hoped that she wouldn't have to deal with anyone else. Once she finished quietly relishing in her success, she moved towards Arya and put her arm around her shoulder. And she rubbed her other arm.

"Are you okay?" she quietly asked.

"I'm fine. I just think I need some space from Maya. Her problem with you is just a bit too much for me."

"I didn't even know she had a problem with me," replied Sadie, with wide doe eyes, playing the victim.

"It doesn't matter right now. I've just had enough of her accusing you of things, it's wrong."

"I know. I can't believe she thinks of me like that. Why would I do any of those things? Absolutely crazy of her to think that" Sadie exclaimed. "Crazy."

Once Arya ran through everything that just happened, she slowly got up, wanting to go upstairs. But before that she needed Sadie to go. However, before she could ask, Sadie spoke.

"What shall we do to take your mind off things? Do you want to go grab some milkshakes, I know you love them. Or we could make some popcorn, or I know of a place that I go to whe-" started Sadie.

"Actually, I think you should go too."

"Wait what? Why?" whined Sadie.

"I just need to be alone, Sadie."

"Bu- but what about the plans we had, with the photos?"

"That was your plan, Sadie. I already told you this morning I was busy today, but you still decided to come over. I'm sorry, but I just want to be alone right now."

Sadie was taken aback. Hurt. Rejected. This wasn't going right at all; it wasn't going according to her plan. They were supposed to spend the day together, her comforting upset Arya, and them rekindling their twosome, loving friendship. Why did Arya want her to go? She hadn't done anything wrong. And who did she have plans with anyway, Sadie wondered. Her mind racing with questions like, why couldn't she just drop her plans and spend time with her? She did all of this for Arya, so they could be together. Why didn't Arya understand that?

Sadie sighed and simply said, "Oh okay."

Arya walked her to the door and waved goodbye before closing it. Sadie seemed reluctant to go, but Arya didn't want to be around either of them. Once the door shut behind Sadie, her head sank, and she closed her eyes.

What went wrong?

Why hadn't it gone how she played it out in her head?

Lifting her head, she glared at the wavering sun, still overshadowed by approaching clouds. She cocked her head to the side, deep in thought about how she needed to work harder to achieve this impossible dream of hers. Then as quickly as the clouds blanketed the sun, she knew what she had to do next.

Chapter 19

As soon as Arya closed the door, she went on a search for her Bailey bear. She found him rolling around in the grass outside of Kiaan's playhouse. Her tearful eyes rested on his bountiful golden fur, pointing in all different directions and basking in the glorious sun that decided to shower her. Maybe the sun knew when Arya needed it. But after looking at Bailey, her eyes blinked away her tears and she felt her broken heart starting to piece together again.

His golden fur was her metaphorical golden sun; it could shine on her and warm her in any shape or form. And before she knew it, her head was resting on his tummy, but he was having none of it. He just wanted to play.

Barking at her to get off, she then chased him around the garden, with Kiaan shouting at them to listen to him. But they didn't, they were having too much fun.

Arya decided to catch her breath and lay on the soft, lush grass. Sprawled out as if she were making a snow angel. Letting the sun grace every part of her, warming her face and allowing her to focus her mind on this moment. This happy and carefree moment. She closed her eyes, hoping to doze off, but then the light suddenly disappeared, and she was left in the shadows.

Opening her eyes slowly wondering where it had gone, she noticed it was just Kiaan standing over her, arms folded on his side, looking like he was ready to tell her off. "Whatcha doing?" he asked.

Arya sighed. "I'm sleeping, go away."

"But you're talking to me, so you're not sleeping. Get up! I wanna play!" he demanded.

"But I don't wanna!" mimicked Arya.

Kiaan sat on her chest, as Bailey did sometimes. She wondered whether her little brother had copied this move from him. But Arya carried on sleeping until Kiaan put his fingers up her nose.

"Urgh! Why would you do that!" she yelled, her nose feeling wet and gross now.

She chased Kiaan round and round the garden until she had to give up, not having the energy of a six-year-old boy. But she only needed a short rest and then it was back to chasing him, Bailey running around and between them throughout. Then when Kiaan finally got bored, he went into this playhouse and shut the door on Arya. She wasn't allowed in, it was the rule, even though she had made it for him.

Fully content in their playfulness, Arya felt like she had let loose, having no thoughts or worries dampening her spirits. And she was seeing Eli later, which sparked those butterflies to bloom again. All she needed was a simple hug from him, and her worries would vanish.

Kiaan caught her smiling to herself.

"What are you smiling at?" he asked, but Arya wasn't listening to him. She was imagining being with Eli; a hug, holding hands. Then Bailey's slimy, wet ball hit her square in the face.

"OW!" shouted Arya. Kiaan was grinning menacingly.

"What was that for?!"

"I asked what you were smiling at, and you didn't listen. This was the only way, you know."

"Very funny. And it's none of your business what I was smiling at."

"Why isn't my business? I'm your brother, after all. You can't hide things from me!"

Arya just laughed at him and pushed him over gently.

"Stop that! Is it your boyfriend? Is a boy making you smile because that's gross and I'm telling Mom."

Arya burst out laughing and pushed him again, which he didn't like. So, he jumped on her instead, then Bailey jumped on him and Arya was squished. But she was soon rescued by the sound of her Mom's voice calling them inside.

"Coming!" shouted Arya.

The three of them all followed each other into the house and saw Aashi unpack her work things. They all crowded around the kitchen table. Kiaan was hungry, Bailey wanted treats and Arya just wanted company. Aashi smiled at them, then she noticed the crumpled-up painting on the table.

"What's this?"

Arya looked at what she was pointing at and sighed, trying to hold back the fresh tears that were now brewing.

"Is *that* from your boyfriend?" Kiaan smirked. "Mom, she has a boyfriend now. Did she tell you? She smiles when she thinks of him. It's so gross."

"Oh, shut up. It's not from my boyfriend. I don't even have a boyfriend. Go away," snapped Arya.

Aashi, seeming to pick up that Arya's mood had dipped and that she was in no mood for this of teasing, handed Kiaan a fruit bag from the fridge and off he went with Bailey in tow, tongue hanging out, hoping for a blueberry as a treat. Ayra sighed with gratitude. Mom always knew how to get rid of them, and that method was usually food.

"So, now that they're out of the way. Is there anything you want to talk about?" she asked.

Arya just sighed again, looking down at her destroyed painting, her bottom lip jutting out. But after a deep breath, she explained what happened. Aashi's face saddened and she looked forlorn. Arya knew it was also her favourite painting. When Arya finished telling her everything, including the fight she and Sadie had before Maya came, her Mom brought Arya into a bear hug. She felt like a small child again, needing her Mom's comfort from the bad monsters. Unbreakable and loving arms wrapped around her like a tight blanket. The familiar smell of her loving Mom loosened Arya's tensions, and she felt soothed.

"I don't know what to do now," Arya whispered through broken cries.

"Well, you're upset, and you're allowed to be upset there's no doubt about that. It isn't nice for one friend to blame another," Aashi said. She paused. "Who do you believe?"
Arya shook her head.

"I honestly don't know. Maya did take a liking to my painting and mentioned a few times how she wished she could have it. But I didn't think she would *steal* it. And after she accused Sadie of trying to poison her too. Which is just-" said Arya, mimicking a 'mind blown' expression. "Sadie isn't crazy enough to purposely do that."

She drummed her fingers on the table, and her Mom instinctively did the same.

"Yeah, I don't buy that either," her Mom said. "I didn't think Maya was the kind of person to throw out accusations like that, it seems almost childish. That's not like her at all."

"I know. It annoyed me. I'm so angry that Maya took my painting. How she destroyed it, and then accuses Sadie of calculating it all? I know she doesn't like her but come on, that's just wrong," sighed Arya.

Aashi just listened.

"But on the other hand, Sadie is being too much again. I thought she was changing when she wanted to spend time all together but then gets mad at me again, about the same topic. It's just frustrating and I feel like I'm being pulled on both ends. Both of my friendships are falling apart, and it hurts."

Aashi brought Arya in closer, tucked her hair behind her ears and stroked her back.

"If you feel this bad then you should talk to them. Do whatever you feel is right, but don't feel obligated to fix everything. It isn't your job. You don't have to get them to like each other, because not everyone will like one another, and you really can't force it." Arya listened to her Mom intently. "And as hard as this may be to hear, friends come and go. When you go away to college, you and Sadie may stay friends, or you may not. It's a part of life and if things aren't working out anymore, then you need to let it go." With that she finished.

Arya was sad to hear this, but her Mom was right. She couldn't make them like each other, but if they wished to remain friends with her, they had to accept the friendship. They didn't have to like it, they didn't have to be around each other, but they needed to respect that Arya was friends with both of them. It really wasn't that hard. The only thing she was certain of was that she needed space from both of them right now. Just enough so she could get her head straight.

She hugged her Mom, and thanked her for her words of wisdom. She had helped clear Arya's mind somewhat, and the first thought to come with that clarity was Eli. She ran upstairs. Grabbing her phone from her pocket, she asked Eli whether they could meet up earlier and go to the pizzeria for dinner on the harbour. He quickly responded with an eager "YES" and Arya collapsed on her bed feeling smitten. She still had a couple of hours yet before they were meeting, so she decided to spend the rest of her time with her Mom before leaving.

They chatted some more while Arya helped her cook and do some tidying. There was a lightness to her Mom's company that she realised she often took for granted. Conversation flowed easily. It reminded Arya of how things had been with Sadie. Before everything. And maybe their friendship really was coming to an end.

But Arya didn't allow herself to go down that road. Instead, she stayed there with her Mom, enjoying the time they were having.

Before she knew it, it was time for her date with Eli. She leapt out her front door as if she were a fleeting gazelle and skipped down her front drive, with the sound of her Mom laughing behind her. Arya carried that sound of home and happiness with her until she reached Gilfoyle Street, where she saw him.

Her heart fluttered a little in her chest and she felt her breath catch in her throat. Blush arose in her cheeks, and she could feel her face getting clammy with a happy nervousness, but she hoped it gave her a dewy glow. No matter how hard she tried not to look like a goofy idiot, she couldn't stop a smile from spreading on her face. She was just so happy to be going to him.

Eli turned around and spotted her. His face burst with glee, but instead of going to her, he leaned against the streetlamp nonchalantly. With a cheeky side grin, gently running his hands through his hair.

Oh boy, Arya thought.

His stance had Arya melting into a puddle. She felt a hot rush coming, so she started fanning herself and saw Eli laugh, which made her smile even more, if that was even possible, now her cheeks were hurting from holding such a big grin. Not being able to wait anymore, they both ran the little distance they had between each other and hugged. That hug felt like it lasted a thousand years. Standing in a spot where the warm sunlight beamed over them. This warm embrace felt like a hundred golden suns had surrounded them.

At first, Arya felt each of their heartbeats, pulsing quickly because they were embracing each other. But then she felt they started to sync, they breathed in together and they breathed out together. When she laid her head on his chest, she felt at peace, she felt serenity, she felt at home. Nothing could take away this feeling, and she never wanted to leave it. This was where she wanted to be.

But in the distance a car was revving, quietly like a lion purring, watching its prey. The car had slowly followed Arya from her street and was now parked up on the opposite side of the road, ready for when the couple started their venture. Hands tightened on the steering wheel, knuckles turning white with the anger that was rushing through her body, Sadie watched them.

There was always something getting in the way of their friendship. She didn't even know he was here, that they were still talking or that they were seeing each other. Arya had kept that quiet! If Sadie could scream, she would. Instead, her insides filled with silent shrieks. Another hurdle in her way, another hurdle she had to knock down. Suddenly, she realised that through her blind anger she missed her cue. They were starting to leave. She was ready to move, she was going to follow them, every step of the way. Her bloodshot, strained eyes were watching Arya, not leaving her sight, she started the car and followed.

She would end this relationship.

Chapter 20

They walked hand in hand, swaying their arms rhythmically. Walking in sync with each other, in their whirlwind summer romance. Arya stole a quick glance at Eli and noticed he was shyly looking down but uncontrollably smiling. His gorgeous face ignited a burning fire in her stomach. She squeezed his hand, he looked at her and blushed, squeezing her hand back. Caught up in their own bubble, they carried on walking to the pizzeria in electric silence that was humming throughout the calm air. But they were at peace with the silence, there wasn't any awkwardness to it at all, and both knew the other felt the same. It was unspoken words.

When they eventually made it to the pizzeria, they were shown to their booth and they both quietly sat down. Arya took a deep breath and was about to apologise for being so quiet, but Eli broke the silence first.

"I'm sorry for not speaking much, I feel quite nervous. I don't know what's come over me..."

Arya sighed in relief. "I'm exactly the same! These nerves just hit me suddenly," she laughed.

Naturally, admitting this instantly relieved them, knowing that they weren't being silly. They both breathed in and looked at each other, boring deeper into each other's eyes. Eventually, they found themselves having reached over the table to interlock their fingers together. Hands perfectly fit in the spaces between their fingers. Smiles broadened upon their faces; their eyes twinkled with the candlelight flickering beneath them. But also, with new love.

They were both bright-eyed and bushy-tailed, thrilled to be in each other's company in a romantic setting, having waited so long for a proper date. Chatting non-stop because they each loved the sound of the other's voice, taking in everything they were saying like gospel. Laughing at each other's jokes, listening to the deeper conversations and becoming lost in each other.

When their food arrived, they completely forgot they were even out for dinner, because they hadn't felt hungry from all their conversations. But once the smell of the food wafted over to them, they couldn't wait to eat. And afterwards, their bellies were full of pizza and hearts full of contentment.

Deciding to make the most of being by the sea and to enjoy the ambience of a summer night, they took off their shoes and dashed to the beach. They walked barefoot along the calm water, sand grains bellowing over their toes, and the rush of the ocean waves singing in their ears.

As she was lost in thought thinking about how this moment was so perfect and she wanted to capture it for eternity, Eli spoke.

"So, because it's a clear sky, I was wondering if you wanted to go on a detour to end the night?" he asked with an expectant smile.

Arya was intrigued but a tad nervous, because she was hoping it meant something other than his place.

"Oh? What did you have in mind?" she replied anxiously.

"Well, the friends I'm living with both study photography, and they wanted to visit Alvord desert to stargaze and hopefully capture the view."

He paused, looking at Arya. She didn't say anything yet.

"Err...so, I was wondering whether you wanted to go, um, whether you want us to go with them. To see the stars...to stargaze. I don't know whether you'd be interested..." He trailed off, hand on the back of his head, laughing awkwardly.

Arya's face burst with excitement. "I would love to go. I've always wanted to go stargazing."

"Oh. OH, okay yeah. Great! Well, they were thinking of heading there in about an hour and they said they can pick us up along the way. If that's okay with you?"

"Sure. Sounds perfect."

Since they had time to spare, they decided to have milkshakes. Luckily the milkshake truck was still open, and one look at each other and they knew what they were thinking. Without a second to spare, they raced to the stall, trying to beat one another. And Arya got there first.

"Beat you! You will always be too slow for me," she winked.

Eli stuck out his tongue in defeat.

Arya spent around five minutes deciding what flavour she wanted. She was stuck between an Oreo and brownie milkshake, or a strawberry, cream and cookie dough combination. Eli immediately ordered the Oreo, which helped Arya reach a decision. She asked the server for two.

"Oh, copying me now, are we?" asked Eli, cheekily.

"What can I say? You've got good taste."

"I definitely have good taste," he replied, looking deep in her eyes with meaning.

Arya blushed as red as the strawberry milkshake she nearly ordered. No matter what Eli said, he always gave her butterflies, and she loved this feeling. Never had she experienced a love like this before; the crushes she had previously seemed like child's play now. This was the real deal, she knew it.

As they waited for their milkshakes, they rested against the wooden fence panels. Eli was holding her hand so gently, rubbing his thumb over her finger, again and again. His touches were soft and warm, like fresh laundry being taken out of the dryer. He was now what Arya craved. From his gaze, his smell and his touch, down to the sound of his voice. He was her heaven. Once they got their drinks, they went back to the beach and sipped on their delicious treats happily.

"Hey, can I have a sip of yours?" asked Arya.

Eli looked at her puzzled. "We have the same flavour, why do you want a sip of mine?"

"You have a big piece of Oreo, and I want it." She shrugged.

Eli bellowed with laughter. "Really?"

She nodded furiously, trying to hold in her own giggles.

"You're not getting it! It's mine!" laughed Eli.

Arya gave him the puppy dog look, with the extra pout.

"Oh, all right, here you go."

Arya giggled. "I'm only joking! Just wanted to see how generous you were."

Eli playfully rolled his eyes and softly nudged her shoulder with his. Arya just smiled and went back to sipping her milkshake. She was glad they could playfully joke and tease each other; it showed compatibility. After they were done, they sat on the sand just above where the tide was coming in, so the waves could wash over their feet, but not bowl them over.

Arya's thoughts settled in since she was surrounded by the tranquillity of the ocean. And she realised that Eli had seemed nervous when he asked her to stargaze. Why, she hadn't a clue. They had already rid themselves of their nerves earlier. So, why did it come back to Eli? Maybe it was because this date felt more personal and meaningful than getting dinner and milkshakes, so it brought a whole load of pressure with it. But she didn't want that, and she was sure he didn't want that either.

"Hey...you seemed nervous then. Do you want me to come along? Or do you not want to go?" she asked out loud.

"I do want you to come along, honestly. It's just... I didn't know whether you'd find it boring. I love looking at the stars and I've always wanted to do it with someone special. Just lying on the ground looking up at the sky. Lost in awe...wishing you were up there..." He trailed off.

"I guess it is quite an intimate date. Quite romantic," whispered Arya.

"Exactly. And I've now found that special person I want to experience it with... I guess I was just nervous to ask you because I didn't know whether you would like it," explained Eli.

"I couldn't be more excited."

Eli blushed, feeling the love rush in his veins, he was completely smitten by Arya. And now she was satisfied with his answer, she rested her head on his shoulders, and he rested his head on hers. They both watched the calm, clear, serene waves wash over their toes, ever so gently. Both wishing they could stay exactly where they were for eternity. Watching the glorious sunset on the horizon. Eli heard that when the sun hits the horizon it creates a quick flash of light, so luminous and entrancing.

He had never been on a beach at sunset before and was eager to witness it his own eyes and there was no better time like the present. As the sun slowly started setting, the beach became quieter, the chatter died down and eventually it was just the two of them left. Anticipation building because they were about to witness something magical. This was so ordinary to some, but for Eli, this would be the first time he would see this.   He put his arm around Arya and pulled her closer to him, his heart racing as he did so. Building up the courage to go in for a kiss, because it felt like the right moment. But just as he was about to tilt her head up, she whispered that it was time.

"Look, the sun's about to hit the horizon."

The way she whispered this in hushed tones while looking out into the horizon in awe, sent chills down his spine. He was mesmerised by her. The way the colours of the sunset swam in her eyes, the peaceful smile lingering on her rose-coloured lips, the way her skin glowed. He didn't want to look out to the horizon anymore; he was already looking at his sunset. Then with a quick flash, the sun hit the horizon. At that moment, the flash glared in Arya's eyes, illuminating the golden pools that swam in her chocolate brown eyes. Eli melted, right there.

"Wow. That was so beautiful. I forgot how mesmerising it was. Did you see it?" asked Arya, still glowing.

"Yeah. I saw it. Beautiful."

Arya didn't know he meant her. Eli wasn't sad that he missed it either, he was looking at something much more beautiful. She then turned to watch Eli, taking in everything about him. Every freckle, every eyelash, the dimple in his right cheek, just wondering what he was thinking about. Because she had noticed he couldn't seem to take his eyes off her but couldn't find the words to ask him why. Then he reached out and tucked her hair behind her ear. Goosebumps erupted all over her as she shivered slightly at his touch.

Alarmed at her reaction, he went to grab his jacket and draped it around her, then he pulled her even closer to him. They were so close now. She could feel his breath on her cheeks and could smell his sweet-smelling cologne. Their eyes were flittering between each other and his hand slowly moved up her arm to her neck. With his soft, unspoken touch he gently caressed her face with his fingers, tilting her head up and moving her face so her lips were close to his.

They almost touched... Then a car horn honked.

"HEY ELI! Come on!"

Two guys were leaning out of a car at the edge of the beach.

Eli groaned. Arya giggled.

"Soon," she whispered.

Eli smiled in agreement and grabbed her hand and made their way to the car. Jonah was a photographer. Very tall with platinum blond hair that was half shaved, he wore a crescent-shaped earring and had icy blue eyes. But he radiated a warmth like that of freshly baked cookies. Then there was Aziel who immediately came across as quite eccentric, with a hyperactive energy.

He had grey hair that accentuated his forest green eyes and brown freckles. But he had awful fashion taste, Arya thought.

They both welcomed her like they were long lost friends. She and Eli hopped into the backseat of the car, and they drove off. As they were driving, Arya asked all sorts of questions to both of them. Why the grey hair, why photography, why come to this city?

They both laughed at her curiosity but answered all her questions. And in turn they asked her questions. What she wanted to do at college, where she saw her life going, and what she liked to do in her spare time. When she expressed her love for painting. Jonah promised her that if he captured any great photos tonight, he would print one out and gift it to her, so she could recreate it in her paintings. Arya was grateful for that.

Instead of following the car's GPS, Jonah took them on a rocky, rugged, butt-aching route to the desert. It was an off-road experience to remember, and Arya felt like she and Eli got the worst of it in the back. They jutted forwards, backwards, up and into each other. The boys laughed and joked at all the turbulence, but Arya wanted to get out. When they turned off the rocky route and onto a smooth surface, she felt a wave of eternal gratitude.

Soon they were at their destination. Out here, away from the glaring lights and sound pollution, they were met with peace. The air around them was still and quiet. As they climbed out of the car, their feet crunched on the dry ground below, and the sound felt like it echoed throughout the barren desert. She saw that there were a couple of other cars scattered around, but the engines were all turned off. No sound or light was emitting from any of the cars until one straggler appeared. But as quickly as it arrived, its engine was abruptly shut off, and the driver was left in the darkness.

One of the other groups that had travelled to the desert, had perched themselves on top of the car, admiring the awe-inspiring beauty above. Everyone that had driven up was now sitting on the floor gazing at the world above. Apart from the car that had just pulled up, no one came out of it, and she couldn't even see it anymore. Not in the desert darkness. Arya thought it was weird. How could someone even see the stars from their car?

While she was left in deep thought, Jonah had been busy setting up his tripod and photography equipment. Aziel was lying on the ground, hands beneath his head and he stared into the abyss, an amazed expression on his face, as if he were lost in space himself. The bright stars reflected in his eyes. Arya then felt a gentle hand on her shoulder, she turned to Eli, and he showed her a spot for them to sit down. He had laid down a plump blanket that his friends had brought with them, so they could lie on it as they stargazed.

Arya and Eli first sat down and leaned on their hands, tilting their heads up, lost in the environment they were in. Their surroundings were quaint and peaceful, with a quiet whoosh of a gentle breeze swooping in every so often. It seemed like every person that was here was all lost in admiring the unknown world just above them that they could never be a part of.

Her eyes were darting in every direction of the night sky, taking in every star. Each and every sparkle in the inky, black darkness that blanketed them. She felt like she would never have enough time to absorb the astronomical beauty she was witnessing that night. Then suddenly, they were all blessed with a shooting star that swam across the sky. A gasp echoed through the desert, from everyone lucky enough to see it. It was a magical sight.

"Beautiful," spoke Jonah. "I think I captured it!"

"That's amazing!" chimed Arya.

They all crowded around his camera and observed his photo, and indeed he did capture the star. Even though it was a single shot, it still managed to look like it was sparkling in the night. It captured Arya's heart. She hoped this would be the picture he would give to her. After the excitement of the picture dwindled down, Jonah went back to taking more photos, Aziel found a new spot to lie down in, and Eli and Arya went back to their blanket.

Arya looked around her, feeling lucky that she was here, that she was with Eli and that she was happy. She turned to discreetly look at him and watched him gaze at the night sky. All she could see was a million stars mirroring in his eyes, as if someone had perfectly placed each star individually, to capture the galaxy in his already gorgeous eyes.

They were aglow with the twinkle of the night sky like it was a portal to bliss. If that was the last thing she saw, she'd be happy. She sighed, catching the attention of Eli. They stared longingly into each other's eyes, smiles spreading across their rosy cheeks, knowing exactly what each other wanted. And without wasting another second Arya moved towards him and they kissed.

Fireworks were going off in Arya's heart, bouncing off in every direction. Butterflies erupted in every crevice of her body. Fingertips tingled, and goosebumps appeared all over her. She daydreamed about this kiss, but it never amounted to the real thing she was now experiencing. It was more than she could ever imagine, it was heartfelt, warm, like a dream. She didn't want it to end; she didn't want to wake up.

But it had to end sometime and when their lips parted, she instantly missed his. They looked at each other and in that sweeping moment, they felt so connected. And as if they were soulmates, they both erupted into quiet giggles. Eli wrapped his arms around Arya, and they fell back onto the blanket, looking up at the stars again. Both wished this night could stay like this forever.

Out of all the empty cars that were parked in the observant area, one car unlike the rest remained occupied, by a very vigilant, irritated, mad and erratic person. It was Sadie.
She had been following them the entire evening and had followed their car from the beach, driving behind them onto the off-road path and into Alvord desert.

She hadn't taken her eyes off Arya all night. She had witnessed the intimacy Arya and Eli had, the bond that had built up between them. How quickly Arya took to the other two unmentionables. It boiled her blood. Arya was so happy to ditch her and be with a boy she had only met and then accompany him and his friends? Unbelievable. Despicable. It made her feel replaceable, dispensable and outraged. Sadie would have to do everything and anything in her power to destroy everything Arya had. Except for her, of course. She could never destroy their friendship.

With that in mind, Sadie quietly drove off, eyes hardened and intense, full of anguish and anger. Enough was enough, she thought. Arya was hers and she didn't like to share.

Sadie had to break up the love that was now coursing through Arya's veins, relishing her with eternal happiness. Sadie needed to remind her that their friendship was her happiness, that Sadie was her happiness, and no one else. This thought grew in her mind incessantly, like an infection spreading, without any signs of halting.

The darkness of the night and emptiness of the road she was driving on, now mirrored her heart and mind.

Chapter 21

A few days had passed since the most romantic night of Arya's life under the stars. Nothing had dampened her spirit in those following days, and she had remained giddy ever since she left his side. It felt like those painful moments of her friendships deteriorating, just like her treasured painting, had all been a nightmare. But after spending her days in sweet denial, she had to face the reality of the dramas she was hopelessly pulled into.

Even though she had spent all her time with Eli, she never once brought up the problems in her social circle. She didn't want to upset the peaceful balance she had created with him.

As she lay in her cosy bed, with the golden sun seeping through her gossamer curtains, she was at peace in her dreams. Eventually, she woke up, feeling the warm light of the morning sun hug her as if they were long-awaited friends. She wished to stay in her dreams a little while longer. Where Eli was, as they were utter bliss. And waking up meant that she would have to embrace the inevitable storm, sometime.

However, as Arya was wishing to delay this storm for as long as possible, Sadie had already been under the thick of it. Sucked into its thunderous, darkening clouds that were swarming around her head. These last few days had her spending hours stuck in those ominous thoughts, planning what she was going to do, waiting for the right time. Because her desperation had reached its peak. She ached to bask in her golden sunshine again. To be with Arya again. She longed for her.

Begrudgingly, Sadie awoke from her sleep and was met again with a cold sun glaring into her room. Sunlight blinding her from the reflections hitting her broken glass chandelier. She stared at the broken sunlight, wondering why she could no longer feel its warmth. The summer that had started so golden and harmonious was now turning blue…

She groaned and turned on her side, pulling the blanket up over her head, burrowing herself in her bed, hoping it would make her disappear. Her chest felt heavy, and her body felt oddly weak and fragile. There was no urgency in her to get up, she just felt like staying in the same position, wrapped up in a ball, forever. But then her Mom came into her room.

"Wakey wakey…time to get up, you have your piano lesson in an hour!"

Sadie groaned.

"Come on, you haven't gone to one in a while. it'll do you some good. Trust me."

"But I don't feel like it," moaned Sadie.

She felt her Mom sit down on her bed, and then her hand as she started to gently stroke Sadie's head.

Getting closer and closer to her with each stroke, till her head was now resting on Sadie's shoulders. Rose then pulled Sadie up from her bed and hugged her. This sudden warmth that grew in Sadie from her mother's love, left her in tears. She always found it hard to talk to her Mom, she never really told her much about her personal life, and she never understood why.

But she liked this hug, she liked this love she was receiving, and she let it unfold. Big crocodile tears were now spilling over onto her cheeks. They were unstoppable, warm and cathartic. But Rose continued to just rock her back and forth, without saying a word. After a little while Sadie dried her eyes and lifted her head from her Mom's embrace and sat back. Taking a few deep breaths in, she was ready to get up, and she let her Mom help her.

Rose took her to the bathroom and washed her face, brushed her hair as Sadie brushed her teeth, and wrapped her up in a dressing gown that was fresh out of the dryer. Sadie felt weird with all the love she was receiving, but she didn't question it because it felt so nice.

After she refreshed herself, Rose and Sadie went downstairs, and breakfast was made. Hot, fresh and spicy omelettes, a savoury treat ready for Sadie to gobble down hungrily, with a side of fruit to give her a sweet pick me up. When Sadie finished and began to tidy up, she noticed a bundle of pictures on the counter. Curious, Sadie walked over to look at them. Rose caught a glimpse of her doing so.

"Those are from our holiday," she said pointedly.

"Oh?" Sadie started to look through them.

Flicking through them one by one, she stopped on a particular captured memory. It was of her and Arya in front of a castle, fireworks lighting up the night sky, the girls hand in hand and grinning like they were two children high on sugar. Just like the painting Arya made. But Sadie liked

Arya's more. She took a shaky breath and touched their heads gently, wishing to be back in that moment.

"I remember you saying that you guys wanted to use them in your scrapbook, right?" reiterated Rose.

Had her Mom left them here for a reason? Were they here to trigger Sadie's desire to scrapbook again? Sadie wondered if it would make her feel better. If it would help her, or if it would help their friendship. Sadie remembered all the incredible moments from their holiday.

She sighed.

The burning desire to immediately start scrapbooking grew in her. But it wouldn't feel right without doing this with Arya. Sadie was about to text her, to see if she wanted to come round, but questions started to fill her head again: would Arya even want to do this with her? Has Arya forgiven her again? And would this be the right way to reconcile their friendship?

Unfortunately, she had no answers to her burning questions, the only way she could find them was to take a gamble and risk it by going to Arya to see for herself. So, no words could be taken wrong over the phone.

Not wanting to be without Arya for a minute longer, Sadie psyched herself up and was feeling very determined now. But before she was about to run upstairs to get ready for her piano lesson, her Mom called her back.

"Before you go, I just wanted to run something by you."

Sadie curiously waited.

"So, me and your Dad were meant to go away this weekend, as you know, but I'm needed at work instead. So, we're unable to go. We wondered

266

whether you and Arya wanted to go to the cabin we booked instead? Might do you two some good to get away in the wilderness, without the distractions of other people or your phones…"

Sadie instantaneously felt elated. A burst of joy rippled through her. This was the perfect activity to mend a breaking friendship. Squealing inside, Sadie felt excited about the idea of being in a cosy cabin.

In sudden haste, Sadie hugged her Mom, rushed upstairs and grabbed her piano notes, then ran downstairs, grabbed the bundle of pictures and set off. Finally, with a spring in her step.

The next hour at her lesson flew by because she was too excited and nervous to see Arya. Although it distracted her from hitting the right keys, she kept making mistakes. Arthur could see that she wasn't entirely focused, so he let her go early and she dashed out of the house.

After all that pumped-up adrenaline, she now stood nervously at the end of Arya's front drive. Her body felt rigid. She didn't know whether she was coming or going. Sadie wanted to go towards the door, but her feet felt like lead. Leaving her stuck to the ground. She was too nervous. Sadie tried to psyche herself up again, encouraging herself and reassuring her troubled mind that Arya would be overjoyed to see her. And once she felt ready, she took one step forward, just as the door opened.

Under the door frame, with the warm, yellow-painted door reflecting off her skin, was Arya. Sadie felt a sudden hot flush flourishing over her and her palms instantly became clammy. She felt her nerves in her stomach doing somersaults, afraid about what was going to happen next.

"Hey," called Arya.

"Hey..."

"Are you just going to stand there or?" she asked.

"Wha-what? Do you want me to leave? I can leave if you want me to..."

"I want you to come inside!" beckoned Arya.

Sadie smiled, feeling relieved. She walked shyly to her, hoping for a hug, but didn't want to push it. It didn't have to be a long one. And as if Arya read her mind, she hugged her.

"Let bygones be bygones?" she suggested.

NO, boomed the voice in her head.

"Yes," answered Sadie.

It was always the voice telling her to do things that ended up ruining their friendship and she couldn't let it keep happening. Sadie needed to learn to lock it away, for good.

Arya surveyed Sadie's face and noticed she looked conflicted, but she brought her into the house in hopes of washing that away. When they entered the house, they ended up just standing awkwardly around the kitchen counter. Neither of them knew how to start a conversation, they were both feeling oddly anxious in each other's presence.

"So..."

"Um..."

"You go first!" laughed Arya, nervously.

"No, no. You go first," encouraged Sadie.

Arya sighed, interlocking her fingers with each other.

"I think we both need to work on our friendship. We've had more fall outs this summer than we've had throughout our lives."

Sadie nodded in agreement.

"I don't think we should go over what happened, like I said, let bygones be bygones. But you need to know that I love you, okay? That won't ever change, no one could ever change that," finished Arya.

Sadie started to well up. All she could muster was a whisper of, "I love you too," and she ran up to Arya and they bear hugged.

In that hug, Sadie's sadness and Arya's grievances both melted away, and they felt like them again. After they separated, Arya asked what was in Sadie's bag.

"Oh! I brought our holiday snaps. My Mom printed them off and told me of a really sweet idea for us…"

"Ooh what is it?" asked Arya sweetly.

Sadie explained the weekend away idea to Arya and as soon as she mentioned that it was a cabin, Arya's face lit up.

"AHH yes! We have to go!"

"Really?" said Sadie, relieved.

"Of course!"

Sadie just smiled in response.

She didn't want to get too excited. Whenever she was excited about something, it never ended up going the way she wished it would. Something or someone would always ruin her plans. Which always left her falling from greater heights. Besides, it was only Wednesday and plenty of things could go wrong before Friday. But she let Arya become more and more excited because she liked it, and she liked seeing her happy.

They both cuddled up on the sofa, flicking through all the picture-perfect moments together, reminiscing their favourite part of the summer. Arya was amazed at how well they turned out, and suddenly she remembered that she had saved a bunch of items from their trip.

Cheerily, Arya took Sadie upstairs, excited to show her the souvenirs she kept. But before Sadie entered the room, a feeling of dread washed over her.

This was where she destroyed Arya's favourite art. The feeling of guilt hit her like a slap in the face. How could she even think about stepping into this room again? It felt like there was a forcefield stopping her from entering Arya's room.

Arya looked around and saw Sadie standing in the doorway looking uncomfortable.

"Are you okay? You look kinda queasy," said Arya.

Sadie could only muster a frantic nod. Her palms felt clammy again, she wiped them quickly on her jeans and pushed herself to enter the room. Once she was in, all the tension just disappeared. She felt oddly normal again. Shrugging it off, she walked towards the bed and plonked herself on it. Arya then pulled out a box that sounded like it was full of things.

Curiosity and excitement started building in Sadie, these were the things that were going to make the scrapbook look immense. Arya always had the best crafting materials.

The box was gently placed on the bed, and every content was taken out a few at a time and placed perfectly on the bed. Arya didn't like clutter, and she liked her things to not look chaotic. The items in the box included: her Disney World and Universal Studios tickets; wrappers from the sweet treats they had in Harry Potter World; a penny-sized squished brass plate that had the theme park logo embossed in it; her wrist bands for the fast passes they had; an assortment of coloured confetti from a parade; a crumpled daisy she picked from a small patch of grass found on International Drive; Disney Character pins and patches; a souvenir picture from one of the biggest roller coasters she had been on; receipts from every restaurant they went to; a keychain of Maggie from The Simpsons, who Arya loved the most (and because it was a gift from Eli on his last day there); and other bits and pieces for crafting, such as sticky ribbons, gems, cards, beads and so on.

"Wow!" exclaimed Sadie. "You've got loads of things here!"

"Yeah… I think I went a bit overboard with taking everything back with us," laughed Arya.

"No, I love it! There will be so much for us to add to my scrapbook, I'm so excited to do this with you."

Sadie then picked up the keychain.

"Where did you get this from?" she asked.

Arya turned to look at what Sadie was holding up and saw it was Eli's gift. Her eyes opened up wide. She hadn't told Sadie she met Eli in the hotel or that they were seeing each other now, and it wasn't the time to bring that up.

"Oh, that's nothing...something I bought from a souvenir shop. I'll just take that..." Arya stumbled over her words.

Sadie thought Arya's reaction was odd. But she gingerly gave it back like it was made from glass and decided not to think any more about it. She couldn't remember going into a souvenir shop there, but she guessed that they hadn't been glued to the hip the entire trip. It was only a keychain; there was no reason to worry about it.

After they gathered what they wanted to use from Arya's box, they decided to go to Sadie's house. Arya hadn't gone there in so long. The whole way to Sadie's was spent chatting about their weekend away at the cabin. What they were going to do there, what to bring with them and so on.

The realisation that they were going away for a second time this summer was just setting in Sadie's mind. They were so lucky to have gotten this chance and being able to be alone this time around made her even happier. Her passport stunt seemed so stupid to her now, she cringed at how dumb she had been.

Finally, they reached Sadie's house and were welcomed with the smell of freshly baked cookies. The smell was so alluring, that their stomachs rumbled instantly. When they entered the kitchen, they saw Rose nibbling on a tempting, rustic looking chocolate chip cookie, while working on some paperwork.

"Hey love, how have you been?" she asked, giving Arya a big hug.

"I've been good! How're you? Feel like it's been a long time since I saw you."

They babbled away happily, all munching on cookies. After they finished, the girls made their way to Sadie's room. From the first step into the room, Arya felt like the atmosphere in the room had changed. It felt strange, like there was a negative aura enveloping the room.

She scanned the surroundings and saw tissues scattered everywhere, clothes dumped in spots around the room, and everything was askew. Arya knew Sadie was messy, but this was different, it was more than messy.

She realised Sadie may have treated her room like this because of the argument they had. But it also seemed too much for just a spat between friends. Arya was about to ask Sadie why her room was like this, but then she noticed something on Sadie's bedside table.

"When did you get a new phone?" asked Arya.

Sadie's face went white as snow as if she saw a ghost. Arya wasn't meant to have seen that. During the last few days when Sadie was in her darkest mind, she thought of a devious way to split Arya from Maya and Eli for good. Which involved this phone.

When Sadie woke up today, the idea was still swirling around in her head, a very prominent thought, but then when she saw the pictures, it melted away. And now...now she was in two minds, does she follow through on her idea, or does she stop now before she ruins her friendship entirely?

"Um, hellooo?" said Arya, waving her hand in front of Sadie's unfocused face.

"Wha-" replied Sadie.

Arya then pointed to the phone. She laughed and asked again.

Sadie had to think fast and think on her feet.

"That's not a new phone. I'm err, selling that. It's, it's...an old phone that I found. Thought I should sell it," Sadie said quickly.

Arya nodded.

"Shall we clean your room?" she asked.

"Wha- what, why?" replied Sadie, defensively.

"Um, so-sorry, but it's such a mess. I think we should tidy it… It can help clear your mind too."

"Why would I need to clear my mind?" she snapped back, now agitated.

Arya saw she had touched a nerve, so she decided to proceed with even more caution. "I find it helps keep me focused, more at ease and less stressed when my environment is tidy and uncluttered. I just thought it

274

might help you if your environment was less…" she did a hand motion to point out the mess.

Sadie looked at her with such detest. Forehead frowning, lips taut with tension and a bitter taste in her mouth growing. But then she remembered who she was looking at, it was Arya, and she could never hate her. She knew deep down, *the voice,* knew that they could never hate her. Shocked at her reaction, Sadie tried to shake it off. Unsure of where this feeling came from but realising that Arya was right. Maybe cleaning her room was the right thing to do. So, Sadie tried to calm her raging thoughts, which were unnecessary and understood that a clear environment would mean a clear mind.

Sadie nodded slowly to Arya. Arya felt relieved. She knew it would help Sadie, and she also liked to organise just about anything. It was a win-win situation.

Arya connected her phone to Sadie's speakers and blasted Taylor Swift. Knowing it would get Sadie dancing. Arya started picking up all the tissues, it was gross, and she hated it. But she knew they were probably from Sadie's tears, and she didn't want her being reminded of how much she had cried.

And Sadie started picking up all the clothes off the floor and dumping them in her laundry basket. Despite only tidying those two things up, her room looked a million times better. One final thing was tying back her curtains and letting the sunshine in, opening the windows and allowing fresh air to swirl around a stuffy room.

Although the sun made Sadie shiver slightly, feeling unhappy and unnerved that the sun had a vendetta against her. But at least it loved Arya. Sadie watched how the sun glistened off her skin like she was a canvas, and the sun was the paint.

After they tidied her books and everything else, Arya decided it was clean enough and they both collapsed on the floor. Satisfied with their day's work. They put a movie on and watched in peace.

Sadie's head finally clearing. She felt oddly balanced for once. Her mind had been clouded by ominous thoughts for so long that it felt weird being empty. But she had a sinking feeling that it wouldn't last for long. Deep down she knew the clouds would come back, stronger than ever. And sure enough, it did.

Arya's phone buzzed and she saw Eli had texted her., asking if she was free. She quickly replied saying she was spending time with Sadie and that they can call later. Sadie noticed Arya was texting someone, but she reassured herself that she needed to stop.

Reminding herself that Arya was allowed to talk to other people. Over and over, she repeated this to herself, and it would have ended fine if she hadn't seen her name in one of the texts. Then she got paranoid. And she couldn't continue reassuring herself, because she couldn't stop the voice from coming back to her and pointing out that Arya was talking about her. The voice echoed in her mind.

Use the phone.

Sadie tried to fight it off, but seeing her name sent her into a frenzy. She had to carry out her plan. All she needed to do was wait for the right moment, when Arya wouldn't be with her phone. But she needed to prepare herself.

So, while Arya was watching the movie, Sadie went to the box that her new phone was in. It had already been set up, so it was ready to be used, she just needed to write down the number. Once she was done, she sat back down next to Arya. She looked up at Sadie and smiled. After thirty minutes or so, Arya yawned and stood up. She did a couple of stretches, took out her phone and dumped it on the bed.

"Just going to the bathroom, I'll be back in a minute," she said.

Sadie's head shot up; this was her chance. As soon as Arya left the room, Sadie grabbed the phone and unlocked it. She opened the contacts and found Eli's number. Hesitation started to creep in, but she didn't have time to rethink what she was doing, she needed to quickly get on with it.

Opening his contact information, she blocked his real number and replaced it with the number of Sadie's new phone. She knew it wouldn't work for both Eli and Maya, because it would merge messages, so she could only block Maya's number and nothing else.

After that, she quickly opened her Mac and logged into Arya's iCloud account so she could read her messages. As soon as she logged in,

Arya's phone pinged with an email alerting her of this new login, which Sadie swiftly deleted. Her heart was thumping in her chest, adrenaline pumping in the secrecy she was committing. Afraid she was going to get caught, she carried this out quickly. She finished what she needed to do and rapidly sat back down, like she hadn't moved a muscle.

This way Arya would have no real contact with Eli and Maya anymore. Instead, Sadie would now be receiving messages meant for Eli from Arya and she would reply by impersonating him in whatever way she wanted to. And if Arya decided to message Maya after their argument, which Sadie was certain she wouldn't, Maya wouldn't receive them. Therefore, creating a giant chasm between them. Which is what Sadie wanted.

Chapter 22

When Arya left Sadie's house and was back in her room, she decided she'd call Eli. She hadn't heard from him since their last text. He hadn't replied. Arya thought that he had just been busy or forgot to reply, it happens. Lying on her bed in her PJs, hair tied in a bun and feeling as happy as ever, Arya called him. Listening to the ringing sound, waiting for an answer. But it never came. She hung up and shrugged her shoulders and decided she'd call back in thirty minutes, or maybe he'd call her back instead.

But even after an hour, Eli hadn't called Arya back. She kept ringing and ringing and to her surprise, it just rang out. Arya couldn't understand why he wasn't answering, let alone texting her to say if he was busy. They had spent days and days with each other and texting endlessly, so why the ghostly silence now? Did she do anything wrong? Arya couldn't carry on pondering over why and decided to text him again, just one last time.

Hey, are you okay? Been trying to call you! Let me know if you still want to talk.

Arya patiently waited. And wondered. It was getting late now, and she still hadn't heard anything from Eli, no text and no call. Her effort was all in vain. And after realising that there was no point staying up any longer, she hopelessly placed her phone by her bedside table and lay down on her pillow. Face turned towards her phone, watching it like a hawk, just in case he called. Eventually, when her eyes were too heavy to stay open and she couldn't stay up any longer, Arya let her eyes close.

While she was sleeping, Sadie was still up watching a movie, though she could barely focus on it. On her side was the new phone that had three missed calls from Arya and unread texts.

She obviously couldn't answer the calls, because she wasn't Eli. Also, she wanted "Eli" to ghost her. It would work, she knew it would. Once Sadie finished the movie, she decided it was time to sleep. Begrudgingly thinking about the obstacles that had been in her way this summer that was meant to be theirs...hers.

The next morning came, and Arya woke up eager to see if Eli had texted. She hungrily grabbed her phone and realised she hadn't received anything from him, absolutely nothing. Her heart sank to the pit of her stomach. Her head started to buzz as if a thousand bees were flying around. It was going into overdrive, overthinking all the various reasons why she hadn't heard from him. But Arya had to reassure herself not to jump to conclusions because she wasn't going to let herself be paranoid again. But she so desperately wanted to hear from him, so she decided to text him again:

Hey...still haven't heard from you. Are you okay?

Naturally, Arya was anxious that something was wrong, maybe she had done something to upset him or maybe he truly was just busy. Trying

280

not to let her thoughts get the better of her, she decided to have a nice relaxing bath. Getting her comfy clothes out of the wardrobe, a soft towel, a book and her phone, she made her way to the bathroom. Arya decided she deserved to use a luscious bath bomb that promised radiance and a soft skin feeling. It was pastel coloured with glitter embellished on the outside, and it smelled luxurious.

Turning on the taps, she let the bath fill up while she brushed her teeth and got undressed. Once it was ready, she dropped in the bath bomb, sprinkled bath salts, lit a few of her tealight candles and played some soothing music. As she watched the bath bomb fizz and the colours leak into the water, she immersed herself in the toasty, liquid gold. Letting the sounds from her anxious thoughts wash over her, instead of swimming inside her mind.

She lay in the bath for a while, with closed eyes, breathing in and breathing out. Allowing the ambience, she created to ease her aching soul. Releasing her tensions and soothing her heart. She let the music flow in her ears until her peace was abruptly disturbed by a buzz. Slowly opening her eyes, she tried to locate where it came from, and from the side of the bath, she noticed her phone had lit up. She hurriedly grabbed it with both hands and saw Eli had texted her. Without drying her hands, she opened the message.

Hey. Can you chill out with your constant calls and texts. You're starting to act a little crazy.

Arya's mouth dropped. Shock had encased her, so much so that she almost let go of her phone from her suddenly numb fingers. She blinked a few times, making sure that she had read that text properly. This seemed out of character for Eli. Extremely out of character. How could he call her crazy? How could he be that brash with her?

She didn't understand where this came from. She suddenly felt sick, her heart started racing so quickly she could hear it in her ears, thumping dramatically. Her fingers started fumbling over the keyboard, trying to think of a response, how would she even reply to that?

She wrote words and quickly deleted them, over and over. Not happy with what she was writing. She was trying so hard not to say anything that could make her seem "crazy", even though she didn't know what that meant. Arya didn't think she was being crazy.

Then the self-doubt started to creep in, going over all the things she said, trying to make out where she went wrong for him to think that. But she couldn't think of anything. They were as good as gold...so what happened?

After spending minutes deliberating on what to reply, she just wrote a simple sorry and left it at that. Her mind wasn't in the right place to say any more. Her body felt numb as it sank into the sudden icy depths of the cold water engulfing her body. The rose-coloured glasses of her whirlwind romance had just shattered into a million pieces...

Rose was now the colour of Sadie's cheeks as she realised her plan was taking shape. Was she feeling adrenaline from hurting her best friend?

Surely not. But she took the feeling and rode with it. When she saw Arya's limp reply to her text impersonating Eli, she decided she'd leave her hanging for a couple of hours and then respond. For this to work, Arya needed to feel the space growing between them. And Sadie can strike the target with her arrow and break the love bond between Arya and Eli. Then Sadie and Arya would be evermore.

She started humming joyously, basking in her premature achievements. And started to pack her things for their weekend trip. First and foremost, she placed her precious scrapbook in her overnight bag, alongside all the crafting material and belongings from Arya.

Then she packed everything else, even her matching PJs that Arya has, as Sadie knew Arya would bring them along too. She had to pack a book or two...just in case, she finished rereading the first one. Sadie felt so elated about their trip, singing at the top of her voice and imagining all the alone time they will have together. Arya was her sun, and she couldn't wait to bask in her golden radiance. This trip meant everything to her and Sadie prayed it would bring her back into the warmth, like a sunrise. A new beginning.

Arya sat on the bed, after mustering the energy to leave the wallowing water and was now soaking in the warmth of the sun shining through her window. Even though she felt low, the sun always wrapped around her like a comfort blanket. But she felt hollow. Despite having made amends with Sadie, there was still a Maya shaped hole in her life and her relationship had hit a bump before it could even start.

283

A feeling of dread started creeping in. What could she do? Having mulled over her thoughts for what felt like an eternity, she knew what she should do. Friendships were precious, fragile, and very breakable. But this was one friendship she didn't want to lose, so she reached out to Maya.

Before Arya messaged her, she thought of a different way to approach Maya. Something imaginative and original, hoping it would bring a smile to her face. Arya quickly grabbed her sketchpad and a pencil and as quickly as the image conjured in her mind, it started to come together.

Drawing a rugged branch, delicate leaves and plump olives, her olive branch had been drawn. Pleased with her art and feeling optimistic, she decided to add colour to it. Using her favourite paint colours, like the earthy green to bring a freshness to the olive branch, as if it was coming to life. Once she was satisfied with her art, she took a picture of it, positioning it so the sunlight danced off the reflections of the fresh, wet paint. Then she sent it to Maya, hoping she understood what it meant.

A notification popped up on Sadie's Mac. Her head snapped up, unnerved at what that message could hold. Having remained logged into Arya's iCloud account, she could see everything. Sadie cautiously walked towards the laptop and glared at the message. Staring back at her was a picture of a branch with fruit on it.

Unsure of what it was, she zoomed in and finally, it dawned on her. *An olive branch*. Anger bubbled through her up to her throat. She slammed the screen down and stormed back onto her bed. After everything she did, destroying Arya's favourite painting, framing Maya, and Arya still wanted her back? Sadie's frustration was ready to explode like boiling magma.

It had been a couple of hours since Arya messaged Maya, extending her hand out. But she received nothing back. She started to feel like she was falling into a hole, losing grasp on people around her who she felt so in tune with. What was she doing wrong? She desperately wanted to call Eli to unfold her emotions, let him in and seek comfort. But she was too nervous to message him now. She didn't want him to call her crazy again, she didn't like that. And she couldn't tell Sadie because she was unaware of their relationship.

Just when she was feeling like she was losing her mind, she heard the all too familiar tippy taps of Bailey's paws. She watched him nudge her bedroom door open with his nose, poking in. Watching his nostrils flare as he was sniffing the air. It's like he could sense when Arya wasn't feeling herself and all she needed was love from her golden Bailey bear. She called him, and he bounded in and stopped at her feet. All he did was place his head on her lap ever so gently and then came the tears that poured out from Arya. From feeling so overwhelmed, that she couldn't hold it in anymore.

But Bailey didn't like this, he jumped up on her and licked away the salty tears that dared to grace her face. Arya started laughing trying to push him off her, but he wanted to jump on her bed instead.

Normally she didn't let him lie on her bed, but just this once all rules were out the window. She lay down and he lay closely next to her. Feeling his warmth, and the softness of his lion mane fur, she rhythmically stroked him, over and over.

Eventually, she felt better, and her head became a little clearer. Determined to at least clear one of her struggling relationships today, she reached out to Eli again.

Can we talk? I feel like you may have misunderstood me… I just wanted to talk to you, and you called me first.

And with a ping, the message was sent. Now she had to wait patiently. At least she had Bailey here to distract her until she got a response, any kind of response.

To pass the time, she decided to sketch some more, which always calmed her down. And there was no better muse to draw than her Bailey. She sat up and rested against her bed railings, propping a pillow behind her. Bailey just watched her every movement, but remained close to her, well at least to her feet anyway.

Arya zoned into her work, drawing the outline of Bailey and building up the picture with fine lines representing his fur, layer upon layer. For some reason, the feeling of drawing these fine lines so delicately and precisely calmed her anxiety down and helped her breathe more steadily. And before you knew it, she finished drawing Bailey and she felt like herself again.

"Look it's you! Aren't you cute?" she cooed.

Bailey just barked and Arya kissed his head. She finally felt like she was okay enough to go downstairs, she was absolutely starving but hadn't felt that hunger feeling until now. As she was about to head out her door, with Bailey in tow, her phone vibrated. Arya felt like her heart had jumped into her throat. This always happened whenever she sent a risky text and now, she received a risky reply. She couldn't explain why she felt like that, but she couldn't stop it either. Arya cautiously approached her phone and opened it.

Arya, you're getting on my nerves a little. You're acting really needy right now. And I need some space.

Arya's eyes brimmed with tears, and she slowly lost grasp of her phone, and it fell to the floor with a thud. Somehow, it felt like her heart was made out of glass, and Eli had smashed it to the ground. Shattering it into a million pieces. She didn't understand where all of this was coming from.

Thinking about how smitten they were with each other the other day, not letting go of one another's hands, the kisses they shared...the moments they shared. Where had that gone suddenly? Where had the love gotten lost to? Arya couldn't make sense of it all and before she sank into a hole so deep that was impossible to escape from, she bolted out of the house to the one person she needed right now.

Sadie sat on her bed in the quiet, secluded from the outside. She spent time with her thoughts and her thoughts alone. Getting lost deeper and deeper until she heard the doorbell ring. Curious, she went downstairs and opened the door, and to her surprise, it was Arya, in tears. *Showtime*, Sadie thought.

"Oh my god Arya, what's wrong? Why are you crying?" asked Sadie, feigning empathy.

Arya couldn't say anything, instead, she just reached for a hug from Sadie. And Sadie embraced her wholeheartedly, loving every moment of this hug, stroking Arya's hair. Again, she asked what was wrong.

"I've driven Maya away, she won't even talk to me and, and now, I've lost Eli too," she cried.

"Why would you think that? Who's Eli?" asked Sadie.

"I texted Maya a couple of hours ago, hoping to put the past behind us, like how we did. But she hasn't replied and-"

"But why would you do that? She betrayed you, Arya," said Sadie, quietly.

"Friendship is more important than a painting, I should have known better before hurting her over it," replied Arya. "And Eli is...well, do you remember that guy I met on holiday?"

Sadie nodded. And Arya explained all about how they met up in the hotel and talked to each other when they could. How they grew to love each other.

"Love? What would you know about love?" exclaimed Sadie, eyes rolling. "You've met him like four times, how can you be in love?"

Arya was taken back by Sadie's bluntness, but she was so heartbroken that she didn't say anything. Maybe Sadie was right, what did she know about love? They did only meet a handful of times, maybe that's not enough to build a strong connection like that. She realised she had been taken for a fool. This gut-wrenching pain had taken over her, having lost a friend and a boyfriend all in one day. It was too much to bear.

"I'm all alone now," said Arya, with a cry that was so hollow and heartbreakingly painful that it stunned Sadie.

She felt so guilty now, as this was all her doing. Look at what she was doing to her best friend. How could she have been so heartless? But she couldn't own up to it, because then Arya would be broken completely, and she didn't know whether she could survive that. Instead, Sadie embraced her with all the love in her body.

"You're not alone. No, you'll never be alone. You have me, and I'll never leave you," reassured Sadie.

Tears streamed down her face too, but she had no idea why she was crying. The girls just sat in the doorway hugging each other until their arms ached.

The next morning arrived, and it was the day the girls would be going away for their short trip. After Arya had left the previous evening, they both had a sinking feeling in their chest, but still looking forward to it anyway. It was a chance for a renewal, and it would take their minds off their troubles.

When Arya had given Sadie the go ahead, she left her house and drove to Arya's. She didn't need any music playing, because the thumps from her heart were more than enough sound. Parking outside Arya's house, Sadie watched Arya walk solemnly to the car, looking lost in her thoughts.

Piling her luggage in the back of the car absentmindedly. But when Arya sat at the front beside her, Sadie's mood lifted. She smiled at her, but she noticed that Arya wasn't looking up from her hands. Sadie wished she could be in her mind; she was curious to know what Arya was thinking about so intensely.

Arya sighed deeply. She thought about how there was still no text from Eli in the morning. A deep ache had set in her heart, and as much as she tried to erase it, it wouldn't disappear. She wanted to reach out to Maya too, she missed her. But she felt like Maya didn't want to know her either.

She felt rejected and lonely. Then she heard Sadie quietly sigh too. And she realised she can't be that lonely, not when she had her best friend with her. At the end of the day, whether they were dancing through the highest highs, or screaming through the worst lows, Sadie was always there. She felt lucky, privileged even, to have such a loyal friend.

When she had gained enough courage to look at Sadie's face, her heart felt like it bloomed a little and her face softened. She grabbed Sadie's hand and squeezed it.

Sadie saw that Arya was wearing the rose gold friendship bracelet she gifted her, and it made her smile. For once, Sadie didn't feel like she needed any more reassurance of their bond, their friendship. Feeling happy, she finally banished those blues away for good.

They waved goodbye to Arya's parents. Arya watched her Mom beaming at her. For some reason Arya felt a little sad leaving her, she hated being away from her Mom. But she'd be back soon, so she mouthed 'I love you', and blew her a kiss to her before Aashi slipped back inside.

Then Sadie drove off, music now blasting and both girls singing at the top of their voices, enjoying the last days of the August sun. This journey was already beginning to feel cathartic for both. They truly felt blessed to be with one another.

The trip to the cabin was only an hour away but travelling through their city took the longest time. Driving through the busy streets of downtown, past the beach, breathing in the salty coastal breeze, and up the storybook hills. It was a long ride. As Sadie was driving up a rugged road on top of the hills, the car started to jolt as the wheels hit the awkward bumps in the road. It reminded her of the night she followed Arya to the desert and that awful road she drove on. As if their minds were connected, Arya was also reminiscing the same memory, but for different reasons. Because her memory was filled with love, amazement and touching moments.

"If this road gets any bumpier it'll be just as bad as that desert route," laughed Sadie. Completely lost in the moment.

Arya laughed, still thinking about that journey too. With Eli and his friends. Her smile then faded, as it dawned on her. Sadie wasn't with her; how did she know about that? Utterly confused, she turned to Sadie and asked a simple question.

"How do you know about that?"

"What?" laughed Sadie, not fully focused on what Arya had just asked.

"How did you know about that desert route?" repeated Arya.

Sadie's face went as white as snow. Having now realised what question had been directed at her. She gulped. The sweat produced on her forehead. Arya saw the colour of Sadie's face turned and knew she was hiding something. The only explanation she could think of was if Sadie had followed them that night. It was an outrageous thought, but not so impossible. Not with everything that has happened recently.

Then suddenly, Arya had a flashback to that night, when the lone car pulled up behind them. No one had left it, which Arya had found weird. The car looked familiar too, it looked a lot like the new car she was in now. Not trying to let her mind run a mile, Arya started to wonder whether that was Sadie. Surely it wasn't. But for some reason, it just fit together like a puzzle. A lump formed in her throat; she had to know whether her intuition was right.

Through the thumps of her heart pounding in her ears, Sadie briefly heard Arya say, "Pull over". And she did as she was told, pulling over on a slip path on a bridge that overlooked a spring. Sadie thought it looked familiar as she approached it but couldn't think why. It wasn't important right now, because she was about to be found out for all her devious crimes.

As the car turned off, they were left in silence. Except for the rush of water from the nearby spring. Sadie could feel Arya's eyes boring into her head as if she could read all her thoughts. But Sadie couldn't look back at her. She focused on staring at the steering wheel, wishing it would swallow her up.

Whereas Arya was breathing hard. Trying to steady it, because she felt like she was going to blow. Right now, she needed to be sure first, that her paranoid thoughts weren't delusional. She couldn't let herself jump to conclusions yet. The only way Sadie would know about the rugged route would be if she had followed Arya on that day. There was no other way Sadie would know it because Arya knew she wouldn't be caught dead in a boring empty desert. Arya's mind continued to race with a thousand questions she wanted to ask Sadie. But she asked her the same question. She tried not to show any emotion to it either, Arya couldn't now be the one throwing accusations around as her friends had.

"How do you know about that route? You've never been to a desert, especially that one."

Arya's voice echoed in Sadie's mind. She fought diligently for an answer for her, that wouldn't show her in a bad light. But her ever-growing, silence just made her look more and more guilty in Arya's eyes, revealing that there was more to it.

As hard as Sadie tried, she couldn't think of a logical reason as to why she would know. She was done for; she had been found out. But she was still going to desperately try to regain her side, Sadie wouldn't go down without a fight.

Sadie forced a laugh. "I heard it from you, don't you remember telling me about it? Surely you remember! It was only yesterday!" lied Sadie, awkwardly laughing.

"Don't lie. I never even told you about that date with Eli. Let alone the trip to the desert." Arya's face now hardening. She was losing her patience. "Sadie. I'm asking you one more time. How do you know about it?"

"I-I...heard it from your Mom!" lying again.

"Stop lying. You followed me, didn't you?"

"What? No! Of course, I didn't. Why would you say that? You're just as crazy as Maya, accusing me of things I haven't done!"

"I'm not crazy!" shouted Arya.

She had had enough of people calling her crazy, first Eli and then Sadie. What had gotten into them? Suddenly, a very prominent thought dawned on her, that sent her mind into overdrive. Was she being crazy or was she actually being forced to think that? Arya felt stupid for doing this, but she needed to make sure she wasn't being crazy. Grabbing her phone out of her pocket, she called a number.

"Wha-" started Sadie, but she was interrupted by a ringing. It was coming from the back of the car.

Arya unbuckled her belt and rummaged around in the back, trying to find where it was coming from. She got closer to Sadie's bag and as soon as Sadie realised where she was going, her blood ran cold. It felt like the breath in her had gone, just like getting winded. All she could hear was the phone, ringing and ringing. Desperately hoping Arya wouldn't find it, but as soon as she thought that it came true.

Arya unzipped a bag and dug down deep until she grasped around a vibrating phone. She pulled it out and saw it was the same phone she saw in Sadie's room. And it was now blaring the name 'Arya'. She couldn't believe it. Then as if she knew what to do, she unlocked the phone and opened the messages and she saw one text thread.

It was all the texts she thought she had sent to Eli. Arya saw the texts that had made her cry, that had made her doubt Eli's love for her, the one where he was calling her crazy. All of it. And it sunk in, that it wasn't Eli texting her...it was Sadie all along.

Arya felt like she had deflated. Falling back onto her seat, still holding the phone but at arm's width, as if it was a bomb. Arya was truly lost for words. However, before she could say anything, Sadie ripped the phone out of her hand.

"What is this? What's it doing in my bag?" she hurryingly lied.

Another thought sprang to Arya's mind as if she was piecing a puzzle together. Grabbing her own phone, she unlocked it and searched for another number. Making sure to thoroughly check it this time and what she found out surprised her. Maya's number had been blocked. But she hadn't blocked it.

Arya's head snapped up and her piercing eyes glared at Sadie. All she felt was nausea, rippling through her. Needing to get out, she hastily pushed open the car door and clambered out. Feeling light-headed and weak, stumbling onto the ground. Arya then stuffed her phone into a pocket and ran to the side of the bridge, trying to gasp for air that couldn't fully find its way to her lungs.

Her body started shaking, she started to feel woozy, she felt like her heart was going to beat out of her chest and her body started to feel numb. Arya felt like she was going to have a panic attack, she needed to try to breathe.

Arya tried to focus on observing the environment around her, in the hopes of it calming her down. From the locks hooked onto the bridge railings, to the shimmer of the gentle water flowing down the spring. But a fog was moving in over the rocks, clouding her vision of the spring, mirroring her clouded mind. Suddenly, she felt someone's hands on her shoulders. Arya ripped herself away from them as if they burnt her skin. Pushing Sadie away from her. Arya just looked at her with such rage. Remembering how Sadie had called her crazy that was the last straw.

"I'm crazy? You've been spying on me; you've gone into my phone and blocked my friends! How do you even know my pin? What the hell were you trying to do?" she shouted.

Sadie just looked stunned, not knowing how to reply. Arya started frantically pointing towards the car where the phone was.

"Answer me! What have you been doing? Why when I call Eli, does that phone ring? Why?"

Sadie was struggling to think of a response.

"How is Maya's number blocked on my phone? I wouldn't do that!"

Sadie looked like a deer in headlights. She couldn't find her voice to reply.

"ANSWER ME"

And like a switch, Sadie roared back.

"STOP SCREAMING AT ME. I DID THIS FOR YOU!"

"Excuse me?! How is this for me?"

"You don't need them! You have me! They were trying to take MY place. I could feel it, and no one can take my place. I had to get rid of them! So, I-I pretended to be Eli and blocked Maya's number on your phone...so they wouldn't get your messages...to push you away."

Arya felt a blow to her chest. She couldn't process what was going on. None of it was registering in her mind and Sadie didn't make any sense. All Arya could do was pace back and forth, trying to understand Sadie's justification for her madness. But she couldn't. There was no logic for what she had done. From that moment on, Arya began over analysing every little thing that has happened recently, every odd thing that's occurred. Then an awful thought popped into her head.

"Did you put those nuts in Maya's food? Please tell me you didn't..." nausea creeping back in Arya.

The air was still and quiet. The only sound rippling through the air was Sadie's ragged breath. That was a clear answer to Arya.

"You're SICK Sadie, sick! You could have killed her. She could have died! How could you do that? What's wrong with you?" she shouted, feeling like she was going to throw up.

"Oh please. If I wanted to kill her, I had the chance to do it way before then."

"Wait, what?" gasped Arya.

"The night you showed her *our* special room…I was furious that you would betray me like that, and I wanted to hit her…to finish her off!"

"Hold up. Were you the one standing outside looking up to my window that night?" questioned Arya. Waiting for the answers to her many questions. "I knew someone was looking at me… I knew it. And to want to hurt someone over that? Sadie, you need help!"

"I had to know how close you were getting! Because she has no right being in your life. I tried to push her out, but nothing was working…So, I-I had to go bigger. And that's when I destroyed your painting and framed her for it. And it worked, it worked! She left for good, and now it's just me and you. No more Maya. You get that right?" babbled Sadie.

Sadie then paused, realising she was continuously digging herself a hole. And now sounded like she was losing her mind, with her eyes wild, body shaking and her breath staggered. There was nothing that could save her now.

298

Arya's eyes widened in complete shock.

"YOU ruined my painting? And framed Maya for it?" she roared.

Sadie had messed up; she stitched herself up. There was no way out.

"Let me get this straight. First, you waited outside my house because she was with me, and you didn't like that. Secondly, after none of your stupid plans worked, you put nuts in Maya's food knowing she's allergic to them. And when that was unsuccessful, you destroyed my favourite painting in the entire world and framed her for it. Then you followed me on my date, *spied* on me, went into my phone and blocked two numbers. And finally, you impersonated Eli. Wow. That's brilliant, Sadie. Really."

Arya started sarcastic clapping while trying to hold back her tears.

Sadie was lost for words. She did do all that. But she wouldn't apologise, because she wasn't sorry for it, and she would do it all again.

"What kind of a friend are you? You're meant to be my best friend! My number one, and instead you deceived me, tricked me entirely. God, I've been so naive, so manipulated...by you! You've kicked out the most important people in my life! You made me feel like I was going crazy by gaslighting me. But it's all been you!" sobbed Arya, now almost breaking down. Tears started pouring from her eyes, her face turning red and blotchy from crying.

"I AM your best friend. I am THE best friend. You see all the things I've done for you; I've done it for us too. Only a true best friend would go through all that trouble!" started Sadie, but before Arya could reply, she carried on. "You were going to ditch me for Eli and Maya. You've barely known them! You've known me your whole life. You even hid Eli from me, from the very start! I saw you getting together at the hotel. I thought it would end when we got back, but then I saw you two together again. And I couldn't have that!" finished Sadie, breathlessly, holding up her phone with the picture she took at the hotel.

Arya's eyes widen in shock. "Oh my god. How long have you been spying on me?!" gawping at the picture.

"It doesn't matter now. They're gone! And now it's just me and you," blurted Sadie hysterically.

"There will never be a "me and you" again. A friend would never do what you've done. Everything that has gone wrong has been because of you, no one else and yet you made everyone feel it was their fault! Maya was right, you are toxic!" exploded Arya.

Arya started shaking her head in utter disbelief, hands thrown in the air, her cheeks glistening with the sadness she felt. But Sadie didn't respond, it was like she was frozen and then she saw Arya start to walk away from her.

Don't let her go, said the voice.

"Where are you going?" howled Sadie.

"I'm going back to Maya. I need to apologise and clear all this up!" shouted Arya, turning away from her. "I need to be away from you."

"No, you can't do that! Please! Please come back-" wept Sadie, following her.

"Don't you dare follow me! I don't want to be anywhere near you!" screeched Arya.

NO! Stop her! Bellowed the voice.

Desperate madness took control of Sadie, blinding her vision. Flooding her mind with so much anger. She had never felt like this before. A surge of power exploded out of her and Sadie screamed, like she was in utter anguish. And before she knew it, she charged toward Arya, grabbing her arm, and trying to drag her back to the car.

"What are you doin-" yelled Arya, feeling Sadie's strong hands get a grip of her.

Sadie swung Arya around by her shoulders, then began to pull her back to the car. Arya pushed back as hard as she could, but Sadie latched on to her wrists and began pulling until Arya lost her footing. She fell forward and now Sadie was dragging her by her wrists along the ground. Arya screamed in pain and kicked out, managing to propel herself into Sadie who fell forwards.

Then Sadie hit Arya, a straight punch full in the face, feeling Arya's cheekbone crack and her own fingers crunch. They both reeled back in pain for a moment before Sadie pushed Arya back towards the barrier by the bridge. Hitting, spinning, then a grab, and a push. Followed with a fall. A scream echoed in the deathly silent air, growing quieter and quieter, falling further down, until with a sickening thud the screaming stopped.

Chapter 23

Sadie woke up in her car, feeling dazed and lethargic. She was trying to settle her head from spinning in circles but couldn't quite calm it down. Moving a little, she sat upright, and her body felt oddly stiff. Sadie guessed she must have fallen asleep in an uncomfortable position. Attempting to readjust herself into a position where she didn't ache, Sadie began to wonder why she was still in the car and not at the cabin.

Looking ahead of her, she saw the bridge, heard the spring grow in her ears and felt her stomach immediately drop. It dawned on her, that what happened here, the argument, the fight and the...

No.

That couldn't have happened. She couldn't have done that to Arya. But the scene kept replaying in her mind over and over. It made her feel sick. She started hyperventilating, not being able to catch her breath quick enough. Frantically looking around, she saw...

Arya was right next to her. Sleeping soundlessly in the passenger seat. And just like magic, every panicky feeling Sadie had, melted away. All that panic was for nothing and everything was okay.

After Sadie settled herself down, it became clear that it had been a nightmare. And what a nightmare it was, it felt so real to her. Erratically trying to shake it off, she stored the nightmare in an imaginary vault at the back of her mind and forgot about it. When she regained her composure, she gently nudged Arya. She then stirred a little, slowly opened her eyes and stared right into Sadie's. Her eyes were piercing, but very much awake.

"Hey, Sades."

"Why did we fall asleep?" asked Sadie, confused.

Arya looked equally confused and just shrugged her shoulders.

Sadie sat back and tried not to think about it. She shook her head again and started the car and headed off towards the cabin, but this time it was in complete silence. Sadie's mind was so far off into the distance, it was unreachable. She spent her journey trying not to think about her nightmare, wondering whether any of it was real and whether Arya actually knew what she had been doing all along. Instead of overthinking, Sadie decided to just ask Arya what they last spoke about.

"Oh, nothing much." she replied.

Arya didn't say much else, so Sadie left it at that. She didn't have the strength to have a conversation, not now. So, she drove in peace, hoping it'll be enough to calm her nerves and anxiety.

After what felt like a lifetime, they finally arrived, and Sadie felt every bad feeling disappear into thin air. Completely stunned at how ethereal the cabin looked and how everything surrounding it was like it had come out of a fairy tale book. A towering willow tree sat beside the cabin, the leaves gently swaying in the soft, summer breeze. Daisies in the grass were fluttering in the air with every rush of the wind and everything else was calm.

In front of the cabin was a big pond, with a rickety bridge built over it. The water was still, adorned with lily pads having bloomed across the entirety of it.

Every so often, Sadie's ears were filled with a buzz of the bumblebees, croaking from a frog and the rustle of the fallen leaves. It felt like time had stopped, that they had entered a bubble where time didn't move, not even for a moment. Sadie breathed in deeply and as she breathed out, a serene feeling washed over her, as if she had entered a dream. A dream that she didn't want to wake up from.

Feeling satisfied she had taken everything in, for now, they made their way to the cabin. The door opened with a slow creak that sounded like it hadn't been opened in a while. But inside was completely spotless, warm and welcoming. There was a real, rustic charm to it. It was homely and woodsy. In the centre of the room were two comfy, wooden sofas that were facing a grand fireplace. A pile of logs was placed beside it, each stacked upon one another, all ready to burn.

But Sadie's eyes gravitated towards the corner of the room, where sitting on top of a brilliant white rug, was a piano. A magnificent piano, one that Sadie always dreamed of playing. Her heart skipped a beat, in the hopes of creating music with it and letting the night wander away with her. As they walked further in, they were met with a rich, red carpet laid out in front of them and the smell of freshly baked goods inviting them in like family.

With each footstep they took, a creak in the floorboards would follow. They both turned around in circles taking in everything about their home for the weekend. When they stopped, they met each other's faces, held hands and giggled, completely elated about their time here.

Running upstairs to check out the rooms, they noticed it was just a one-bedroom cabin, but they were happy with that. The bedroom was also cosy, with macrame tapestries that carried plant pots hanging in each corner of the room and right in the middle laid a luxurious wooden bed.

Each corner of the bed had magnificent wooden posts reaching toward the ceiling, which were carved with etchings of vines, leaves and flowers. They were painted gold and glistened when they caught the sunlight. And draped between the posts were gossamer white curtains. The beddings looked like a soft marshmallow, smelled like fresh laundry and felt like cotton. Sadie felt like this cabin was made for couples, but she liked that because it made it cosier. Just as if they were reading each other's minds, they simultaneously jumped onto the bed and rolled around.

After they had settled in and brought in all their belongings, Sadie felt like stretching her legs and suggested going for a walk together. Arya happily complied and thought it was a great idea. They walked outside and breathed in the fresh, open air and felt tranquillity surrounding them. Once Sadie stepped on the grass, she saw her shoe sink slightly in the soft moss, like it was a bed and had an idea.

"Hey, let's go for a walk barefoot. I want to feel the grass on my feet!"

Arya nodded and their shoes were now chucked to the side, as they ran in the grass, feeling the soft moss and tiny prickles of grass touch their feet. They cartwheeled, did handstands, spun around in circles and made daisy chains under the golden sun.

But no matter how hard Sadie chased the sun, wishing for nothing but it's hot gaze, she still felt its icy glare. Although, this time Sadie didn't care, she was over it. It didn't bother her how much her summer had changed, how the sun no longer hugged her because she had someone more important to hug. Her Arya. And now she was once again with Sadie wholeheartedly, Sadie didn't need anything else, she only needed Arya.

So, she laid back, spread out like an eagle and enjoyed the beauty she was surrounded with, accompanied by her best friend. She noticed Arya lay down next to her and did the exact same. Both now looking up into the blue sky, watching tiny wisps of heavenly clouds fly by.

While Sadie was peacefully lying on the bed of grass, she saw Arya get up and take a daisy that they had plucked to make their chains and wander away with it. Curious about where she was going, Sadie sat up and watched Arya walk towards the pond. But she just stood there for a few minutes not moving.

Finally, she stepped on the rickety bridge and gracefully walked on it. Sadie expected to hear the bridge creak, and whine with every step Arya took, but it didn't. She instinctively wanted to follow Arya now, so she did. Oddly though, when Sadie stepped on the bridge the wooden planks let out a huge cry, so loud it made her jump. Maybe the bridge couldn't hold both of them, thought Sadie.

While she gazed at Arya, she noticed a glorious glow radiating around her. It entranced her. Having the sudden urge to move closer, Sadie stopped and noticed the glistening of the stone in Arya's bracelet shimmer in the sunlight. It made her heart soar, Sadie looked at her bracelet and brought it closer to Arya's. But she accidentally bumped Arya's arm, and the daisy she was holding dropped into the water. They both watched it float under the bridge and disappear.

They stayed outside for the rest of the day and when it started to cool down, they retreated inside. The fire had been lit, and a few logs had been thrown in the fireplace to keep it going. Within five minutes, the cabin was warm and toasty.

For food, Sadie's Mom had arranged for the owners of the cabin to stock the kitchen with all the food and snack items that they could ever need. Sadie was very impressed at the effort they had gone to. There was even a basket in the kitchen with mini muffins, fresh eggs, fresh orange juice and tiny glass jars of strawberry jam. It was too adorable to even touch, but Sadie was looking forward to tucking into it for tomorrow's breakfast.

They ate their food and retreated to the sitting room to relax with some spa stuff Sadie brought from home. Face masks, foot masks and eye masks now on, they were in relaxation mode, listening to music and filling the room with their chatter. Reminiscing about their childhood days and girly sleepovers. Then Sadie remembered one of the main reasons for coming here.

"Ooh shall we start on our scrapbook?" she said eagerly.

"Yes!" replied Arya in an equally eager tone.

Sadie hurried upstairs to her bag and pulled out the scrapbook and the box of Arya's crafts. As she was rummaging through her bag, she noticed she couldn't find her second phone. It was meant to be in her bag with the scrapbook, but it wasn't there. She searched all her bags but couldn't find it. Worried that she had misplaced it and anxious about it ringing if Arya decided to call Eli unexpectedly, she checked her phone and saw that it had no network. She breathed a sigh of relief. Wherever it was, it didn't matter because there was no signal anyway. Arya wouldn't be calling anyone.

Satisfied with this thought, Sadie went back downstairs. Now she was finally doing what she wanted to do and something she longed for. Feeling super thrilled and ecstatic that no one would be able to ruin this for her, with no interruptions and no unexpected delays. As Sadie reached the last step, she saw Arya smile upon her arrival, a true smile. She walked over to help Sadie lay it all out onto the great, oak table in the room and they both perched themselves next to each other.

They spent a few hours crafting. Deciding on what pictures to use and then laying them out in order of when they were taken, this took the longest. After that, they laid the pictures out on the pages they were to be stuck to, just to see what it would look like before it was permanent.

But even then, they weren't ready yet. First, Sadie wanted to layout the page with the craft materials and Arya's collection of stickable holiday souvenirs, just to be absolutely sure that it looked just right. Scrapbooking was a very serious job. After being fully happy with how it looked, they decided they would take a page each to decorate, Sadie took the left side and Arya took the right.

After three hours of doing this over and over, their scrapbooking was complete. From pictures on the plane with their tickets stuck on the corner of the page, to pictures outside every theme park entrance. There was even a picture of Sadie crying when she was outside the Wizarding World, which she and Arya laughed at.

The scrapbook was now like a work of art bursting at the seam. An illustration of their lives together. There was far too much in it, but every single piece that was stuck or written in there was precious to Sadie. She couldn't take anything out or let go of it. The scrapbook was a memoir of their friendship and held all their memories ever since they first met. It was Sadie's most valuable possession.

In full contentment with their finished product, Sadie went into the kitchen and came back out with a load of snacks held in her arms. The most important snack she carried was a bag of marshmallows. Sadie saw Arya's face light up, upon seeing the soft pillows of sugar. She knew what Sadie was thinking of. Roasting marshmallows.

It was a childhood treat they would always do on their camping trips. They loved the ooey-gooey stickiness and the toastiness of the marshmallows. And since they had a roaring, open fireplace here it was the perfect opportunity.

They sat in front of the fire, letting the heat hug them and the warmth bring them closer together. They were now cuddled by each other, cross-legged with their knees and shoulders touching one another. Like they were in sync. They both then stuck their forks in the fire slightly, watching the marshmallow slowly melt. Sadie's marshmallow was ready before Arya's, and she felt playful, so she whacked it on Arya's nose. Leaving a sticky mess on her face, and thus, started the "marshmallow wars".

Roasted marshmallows hit cheeks, noses, foreheads, and even hair. When they surrendered their battle and finished playing around, they finally ate the pillows of goodness and it was oh, so good. Sadie daydreamed about their camping nights again when she took her first bite of the warm, sweet, caramelised marshmallow. The simpler days, where it was just them two against the world. It was like heaven. She was in heaven. And her head remained above the clouds for the rest of the night.

The next morning, Sadie woke up to the sound of birds chirping at the window. Her eyes slowly opened, and she was welcomed by the morning glow illuminating their room. Eager to spend more time with Arya, she turned around and saw she was still asleep. Arya's hair was messily covering her face. Sadie's nimble fingers gently brushed it behind the ears, and she gazed at Arya. Not wanting anything to change this moment. Because it was more than perfect.

Sadie watched the way she silently breathed, her lips slightly puckered and her eyelashes moving with every flicker of her eye. Sadie was transfixed but she didn't know why. Something about Arya was different, but before she could think about it, her eyes fluttered open. Her chocolate brown eyes were fixed on Sadie's emerald, green eyes. Sadie felt like electricity had travelled through her. But before she could think why, Arya pulled a funny face and hit her with a pillow and the feeling vanished.

"What was that for?" cried Sadie.

"You were looking at me funny, so I hit you," smiled Arya.

The girls lay in bed for a little while longer, too warm and comfortable to move. But Sadie wanted to explore the woods that were behind the cabin. She enticed Arya by suggesting various things she could sketch and before you knew it, Arya was quickly sold on the idea. Before they left for their walk, they ate breakfast: omelettes made with fresh eggs and some organic vegetables. To wash it all down they had the freshly squeezed orange juice and now their bellies were full, and they were raring to go.

Their walk started from behind the cabin, where a path had been outlined by various sized fir, pine and birch trees. Each winding around the path, each in its own spot, standing out from the rest but also connected. Their leaves spread out but didn't touch another's leaves. And between those gaps, the light seeped through, and Sadie felt like she had entered a magical enchanted wood.

The girls explored the woods for hours. Finding holes in trees big enough to hide them both in and built forts with old tree branches they found scattered on the ground. Feeling like they were lost in Neverland, Sadie took pictures of everything unusual and beautiful and took about a hundred of her and Arya. Smiling, laughing and falling over tree roots. They wandered by the pond, sat on the grass and made flower crowns from the surrounding twigs, branches and flowers that were scattered around them. Watching the dragonflies flutter effortlessly around the calm water.

Knowing they wouldn't visit any place so magical and this quiet for a while, they decided to be incredibly silent and listen to the sound of the woods come to life. They perched themselves comfortably, held hands and opened their ears to nature. All Sadie could hear was the sound of her breathing. But after a while, her ears pricked at the sound of something scurrying along the wood floor, brushing through the falling leaves and scratching against the bark of the trees.

Then out of nowhere, a red squirrel crawled by the entrance of their fort. Sadie waited in bated breath, not wanting to scare it off. She'd never seen a red squirrel before; it was always the grey ones. She was fascinated at how scarlet red their fur was, how bushy their tails were and their cute tuft ears. The squirrel then scampered away, and they were left in the silence again, but it wasn't for long.

Their ears were filled with the songs of birds, sounding like they were in a choir performing a show. Then there was a rush of the cool summer breeze, blowing their hair, rustling through the leaves, making sure everyone knew the wind was there. The woods breathed. And it was enchanting.

After a while, Sadie felt like going back and Arya followed, it was getting late now. They skipped through the towering trees, straying from the path like rebellious seven-year-olds. A few minutes later, Sadie felt Arya let go of her hand, which she didn't mind. She carried on walking, thinking Arya was following, but she couldn't hear any footsteps behind her. She turned around to see where Arya had gotten to and noticed her lying down on the ground. Arms outstretched in front of her, hands holding her sketchbook, drawing.

Excited, Sadie joined her on the ground to see what she was drawing. To her shock, she saw it was a replica of the painting she destroyed, that she had framed Maya for. Suddenly, she felt queasy about how accurate this sketch was to the real thing, and she didn't like it. Feeling unsettled, Sadie gently knocked Arya as she was getting up, leaving a massive line in the middle of it.

Arya just sighed and stood up, looking lost and disconnected for a split second. But then Arya changed upon looking at Sadie, and she looked normal again and followed Sadie once more. They walked back to the cabin in silence, kicking pebbles as they went. Sadie needed to get her mind off her thoughts, so she started singing to block it out, and not even a word into the song, Arya started singing the same song.

A cheery Sadie turned to Arya and grabbed her hands with so much joy and danced with her, under the towering trees, with the leaves spinning in circles dropping to the floor. Their dance moves mirrored each other exactly, every move Sadie made, Arya followed without a second beat. Sadie's happiness flourished realising how much they were in sync with one another again. She didn't worry about their friendship anymore. It was solid.

When they finished dancing and were back inside, they changed into their matching PJs and enjoyed their last night together. They cuddled in front of the roaring fire, ate pizza, nibbled on muffins and sang their favourite songs. Sadie then remembered the piano in the room, how could she forget that!

She quickly walked over to it and stroked it; Sadie was in awe of how magnificent it looked. Cautiously, she sat on the piano bench and gingerly touched the keys, playing a note from one end to the other. And then she turned the musical notes into an elegant, but an enchanting song. Playing it beautifully and so effortlessly. Arya was now perched next to her on the small bench, swaying in tune with the music. And Sadie didn't play one note off-key. It was absolutely perfect.

They lived in this moment, listening to beautiful music and relishing in each other's company. Sadie didn't think about what would happen when they got back, she didn't think about how she would carry on the charade or how she could continue to keep Arya to herself. She only thought of them now and she was happy about it.

Chapter 24

When Sadie woke up, she felt a heaviness in her chest. It was time to go home and face reality, but she didn't want to leave. She had worked so hard over the weekend not to think about what she had done and if she would ever have to face the consequences of her actions. But this morning, it all came flooding back to her and there was no escape. Should she own up to Arya before they left, or try to continue her charade? She was unsure and decided on the latter.

As soon as she was ready to accept whatever fate awaited her, Sadie opened her eyes slowly, as if she had been asleep for a hundred years. Gradually, she felt the weight of the world slowly creep up on her shoulders. She sat up and tried to stretch it out, but instead, a sharp pain panged in her right shoulder, and she slouched again, her body aching. Sadie sighed, got out of bed and walked solemnly to the bathroom. Hoping a hot shower would wake her up and relieve her of her aching pains. Physically and emotionally.

When she entered the bathroom, she caught her reflection in the mirror hanging on the wall. She looked strange. Her eyes seemed bloodshot, she had dark circles clinging underneath and her skin looked dry and drained. What happened to her all of a sudden? She stood at the edge of the sink, resting on her arms that tried to keep her body up and stared at her reflection. Breathing in and out.

Then she turned the cold water tap on and let the sink fill up with water. Once it was full she plunged her face into the pool of iciness. Feeling the piercingly bitter, cold water cut deep into her pores and wake her skin. When she couldn't take it anymore, she thrust her head back up and stared into her reflection once again. Her breath was now rugged as she glared at her reflection's face, but it didn't look any better.

A vague thought popped into her head, recollecting how Arya from her recent nightmare said she didn't know who Sadie was anymore. And now Sadie felt like she was right. Despite it only being a nightmare, it seemed to now slowly become reality. Even Sadie didn't know who she was anymore. She looked deranged and felt unstable.

Looking back at her reflection, surveying her tired eyes, uncontrollable tears started pouring from them, and gut-wrenching cries tried to escape her mouth. What had she done? Who had she become? Why had she hurt Arya so bad? When did she become so deceitful...
But as quickly as her sobs came out, she stifled them. Not wanting to awaken Arya, as she didn't want questions. And Sadie was dead set on not letting her nightmare come true.

Quickly scampering back to the room to check on Arya, she found herself fast asleep still. Sadie didn't want her to wake up, because it would mean they'd have to go back, and she didn't want to go back to their normal lives. Maybe they could run away, she thought. No one would know where they would be, she wouldn't leave a trace, they could drive to a different state and start life anew. Sadie was getting so caught up in her head with the idea, but her dream shattered like glass when she realised that Arya wouldn't want that. Sadie's hopeful mood dropped and returned to her depressive state. She was about to lie back down in bed when Arya stirred and woke up.

The sunlight was shining so intensely on Arya, that it blinded Sadie and she couldn't see Arya's face. But then she emerged from the light and sat upright. All she did was smile at Sadie and she couldn't help but smile back. Truly smiled, as if she hadn't just spent her morning worrying. They sat in bed for a little while, not speaking a word. Just listening to the outside world. The peace and quiet were something special, something you couldn't experience during the day in a bustling city. If it was up to her, Sadie would stay here forever, in her little bubble with Arya.

When the chatter of the outside naturally died down, and the sunlight moved away from the window, Sadie concluded it was time to start getting ready. She started first by repacking her bag and heard Arya mumble something and retreat to the bathroom. The only reply Sadie could muster was a feeble "Okay" and carried on packing her things. When she finished with her clothes, the last item to pack was their scrapbook.

Her only treasure. A priceless artefact that she held like it was made out of gold. Sitting down on the bed, she opened the book to the most recent addition and gazed at each and everything that was stuck down. As she turned each delicate page, she took a breath in and breathed out as she stroked the pictures of the two of them, interacted with folded pieces of paper and laughed at her own jokes that were written in them. When she closed the book, she had a full heart.

It was like the clouds had cleared and Sadie finally believed deep down that everything would be okay. It had been drilled into her that no matter what relationships or friendships Arya had, the friendship with her could never be replaced.

They had gone through so much, as illustrated by the scrapbook they lovingly added to. This was concrete proof that they were bonded for life, tied together with an invisible string that could never be cut. Having realised this after weeks of immense doubt, she was instantly relieved of so much tension. She felt the weight of the world lift off her shoulders and the feeling of clarity welcomed her once again.

But it was too soon to celebrate this self-enlightenment because she had one more thing left to do. That was to undo the actions she carried out on Arya's phone and also remove all traces of any conversation with "Eli". But she couldn't see the phone anywhere, so she searched Arya's bags, jacket, everywhere downstairs and even her clothes from last night. But there was no sign of it. Frantically worrying she wouldn't be able to rectify her misdeeds, she knew she had to ask Arya straight up where her phone was.

Patiently waiting for Arya to finish her shower, nerves started creeping up on Sadie and she tried to calm herself down. Before she was about to conduct a second search, the bathroom door opened and out came Arya fresh from the shower, dressed in her casual clothes. Just as Sadie was about to ask for the phone, Arya said she was hungry and went downstairs, so Sadie reluctantly followed. They then spent an hour making their last breakfast together and leisurely eating it. But it had to end sometime, and they had to clean everything up, as if they had never been there and marking the end of the trip for Sadie.

As Sadie stowed their dishes in the dishwasher, Arya threw all their rubbish away, and Sadie's eyes saddened as the marshmallow bag disappeared into the garbage bag. Once they were satisfied with how clean it was, they went back upstairs to finish their packing since Arya was still left to pack. Again, Sadie tried to think of a way to bring up the phone, but she couldn't think of a real reason to ask for it. However, she desperately needed it, and she couldn't let Arya leave this cabin until she fixed her mistakes. Then she had an 'aha' moment and snapped her fingers.

"Can I borrow your phone? I just need to text my Mom saying we'll be leaving soon. I don't have any network," she called as Arya went back into the bathroom. She watched Arya come wandering back into the room and simply said.

"I don't have it. I have no idea where it is, it's probably in the car."

Sadie was taken back. She thought it was so strange that Arya seemed so calm and unbothered about her phone not being with her. But maybe she was just different to Sadie. Leaving the bedroom in a hurry, she ran outside the cabin and into the car. She searched for Arya's phone but couldn't find it. Although, she did find something else; her second phone. It had been hiding under the passenger seat, but she had no clue how it got there. It was meant to be in her bag. Getting lost in her thoughts trying to rack her brain, she hadn't noticed Arya had come behind her with her bags.

"What are you looking at, Sades?" called Arya.

Sadie jumped out of her skin and threw the phone in the air. She swiftly caught it and threw it under the driver's seat and resurfaced like it was nothing.

"Oh...just ch-checking the car. Nothing else," she stuttered nervously.

Arya fluttered away and stowed her bags in the back of the car. and then shouted to Sadie that she was ready to go. But Sadie wasn't. She still hadn't found Arya's phone. and what was weird, was that Arya didn't seem one bit bothered about it. It seemed like it was lost.

All of a sudden, Sadie stopped bending over in the car looking for the phone and straightened up. If Arya's phone was lost...the evidence of what she did would be lost with it. If it was lost no one would find what Sadie had done. If it was lost...Eli and Maya wouldn't believe Arya when she confronted them about their texts, and she wouldn't be able to prove anything. All the evidence would have vanished, and no one could accuse Sadie of anything. She would be totally off the hook. A smile crawled on Sadie's face. It was brilliant.

Knowing that she could no longer be caught for her devious deeds, she felt lucky and spritely. She headed back into the cabin to grab her bags and said goodbye to the place where she finally felt reconnected to Arya. She sighed and walked solemnly out of the cabin. As she turned around, she watched the darkness slowly envelope the room as she closed the heavy, wooden door. And with a loud thud, it felt like something had changed in the air. Like it was the end of something.

Heading towards the car she saw Arya sitting in her seat smiling at Sadie, with the light beaming through the window of the car, not a care in the world. Sadie shuffled slowly to the car and sat in the driver's seat, hands on the steering wheel, not moving a muscle.

Earlier she had felt happy and content with her friendship and she knew it wasn't threatened anymore, nor was she threatened by anyone else. She had gone through a turning point of now becoming unphased about going back to their reality and having to share Arya. But now that she was in the car and was ready to drive home, she suddenly didn't feel like going anymore.

Something was stopping her from starting the journey home, and something kept telling her not to go back. It wasn't the voice this time however, surprisingly she hadn't heard that the whole time they were at the cabin. But it was a nagging feeling at the back of her mind that she just couldn't shift. The question of running away dawned on her again, but it was a stupid idea. There was nothing wrong with going home, it was home. Sadie would just have to adjust to this new life. It was the only way she could keep her forever.

"Ready?" she asked Arya.

Arya nodded her head, smiling and off they went.

The drive home was mostly smooth sailing. They passed the high trees that stretched out for miles and open fields with sheep grazing. The

322

weather started to change though, it became cloudy, and they were about to reach the bridge where her nightmare occurred.

But before they reached it, they noticed it was blocked off and a diversion had been put in place, so they couldn't drive over it anymore. As soon as she turned back on herself and carried on the diverted route, her phone instantaneously started going crazy. It felt like a hundred pings buzzed all at once, texts coming in one after the other and constant vibrations.

Sadie realised that her network had probably come back, but she couldn't think of anyone who wanted to get in contact with her that much. Clearly, they were desperate.

As they were nearly home, Sadie didn't want to pull over and check her phone, nor did she bother Arya to check either. She wondered whether Arya's phone was also getting the same treatment, wherever it was.

After passing through the city, the hills and the beach, Sadie was now turning into Arya's road. It was eerily quiet. A shiver ran down Sadie's spine, she felt like something was wrong and it caused her to slow the car down into a creep. As she inched closer to Arya's house, she noticed police cars parked in front. Her eyes widened in horror. What had happened? Were Arya's parents okay? Or her brother? Sadie quickly turned to see if Arya had seen, but she was just staring blankly at the house.

Sadie thought that she must be in shock, so she decided to squeeze her hand, to let her know that she was there for her, whatever had happened. Then she noticed her parent's car was there too. Worry started to cloud her mind, and she started to feel sick.

Finally reaching her spot, she turned the car off and both the girls stepped out of the car. Not knowing what they were walking into. As Sadie was walking towards the house, behind Arya, she felt like time had weirdly slowed down. She felt like the steps she was taking were in slow motion, that she was walking into something devastating, but she couldn't understand why she felt like that.

The front door was left unlocked and there was a collection of voices coming from inside. When she followed Arya into the house, she saw Arya had casually walked upstairs, not even acknowledging anyone in the room. No one had even blinked an eye at Arya walking in, but as soon as she did everyone looked at her and the room fell deadly silent. All of a sudden out of nowhere, Aashi launched at Sadie, screeching with anger seething from every fibre of her body. Her face contorted with pain but had a river of tears streaming down her face.

"HOW COULD YOU?!" she shrieked.

Chapter 25

Sadie was thrown back onto the floor, trying to shield her face. But as quickly as she was knocked down, the weight of Aashi was lifted off her. Uncovering her eyes from her protecting arms, Sadie saw her parents and police officers picking Aashi up and sitting her back down on the chair. Sadie was left on the floor reeling at what just happened. Her face was in complete shock and her body shook uncontrollably.

All she was thinking about was why Arya hadn't come back downstairs, why wasn't she troubled at what just happened? Why didn't she shout at her Mom for attacking her? Rose then slowly walked towards Sadie and helped her up, but the way she was holding her daughter was as if she was scared of her. Sadie could feel the distance, how wary the touch was, and it concerned her. Why was her Mom being so cautious around her?

Sadie looked up at her trying to gauge what was wrong, but her Mom was trying really hard not to look at Sadie. Eyes forward, but fingers firmly gripped on her shoulders, as if she couldn't let her go. Bad feelings started to sprout in Sadie's stomach, growing like a disease swarming through her body. She nervously glanced over at the officers and was immediately taken back by the very hard and intense glares they were giving her. Looking at her like she was a criminal.

Starting to feel scared, she went to hide behind Rose who flinched slightly at this. Finally, Sadie found her voice and spoke.

"What's going on? Why is everyone staring at me?"

She felt like her voice echoed around the room, bouncing off the walls. Now noticing that Kunal's fingers had tightened and turned white as he clenched his armrest, she heard the ragged breathing of Aashi's breath and felt her Mom's presence beside her, though strangely twisted away. The officers looked at each other like they were conversing in their minds or with their eyes. Then as if they had come to a mutual agreement, one slowly approached Sadie.

"Why haven't you been answering your phone?" he asked.

"I had no network this weekend…"

"Ok. Do you know why we're here?" he asked.

Sadie looked at him dubiously.

"N-no, I don't understand what's going on here. Is everyone okay?"

Rapid sniffling came from Aashi, her eyes were so bloodshot like she had been crying for days. Sadie looked around for Kiaan and Bailey, but couldn't find them, she hoped that this wasn't about them and that they were fine. Cautiously she looked back at her parents, but they couldn't meet her eyes and stood there like they were statues. Even they looked exhausted and drained. Sadie was now getting frustrated at everyone and at why was no one telling her what had happened.

"Can someone please tell me what's going on?!" she snapped.

Her parents flinched and Aashi looked like she was ready to lunge at her again, the anger seething in her eyes. But the officer put a hand to her, to tell her to stop. He addressed Sadie again and told her to sit down. His voice was quiet and so serious, that she obeyed instantly. He then pulled out a photo that Sadie knew very well because it was always displayed on the wall behind them.

"Do you know this girl?"

Sadie looked at him with utter confusion, she thought that he must be stupid to ask that question.

"Uhh...yeah. That's Arya? What kind of question is this?"

She laughed awkwardly, looking at her parents, who still weren't looking at her. The officer ignored her and asked another question.

"Do you know where she is?"

"Um... Is this a joke? Did you not just see her walk upstairs as we came in?" she replied.

He turned around to look at Arya's parents who glared back at first but now looked slightly confused and curiosity was written on their faces.

"What do you mean Sadie?" he asked.

"We've just come back from the cabin together... We've been together this whole weekend. These guys know that! And Arya is literally upstairs. I don't understand how you didn't notice her," rambled Sadie.

Then she got up and walked towards the bottom of the stairs, with the officer closely behind her.

"Arya! Come back down! These officers are asking dumb questions about you, it's completely ridiculous!" she laughed.

But there was no answer. She waited anxiously, looking up and waiting for Arya to come downstairs, but she didn't. Sadie was then about to walk upstairs, but the officer took her arm in a strong grip and moved her back on the chair. She stared at him, his eyes bore hard into hers, then she looked at Aashi and saw fresh tears protrude from her eyes.

"Sadie, Arya is dead." came the second officer, crouching by her.

His words echoed in her mind as if her head was completely empty. Her heart dropped into the pit of her stomach, and she felt like time had stopped. She saw Aashi drop her head in her hands, completely breaking down and she saw her Mom bury herself in her Dad's chest. She didn't know where to look, everywhere was filled with anguish and pain, but she still couldn't comprehend what he had just said. They must have been completely mistaken because they were together all weekend, Sadie thought.

"This is a sick joke. She was with me the whole weekend, why would you lie about something like that?" she said with a voice as hard as stone.

"You're lying!!" shouted Aashi. "Stop this! You know what you've done! Admit it!"

Sadie stared back incredulously.

"Her body was found on the bottom of a spring. She was badly injured and most likely died upon impact," stated the officer.

"Impact from what?" asked Sadie.

"From hitting the rocks after being pushed over the bridge. By you."

More anguished cries erupted from the room, both their parents sobbing uncontrollably. This didn't make sense to Sadie at first, but then she suddenly remembered her nightmare. How the ending of her dream made her feel sick. How she was sent into a powerful rage that made her push Arya to her death. But that was just a nightmare...it wasn't real.

"What makes you think it was Arya? As I said, she was with me the whole weekend, why aren't you getting this?" whispered Sadie.

"Her phone was found in her jacket, with her ID in the phone case. Her body was discovered in the early hours and was identified this morning," responded the officer, without a second beat.

Sadie felt like she had been sucked into a black hole. Her ears started to ring, and her palms became hot and sweaty. She held them against her ears and was trying to block everyone out.

"No. No, no no. No, this can't be real. Arya is upstairs, I will prove it to you!" She ran towards the stairs again. "ARYA! Arya, please come down! Arya!"

But there was no response from her. All Sadie could hear was Arya's parent's cry. Feeling impatient, she ran upstairs into Arya's room and was instantly blinded by the sheer amount of sunlight gleaming in the room. Once her eyes adjusted to the sudden brightness, she realised it was empty.

Starting to shake her head ferociously, she clambered up the spiral staircase into Arya's art room, and again she was met with emptiness. So, she ran and searched the entire upstairs but to no avail. Arya wasn't there. A thought struck Sadie, and she ran back downstairs and towards the front door.

"I have proof she was with me and that you're lying!" she called, as she was leaving the house.

One of the officers was about to chase after her, but the other stopped him and told him to wait. They saw Sadie run to the car, open the back and rummage in a bag. She grabbed something and ran back to the house. Everyone was just looking at her like she had gone crazy because she was carrying their scrapbook.

"We added to this on the weekend. She took one page, and I took the other. You'll see all her artwork, you'll see it all here," she said, slightly high pitched.

She ripped it open and flicked to their latest addition, but something was wrong. When she looked at the pages, only the left side had been filled in. The right side, where Arya worked on, was empty. There was no trace of any pictures, ribbons or glue. Sadie ran her hand across the right pages, wondering where everything was and then she fell to the floor. She flicked through every page they added to, looking for a scrap of something that Arya did, but all the right pages were blank. There was no trace of anything made by Arya. She fell silent.

Then an unexpected noise came from the officer's radio. They said that they had searched the cabin and found it in a mess, with empty food packets lying around the living room, but no evidence of two people staying there, even after checking the entire cabin. How did it become a mess again? "What is he talking about? Arya cleaned up, she did that while I filled the dishwasher. Ask them, ask them to check that. There will be loads of dishes in there!" she argued, pitifully.

"Sadie. There's no evidence to prove there were two people there. You were there alone."

She didn't take this in, still believing that Arya was with her. Ignoring the officer again, she grabbed her phone and started looking for the pictures they took together. But all she saw were pictures of her, only her. Sadie in the cabin, Sadie's face by the roaring fire, Sadie's face in the enchanted woods. Just her. There was no Arya.

"What are you looking for?" asked Noah, in a quiet voice.

"Arya. A sign of Arya. We were together this weekend, we had fun, we scrapbooked, played the piano, roasted marshmallows, danced, took pictures...we did everything together. I don't get it...it was all here before," she whispered sadly.

She felt like she was falling through the floorboards. Totally unbalanced, woozy, like she was about to throw up and she started to feel herself slip to her side slightly. Her Mom rushed over and steadied Sadie as she slowly dropped down to the floor. Rose hugged her stiffly.

In broken breaths and heavy tears, Aashi whispered, "How can you hug a monster like her? She killed our daughter!"

"She's my daughter! She wouldn't do that, there's something we're not understanding here!" replied Rose, defiantly.

"We have concrete proof it was her!!" screamed Aashi.

Sadie woke up from her mind trap. "Wha-what? Proof? How?"

The officer walked up to her and held out a tablet that displayed a video. It looked like it was CCTV footage. Sadie hesitated, but she finally pressed play. She had no idea what she was about to see. At first, it was just the bridge that they had driven over, nothing was happening, and she was about to give the tablet back, but then a car pulled up. It was her car. She saw Arya get out of it and walk angrily towards the edge of the bridge and then was closely followed by her.

What followed was everything that happened in her nightmare, she couldn't believe what she was seeing. Their arguing, their fight. Sadie pulling Arya back, it was all there. Caught on video, scene for scene, as if it had been extracted from her nightmares.

Tears started to form in her eyes as she saw herself charge at Arya, witnessing their scuffle, the slaps and the fists flying through the air. Sadie felt like this wasn't her, it couldn't be. And then she saw the most horrific thing she has ever seen... herself pushing Arya over the edge.

"NO!" she screamed.

She threw the tablet on the floor and scurried away from it. What followed was heart-shattering cries and tears pouring down her face because

332

her heart had just been ripped out. She started to hyperventilate and whisper "No" over and over again. Rocking forwards and backwards.

"We need to know what happened. What led to this? Why did you push Arya?" the officer asked.

"I didn't push her! I wouldn't kill her! She's my best friend!"

Aashi scoffed. "You wouldn't let her have other friends. You controlled her and now look at what you've done!"

"No! I wouldn't, I didn't..."

"She loved you like a sister. And this is how you repaid that love... You never deserved her. And now she's gone forever." Fresh sobs escaped her, a broken woman, a broken mother.

Sadie just looked at Aashi crying, how her chest was heaving trying to take in the deepest breaths, tears constantly emerging from her red eyes and her body curled up in a ball on the chair. Sadie still couldn't believe what happened, nothing made sense, it didn't matter what anyone told her or shoved under her face. Arya hadn't died at the hands of her and that everyone was mistaken because she couldn't do that to someone she loved.

Feeling a desperate need to prove herself, she needed to think of a way to make them understand that Arya was alive and that she hadn't done anything. The footage must have been fabricated. Arya was still alive, somewhere. Sadie just needed proof. And that the only way she'd find out is by going back there, to the scene of her worst nightmare. She just needed a way out from here, an escape.

And as if her prayers had been answered, there was a barrel of sounds bounding down the hall where Bailey ran into the room, startling everyone. He was meant to be in a room with Kiaan, but they both had enough of being in there. Bailey ran to Aashi and tried to lick her face and bark at her and Kiaan started screaming saying everyone was ignoring him. Amid this chaos, Sadie sprinted out of the house and ran into her car and sped off. Her heart in her throat, pumping ferociously and adrenaline infiltrated every fibre of her bloodstream as she sped off.

She caught a glimpse of the officers sprinting to their car and the parents following them. But Sadie was too quick for them, she drove as fast as she could, narrowly missing other cars as she sped down every road. Twisting and turning, trying to lose them and it was working. She knew shortcuts that they didn't, and this ran in her favour because soon enough she couldn't see them behind her anymore. But she didn't dare slow down. Continuing to drive at a flying speed she finally made it. The car came to a halt.

Surprisingly, there was no one else there, no other officers, no one. This was her only chance to find something in her favour, anything to prove Arya was here. Clambering out of the car, she shut the door with a thud. As she walked closer to the area, she saw the yellow police tape sectioning off the bridge. Lifting it, she ducked under and walked on the bridge, and it instantly felt like she had walked on ice. It felt delicate like she shouldn't be stepping on it as it could crumble beneath her. But it was just a feeling, she reassured herself. Suddenly it had become windy, her hair was flying around her face, covering her vision but she quickly tied it up, so she could see clearer. Searching high and low for something, she fanned herself around trying to find anything.

Slowly, she walked over to the railings where the apparent end of Arya's life was, and she crouched down. A glint of something caught her eye and as she got closer, she realised it was Arya's bracelet amongst the locks on the railings. It was caught on the barbed wire; the wind was blowing it up for Sadie to see. But she couldn't reach it from the side she was on. Feeling perplexed as to how it got there, she wanted to retrieve it.

Looking around making sure no one was approaching her, she started to climb over the railing, carefully. She knew how risky this was, being high up from the ground and having just rocks and water below her. But she needed that bracelet. It was Arya's and she had to give it back to her.

After mustering all her courage to climb over, she finally was on the other side. All she could hear was the rush of the water flowing below her and the wind coursing through her ears. She looked up at the ominous clouds above her and clamped her hands tighter onto the railing, with her feet carefully placed on the edge. She was about to reach for the bracelet when a barrage of voices came from behind her.

"SADIE DON'T!"

"Please climb back over, Sadie!"

"You don't need to do this!"

All the voices came at once and it startled Sadie that she almost lost her grip; she had no idea what they were shouting about. She looked over her shoulder and saw the white stricken faces of her parents and Arya's parents, shouting at her to come back. The police officers were talking into their radios and cautiously coming closer to the railing, trying not to startle Sadie. Then it clicked and she realised they must have thought she was going to jump.

"I'm fine! I'm not doing anything! I'm just trying to get this bracelet. Arya can't be without it, she needs it!" she shouted back.

"Sadie, please climb back over!"

"Someone else can get that, don't worry about it, it's not safe!"

But Sadie didn't listen, and she began to crouch down to retrieve the stuck bracelet. Inching closer to it but keeping a firm grip on the railings, she reached out for it, but she couldn't quite get it.

"Sadie please, you don't need to get that. Please forget it!" said one of the officers.

But Sadie didn't listen, she kept getting distracted by the cries from her parents, their hushed voices telling her to come back and seeing the officers slowly approaching her from the corner of her eye. She couldn't concentrate.

"PLEASE STOP!" she screamed.

The officers stopped in their footsteps. Everyone fell silent and she was left in peace, finally. She mustered up the courage from within to speak, feeling scared now, but still just as determined.

"I need to do this. I need to get this for her, she needs it. I bought it for her, it's important to her and me. Once I get it, I'll tie it back on her wrist because I know she'll be missing it. Just be quiet, please," she pleaded with a shaky voice.

No one said anything. They watched her try her hardest to retrieve the bracelet, watching her grip the railing with one hand that was turning white from withstanding the pressure of her body. She slowly crouched down and extended her fingers, swaying them around trying to get even a tiny bit of the chain within her grasp. She missed it a few times, just ever so slightly, but she didn't give up.

The wind was picking up again, getting stronger and wilder. It was starting to make her eyes water, but she blinked what felt like a hundred times to wash away the tears. The current of the water below was turning choppy, and wisps of hair started to fall out of place and started to impair her vision. But she didn't let it phase her; she was determined not to let anything get in her way. Pushing through the wind and her hair, she conjured up all her strength and made a final attempt.
Stretching out her fingers, she finally felt the cool sensation of the chain in her hands, and she yanked it out of the wire. Holding it up like it was a prize she just won, a smile spread across her face and a collective sigh rang through the air from the adults.

"Okay now please carefully climb back over, we're here to help you." called the officer, approaching her again.

"Bub, please listen to them. Please come back over where you're safe," cried Rose.

"Mom please, I'm fine. Nothing's going to happen to me. I can't wait to give this back to Arya, she must be going crazy looking for it!"

After Sadie gathered the courage to move again, despite the wind acting against her, a sudden downpour of rain erupted from the overshadowing clouds. She now started to feel unstable and unsafe. The rain was relentless and showed no signs of stopping, it was as if nature was against Sadie. It had made it that more difficult for her to move now, as the railings were now drenched and slippery.

Sadie began to feel more and more afraid of what she was doing, but she had no other choice but to slowly move. Her body was now shaking profusely, paranoid that she was about to make a wrong step. Then she slipped, panicked and, after righting herself, retreated to her previous position.

Feeling frustrated, she tried again and broke through her fear after readjusting herself. But as she moved, she drastically disturbed her grip on the railings that were bitterly cold and wet, and her hand slipped. She couldn't grasp the railing in time and her feet lost their balance on the edge.

Within an instant second, she lost control, and she let go. Screams rippled through the air. Cries rang from every person there. But Sadie fell, still holding onto Arya's friendship bracelet and she hit the rocks below with a sickening crunch.

Sadie woke up slowly, greeted by the warm, gentle sunlight showering her with radiance. She didn't know where she was at first, but as she became more aware of her surroundings, she found she was lying on a bed of soft grass and flowers. Slowly sitting up, she felt like she had been here before, it felt so familiar.

The buzz of the bees filled her ears; the wisps of the gentle breeze rushed through her hair and the smell of fresh grass filled her with glee. After rubbing her eyes, a little, when she opened them again, she realised where she was. She was back by the cabin, in the enchanted woods that took her heart.

Recognising the towering trees surrounding her, the rustic charm of the cabin and the willow tree sitting proudly besides, billowing in the breeze. She stood up wondering how she had gotten here and took a few steps in the grass. The light followed her with every step she made, and then she spotted the small wooden bridge over the pond. Standing in the middle of the bridge was a figure, but she couldn't make out who it was.

Cautiously she walked toward it, and within a couple of seconds, she was overwhelmed with happiness and tears at the same time.

It was Arya. Smiling at her, holding her arms out for her.

Arya looked absolutely radiant. Sadie was transfixed and ran towards her, wanting a hug more than anything. With a rush of emotion, they embraced each other with love so immense, Sadie felt like she was home, where she was meant to be. All she felt was Arya and the warm sunlight wrapping around her body. Oh, how she missed that warmth, how she missed the sun being her friend, greeting her with its gloriously enchanting, incandescent glow.

After they pulled apart, Sadie suddenly became aware that she was holding something. She looked down at her hand and realised she was still holding Arya's bracelet and Sadie sighed in relief. Bringing it closer to her heart, but then Arya touched her hand gently and held out her wrist, waiting for Sadie to tie it back on her. Sadie happily obliged and tied the beautiful bracelet that represented their bond.

"Together forever, right?" asked Sadie.

"Together forever."

Acknowledgements

I want to say thank you to my husband, Kallum, who read each and every chapter as I finished writing them. Who gave me undeniable support throughout the difficulties I faced with publishing this book and for being there every step of the way. From idea conception to the cover design. This wouldn't be possible without you.

And I would like to thank Taylor Swift, who on August 2nd, 2019 at the *Lover Secret Sessions*, showed so much enthusiasm and excitement for my book, that she inspired me to continue writing, even when I was in my darkest days and felt like giving up. It meant more to me than anyone will ever understand.